UNNEUTRAL
MURDER

AN AMOS LEE MAPPIN MYSTERY

UNNEUTRAL MURDER

AN AMOS LEE MAPPIN MYSTERY

HULBERT FOOTNER

COACHWHIP PUBLICATIONS

Greenville, Ohio

CONTENTS

CHAPTER ONE

THE TIME WAS AUGUST, 1943. Embarking passengers on the Portuguese ship *Dom João III* had been instructed to go aboard before 11 P.M. In wartime guests were not permitted on the ship, and since the bar was closed there was nothing for the passengers to do but turn in. Sometime during the night, the trim ship quietly cast off her lines and slipped out to sea. As a neutral ship she required no escort. Along her sides in gigantic letters appeared her name and her nation, together with the Portuguese flag, the whole brilliantly displayed under floodlights.

Having been forced to go to bed early, most of the passengers were out on the promenade before breakfast. They found the ship gleaming with fresh white paint, the attendants solicitous. It was better than they had expected in wartime. The American coast had already sunk below the horizon astern; the ship was alone on the sea. It was a rare morning; the sun shone gloriously on the blue expanse; the breath of the sea was as exhilarating as wine.

"Man litters up the earth," remarked little Mr. Mappin to his secretary as they stepped out on deck, "but he cannot spoil the sea."

"Yes, sir," said the secretary impassively. His name was William Miller, a big, blonde, pink-skinned fellow with thick spectacles that gave him an owlish appearance. Helped by the spectacles, he cultivated an absolutely dead pan.

Mr. Mappin went on: "I'm glad we chose the ship instead of a plane. We'll have a blessed interlude of peace at sea before plunging into the mess over there."

The younger man looked out across the sea, scowling. "The ship is so slow!" he murmured. "It's hard to wait!"

"As for me," said Mr. Mappin, holding up his glasses to the sky and peering through them, "I'm not naturally a man of action. Haven't got the figure for it. So I'm willing to put off what is before us as long as possible."

"You were a brave man to volunteer for it," said Miller gravely. When he spoke softly his voice rumbled.

"Not at all," said Mr. Mappin, adjusting his glasses. "I was too cowardly to refuse the job."

"What's the difference?" said the other, shrugging.

"Well, anyhow, if we had taken the plane we should have been marked from the start as important travelers. This way we may escape notice."

"Not much chance of that," said Miller somberly.

Even here on the peaceful, sunny sea the ship's company reflected the troubles on shore. All the passengers were supposed to be on the side of the United Nations, or what would they have been doing in the port of New York? But it was clear from their sidelong glances that they doubted each other. A cloud of suspicion hung over the promenade deck. Passengers were guarded in their approach to others, and some pointedly kept to themselves. The featherbrained women and the garrulous old men of peacetime voyages were conspicuous by their absence. Everybody aboard the *Dom João III* was *on business*. For instance, a trim, smartly dressed young woman with magnificent black eyes.

"It's not natural for such a one to keep such eyes lowered as she walks the deck," remarked Mappin to Miller. "Who is she?"

"Down on the passenger list as Miss Kate McDonald of Dundee. Has a British passport. The purser told me."

"Could be forged."

"If so, it's a good job. Bears the stamp of a dozen British consulates including New York."

"Maybe so," said Mappin, "but don't tell me those eyes opened for the first time in Scotland."

One young man, an exception to the other passengers, was making up to all and sundry. A good-looking, smiling young fellow, as blonde as Miller, but livelier, he seemed to be of a type that is to be found on shipboard during peace or war.

"Name of Ronald Franklin," said Miller in response to Mappin's question. "An American; agent for Swiss watch movements in America. As they are doing an enormous business during wartime, he has to make continuous trips back and forth."

"Hm!" said Mappin. "Why can't he transact his business by cable?"

"Looks like a harmless fellow," said Miller indifferently.

"Look again," said Mappin. "Notice that while he grins and jokes with everybody his handsome blue eyes are sharp and wary."

"You're right, sir."

William Miller drifted away and plump Mr. Mappin toddled around the promenade alone. In a sheltered open space astern, a ping-pong table had been set up. Young Franklin was bouncing a celluloid ball as Mappin came along.

"Like to play?" he asked, with the winning smile.

"Not with you," said Mappin, glancing at Franklin's long legs. "Give me somebody my own size."

Franklin laughed and fell in beside him. "Ronald Franklin," he said, offering his hand.

"Walter Brown," said Mappin, taking it.

Franklin's conversation flowed as smoothly as a tidal river. Before they had made two rounds of the promenade Mappin was in possession of all the salient facts about him.

His job of selling Swiss watch movements in America; his headquarters at the McAlpin Hotel; unmarried; born in Elyria, Ohio, where his parents and younger brothers and sisters still lived; educated at St. Paul's School and Yale. He embarked on a lively description of his youngest brother, Johnny, who not only had the makings of a good athlete but was smart at his books too.

"I'm going to take charge of that kid's education," said Franklin. "He deserves the best and he shall have it!" And so forth and so forth. "You may think it funny that a husky-looking guy like me isn't in the Army," he said with a sidelong look, "but as a matter of fact I only have one lung."

"So," said Mappin sympathetically.

After completing two rounds of the deck, Franklin said with a charming, deprecating laugh: "But I must be boring you with these personal details."

"Not at all!" said Lee. "I am never bored."

A pause followed which Lee Mappin understood was to give him a chance to talk about himself. This young man was too smart to ask leading questions. "I envy you your life of usefulness," Lee said with an innocent air. "I inherited a bit of money and I've never done any work at all. Just traveled; It was pleasant enough until Pearl Harbor, but then it got on my nerves. I was too old to serve in the Army and I had had no business or professional training. There was absolutely nothing I could do in the war. So I decided to write a book. I always wanted to write a book. I'm going to write a history of Portugal. That's what I'm going to Lisbon for."

"How interesting!" murmured young Franklin. "Who's the young fellow who's traveling with you?"

"My secretary, William Miller. He will do the necessary translating for me. Speaks Portuguese and Spanish and all that."

"A fine-looking fellow. How did he get exempted from the Army?"

Mappin blinked mildly through his polished glasses. "Defective eyesight, poor fellow."

When Mappin finally dropped in his deck chair, William Miller looked at him inquiringly. "We lied to each other fluently," said Mappin. "And neither believed a word. It was good comedy."

THERE WAS ONE COUPLE among the passengers who were above suspicion because everybody knew who they were and what their business was. This was John Stanley and his young wife. It had been announced in the papers that Stanley was going to Lisbon as Fourth Secretary to the hard-pressed United States Legation. He was nearly seven feet tall and broad in proportion, and, as is so often the case, his pretty little wife stood scarcely breast-high beside him. They had only recently been married. She was Vera Whittier, daughter of the tobacco nabob.

When the chimes sounded for breakfast the Stanleys and Mr. Mappin came face to face on the landing where the two branches of the descending stairway came together. "Why, Mr. Mappin!" said Mrs. Stanley, "what a delightful surprise!"

Mappin blinked at her mildly from behind the polished glasses. "I beg your pardon! My name is Brown."

The girl became red with embarrassment. "Sorry," she said stiffly; "my mistake." She ran down the rest of the stairs, followed by her lumbering young husband.

When the couple faced each other across a little table in the dining saloon she was seething with anger. "I've never been treated so rudely in my life! Certainly that is Mr. Mappin. He's been to our house to dinner! There's nobody else could look like that, the ugly little toad!"

"Easy, my pet," said Stanley. "Remember this is wartime, and he probably has good reasons for not wanting to be known."

"Well, he didn't have to stare me down, did he? Such rudeness!"

"You should have waited for a sign from him."

"Not at all! My mother said it was the woman's place always to bow first."

"We have left the comfortable, easygoing States behind us," said Stanley seriously, "and now we will have to watch our step and weigh every word."

"And do I have to submit to a lecture from you into the bargain?"

"No, my pet. But, God knows, all this has just been rubbed into me down in Washington! Be very careful not to mention to anybody that Mr. Mappin is aboard."

Mrs. Stanley tossed her pretty head.

At another little table across the saloon, Miller murmured: "Unfortunate you were recognized, sir."

"It hardly matters," said Mappin.

Miller glanced across the saloon through his lashes. "She is angry. She's giving her husband hell about it."

Mappin shrugged. "Poor young devil! He *would* marry an heiress!"

"Hadn't you better get her aside and square yourself with her?"

"Not at all," said Mappin calmly. "If I did, I'd have to bear with her meaning glances and secret signals during the whole voyage."

"She is likely to gossip to the other passengers."

"Let her gossip. We are safe away from port. It was advance information of our sailing that was dangerous."

"The ship's wireless is working, sir."

AFTER BREAKFAST, when young Mr. and Mrs. Stanley resumed their promenade on deck with cigarettes, they were presently joined by the agreeable Ronald Franklin. The young man's charming manner and smile recommended him to both husband and wife. They continued their stroll with the little woman in the middle. Franklin was able to give the budding diplomatist much valuable information about the complicated situation in Lisbon. He had left there only six weeks before.

"Rather like a madhouse," he said, "but conducted with the most punctilious regard for diplomatic procedure."

By and by a cabin boy presented a radiogram to Stanley. It required an answer and the tall young man hastened away to the radio cabin on the bridge deck.

When he was left alone with the bride, Franklin's conversation assumed a warmer tone. Vera Stanley, who had been around, was instantly aware of it, but since she was in love with her giant husband, she felt safe in leading another man on a little. In fact, she rather admired his cheek.

"How delightful to find anybody like you aboard this stuffy ship!" Franklin said.

"What good will that do you?" she asked pertly.

"Oh, don't misunderstand me," he said, turning a pair of blue eyes on her that seemed to beam with deep (but modest) admiration. "I know you're just married and all that. For me, it will make the voyage pass more quickly just to have you to look at!"

"Really!" said Mrs. Stanley, dimpling.

There was considerably more of this as they circumnavigated the promenade. Vera Stanley enjoyed it. This young Franklin, she told herself, had a continental finish you never found in an American boy. It was one of the things she had looked forward to in Europe.

"A fast worker," murmured Mr. Mappin to William Miller as the couple passed their chairs.

"What an odd-looking little man!" said Franklin to Vera casually, when they had passed out of hearing of the chairs. "With his white vest and spats and neat Panama. I saw you meet on the stairs at breakfast. So odd-looking and so distinctive, you feel that he must be somebody."

"He is," said Vera dryly. She had forgotten her husband's warning. "It's no less a person than Amos Lee Mappin."

"Mappin," said Franklin carelessly. "Sounds familiar, but I don't seem to connect it with anything. Who is he?"

"Why, he's one of the best known men in New York. It's considered quite a triumph when you can get him to come to dinner. He's been at our house, but I couldn't see the attraction. Never spoke a word to me."

"What has he done to become so famous?"

"He writes books. The history of famous crimes and how they were solved and all that. And once in a while he solves a case himself. Don't you remember the boardinghouse for ex-convicts on Henry Street a couple of years ago? The house with the blue door, the newspapers called it."

"I must have been out of the country," said Franklin. His smooth face had stiffened. "A detective, eh?"

"Oh, it makes him mad to be called a detective. He poses as a psychologist or a criminologist, or something high-sounding like that. They say he charges a terrific fee, and won't take a case at any price unless it happens to interest him. Horrid little man! Did you see him try to stare me down? I detest him."

Mr. Franklin, treating the subject as of no interest, allowed it to drop.

When John Stanley returned, Franklin, with his charming deprecating smile, handed over his wife and, leaving them, made his

way in turn, nonchalantly and by a circuitous route, up to the
radio shack.

SOME MINUTES LATER, Captain Gonçalves came striding aft along the
starboard promenade. A handsome man with a firm, seaman-like
expression, he was rendered magnificent by the lavishness of his
gold braid. By this time the sea was heaving gently and there were
only a few passengers left in their chairs. When the captain came
opposite to Mr. Mappin's chair, he stopped suddenly and pointed
across the sea.

"Look!" he said dramatically.

Mappin and William Miller scrambled out of their chairs and
approached him. Still pointing across the sea, he said swiftly: "Sir,
I have need to speak with you without being observed. Please to be
waiting for me in your cabin at eleven."

"Why, of course!" murmured the astonished Mappin. Other
passengers were crowding up. "What is it, Captain? What is it?"

"A whale spouting," said the captain coolly. "But now he has
flipped his tail and sounded. You will not see him again."

"What is 'sounded'?" asked a lady passenger.

"Dived to the bottom of the ocean, madam." The captain bowed
and continued down the deck.

"What do you suppose is biting milord?" said Mappin to William as they regained their chairs.

"Very mysterious," said William.

"Even an honest seaman soon learns to put on a conspiratorial
air in these bad days!" said Mappin.

It lacked less than half an hour of eleven, and Mappin and
Miller presently descended to their cabin. They had one of the two
de luxe cabins of the *Dom João III*, a pleasant room, gay with cre-
tonne covers and curtains, having two single beds, a sofa, and a
whole row of big portholes looking out on the blue sea. It was
entered by a short passage with a bathroom on one side and a trunk
room on the other.

Promptly on the hour, there was a knock on the door and the
magnificent captain entered with his gold-laced cap under his arm.

He was accompanied by a room steward, but at a glance from the captain, the steward remained in the little passage. The captain closed the inner door of the suite, and after bowing to Mr. Mappin and to Miller, looked inquiringly at the latter.

"This gentleman?" he inquired.

"My secretary, Mr. Miller. He enjoys my entire confidence, Captain. You may speak freely."

"Gentlemen, you must have been astonished by my method of address on deck," began the captain.

"Nothing astonishes me nowadays," murmured Mappin.

"The fact is," the captain went on, "one suspects spies in everybody during these unhappy times. My ship's company is selected and investigated with the greatest care, but alas, I have only too much reason to believe that there are spies among them." The captain laid his hand on his heart. "The people of my country are on your side, gentlemen, never doubt that; but there are corruptible ones among them as among all peoples, and the enemy is lavish with his money."

Mappin interrupted this little speech with just a shade of impatience. "Quite so, Captain. But what is the particular trouble?"

"I know that you are Mr. Amos Lee Mappin," the captain went on. "The New York office of the line—how do you say it?—tipped me off. But of course I shall respect your decision to travel incognito. I am entirely at your service, Mr. Mappin." Another bow.

Mappin matched his bow. "I am extremely obliged, Captain. I see by your face that there's something else you had to say."

"Yes, sir, I wanted to convey a warning. Have you noticed a passenger who calls himself Ronald Franklin?"

"I have."

"I suspect him of being an enemy agent. His papers are all in order, so I cannot take action. But he travels back and forth on our ships with suspicious frequency."

"Very good, Captain. I'll act accordingly."

"I mustn't appear to single you out during the voyage," Captain Gonçalves went on, "but I entertain all the first-class passengers from time to time. There is no reason why you shouldn't drop in at my quarters on the bridge deck if you wish to speak to me. Or better still, I make my inspection of the ship every morning at eleven, and if you happen to be in your cabin at that hour . . ."

"I get you. And thank you again, Captain."

With more bows the captain retired, and presently they heard him enter the next stateroom.

"A little long-winded," remarked Lee Mappin, "but his heart is in the right place."

AT THE LUNCHEON TABLE William Miller reported to his chief: "I've been talking to Franklin. Or rather I let him talk to me. He's German."

"So," said Lee. "Did you hear it in his voice? I couldn't."

"No. He speaks good American plus slang, correctly used. No trace of an accent."

"Then how did you know?"

William smiled a little bitterly. "It takes a German to know a German."

"Quite," said Lee. "And if you spotted him for a German, he must have spotted you for the same. It increases your danger."

William shrugged off the suggestion of danger to himself.

"Also bear in mind that if he's smart, he now knows that you know he's German. So watch your step."

"I'll do that," said William grimly.

As they were finishing their lunch, a cabin boy handed Lee a radio envelope. Inside, it bore a cryptic message written on the radio operator's typewriter:

"Please go to your cabin in ten minutes."

Lee smiled. "Another mystery!"

William murmured: "Sir, you treat it too lightly!"

Lee answered in the same tone: "Perhaps I take it more seriously than I let on."

In their cabin Lee tore the message into small pieces and tossed them through the open port. Presently Captain Gonçalves walked in without knocking. He said:

"I take some risk in visiting you at this hour, but the matter seems important."

"Why are you reluctant to meet me openly?" asked Lee mildly.

"I am in your hands, Mr. Mappin. My orders from my government are that I must not under any circumstances favor either one side or the other in this war. Portugal's very existence depends on maintaining the strictest neutrality."

"Good man!" said Lee, shaking hands with him. "What's the trouble?"

The captain handed him another radiogram form. It bore a message written in pencil in a flowery hand. "When I returned to the bridge after inspection, the radio operator gave me this, saying he thought I ought to see it. Ronald Franklin handed it in to be sent."

The message read:

> James A. Dryden,
> — West 32 St., N. Y.
> Grand Weather. Regards to all.
> (Signed) Amos Lee Mappin

"What do you make of it, Mr. Mappin?"

"Very ingenious," said Lee, smiling. "Naturally the ship does not accept messages in code during wartime, and so our enemy has been forced to construct a code out of innocent-sounding phrases. He wouldn't have a code phrase for my name, of course, so he had to write it out in full, and it appeared most natural as the signature. The purport of this message, Captain, is simply this: Amos Lee Mappin is aboard this ship."

"I wasn't sure what it meant," said the captain. "but it is obviously unneutral and it has not been sent."

"Thank you, Captain. I'll give you a message now." There were forms for radiograms in the cabin desk, and Lee wrote quickly: "Stan Oberry, — W. 42 St., N. Y. Look into activities James A. Dryden, — W. 32 St. N. Y. (Signed) Lee."

"For your information, Captain, this Oberry is a private detective whom I sometimes employ. If he turns up anything suspicious, he will pass it on to the F.B.I." Lee handed back Franklin's faked message. "Let Sparks file this with his other transmitted messages," he said, "because it is likely that Franklin may use some pretext to assure himself that it has been filed. At the end of the voyage it can be returned to me for evidence."

"Very well, Mr. Mappin."

CHAPTER TWO

DURING LUNCH on the sixth day after leaving New York, an electrical impulse suddenly went through the dining saloon of the *Dom João III*, and the passengers started jumping up and running to the portholes. From table to table the word traveled: "The Azores!"

Like a magical apparition, while they ate, the silhouette of an island had arisen from the empty sea; startling, inexplicable, there in the middle of the great waste of water they had become accustomed to, a bundle of mountain shapes tied together.

On deck after the meal, the island had drawn appreciably closer. The lower slopes now showed a delicate green verging upward into misty blue summits. Ronald Franklin, standing with his friends the Stanleys beside the rail, gazed at the island through his expensive binoculars.

"That's not Sao Miguel where we're supposed to be bound for," he said, lowering the glasses. "Looks to me like the island of Flores to the north. We're off our course." The young man's face never lost its smooth look, but there were moments when the flesh seemed to harden under his shaven cheeks.

Lee and William Miller were not surprised by the appearance of Flores out of the sea, because during inspection that morning Captain Gonçalves had told them he was altering his course.

"I have been instructed by my office to put you ashore at the town of Horta for a brief visit," he said.

"That's right," said Lee. "Please radio Horta the expected time of arrival so I can be met."

"I have done so."

"What about the other passengers?"

"I shall allow no other passengers ashore," said Gonçalves. "Mr. Franklin, I fancy, would be only too glad to cable Lisbon. I'll tell them there isn't time."

"Very good," said Lee. "I shan't be gone more than an hour or so. Just have to see a man and . . ."

Gonçalves held up his hand. "Please don't tell me what your business is, Mr. Mappin. I am neutral."

Lee laughed and clapped his shoulder.

During the afternoon the passengers had the pleasure of seeing the panorama of Flores roll by with its vivid green slopes and bold cliffs. It disappeared astern and they were alone on the sea again. But when they issued out on deck after dinner that night, they found a brilliant light blinking off the port bow. Then more lights appeared and dark shapes of land loomed in the night. Upon rounding a headland, a whole sparkling necklet of lights was revealed which disappeared suddenly as a high island intervened, and reappeared again.

The engines stopped, the ship lost way, and finally with a roar of slipping chain, the anchor was let go. A charming doll-size town lay spread before them with a cute little fort mounting guard over it. This was Horta, on the island of Fayal. A launch came chugging out of the harbor, and a Jacob's ladder was dropped over the ship's rail. There was considerable grumbling about "favoritism" among the other passengers lined up along the promenade when "Mr. Brown's" short legs twinkled down the ladder and dropped into the launch, followed by William Miller's long legs.

It was less than five minutes' voyage to the quay. Not many transatlantic ships call at Horta, and apparently the whole able-bodied population had come down to see her. Lee and William climbed some stone steps and found themselves surrounded by a gaping crowd. They received a fleeting impression of stucco warehouses in the background, a little customhouse.

Through the crowd pushed a burly, red-faced man in tweeds. "Ha! Brown," he cried, thrusting out his hand. "I'm John Westerholm. This way! This way!"

Close at hand he had a car with the top down, and a Portuguese chauffeur. The three of them climbed into the rear seat and, with a continuous squawking of the horn, the car turned into the little main street of Horta. A brief glimpse of charming little stucco houses in pastel colors, with elegant second-floor balconies, and then they were out in the country climbing a smooth road lined with hydrangea bushes. They turned into a private driveway and drew up before a long, low house with a superb vista of stars and sea. Over the entrance was fixed a little shield bearing the United States coat of arms.

"Come in! Come in!" cried Westerholm, jumping out of the car and flinging open the door. Everything about him was big and noisy. He exuded good humor.

Inside the house the immense, bright living room with its parchment-shaded lamps, easy chairs, and shelves of books was like a room from home transported intact across the sea.

"So this is what you're like," he said, looking little Lee over in the light. "I've heard so much about you!"

Lee's glasses twinkled. "I take it you were expecting something bigger," he said.

Westerholm waved his hands. "No sir! I don't measure a man's value by his inches!" He led them across the big room into a study. "Sound-proof!" he said dryly. On the table stood a bottle of Scotch and glasses, and from a small refrigerator appeared soda and ice cubes as if by magic. "I knew the captain wouldn't want you to stay long," he said, "so all is ready."

"I promised I'd be back within an hour or so," said Lee. "It will be enough. I wanted to have a look at you and to have you meet William Miller. I want to ask you a couple, of questions, and to answer any you may wish to ask me. But my principal objcct in coming here is to instruct you in our new code. Invisible writing is no good; our previous code is in the hands of the enemy. This has never been written down. So listen well!"

Their heads drew close over the table. After Lee had explained the principle of the code, he said: "The first and the last paragraphs of your letter are not to be coded, you understand. The essential part of the communication is in the middle, and that must be made to sound perfectly harmless."

"Boy! that's quite an order!" said the big man ruefully. "I never was good at puzzles. This is worse than acrostics!"

"You need use it only when some poor devil's life or liberty is at stake," said Lee. "It's worth going to a little trouble for!"

Westerholm made some notes on a scrap of paper. "I'll study this for a couple of hours and destroy it before I sleep," he said.

"Okay," said Lee. "But don't neglect to burn it. If it should fall into the hands of the enemy we're sunk! I suppose you have spies, even on the island of Fayal."

"And how!" said Westerholm.

They passed to lighter matters. "How long have you lived on Fayal?" asked Lee.

"Nearly ten years, Mr. Mappin. The consular duties here are nothing. I chose the post for the opportunity of doing some work of my own. After Pearl Harbor I sent the Missus and the kids home. I would have gone with them had I not received a hint that I could do a bit of really useful work here."

"I know of what you have done," said Lee, lifting his glass to him.

"Nothing at all! Nothing at all!" said Westerholm. "What about your two questions?"

"What are the communications between the islands and Lisbon?"

"The ships on the line you came on, to and from Ponta Delgada about every fortnight. They do not call at Horta unless ordered. Also the Island mail-steamer from Lisbon every other week. That calls at all the islands."

"Can we use the mail-steamer in our work?"

Westerholm spread his hands. "Doubtful. The captain is incorruptible. The purser is a good friend of mine and you can approach him safely. It would be difficult, though, to smuggle anybody aboard the ship without the captain's knowledge."

"Is there any other means of getting our friends through?" asked Lee.

"In case of emergency you could send me passengers by one of the Lisbon fishing boats. There is one skipper that you can depend on absolutely. His name is Pedro Chavez. The boat is the *Enguia*.

Chavez lives in Lisbon. I'll give you his address. His vessel has an engine. The voyage would be uncomfortable, but not dangerous at this season."

"The second question is, what is the chance of catching an American or Allied vessel homeward bound?"

"Can't give you exact dates, of course. A homeward-bound convoy will be leaving Algiers after September tenth. They'll be passing to the south of these islands say a week later. I'll be in radio communication with the convoy for ten days or more. In case of need, I can summon one of the faster ships to call at Horta."

"What about submarines?"

"None in this part of the sea at the moment. The passage of the convoy may bring them here, of course. As to later sailings, I'll have to let you know. What about coding such messages?"

"In a cable where you are limited to a few words, you must use your ingenuity. In this case you would cable: 'Mother will be ready to go home after September fifteenth'."

"I get you."

"Have you any questions?" asked Lee.

Westerholm shook his head. "Only your address in Lisbon."

"Lisboa Palace Hotel until further notice."

"Have you a trustworthy Portuguese servant or messenger?"

"Not yet. William speaks the language, but he could hardly pass for a Portuguese."

"I'll see what I can do for you from this end."

After a little more talk, Lee looked at his watch. "We must start back."

They left the house.

At the quay the launch was waiting. They shook hands with Westerholm, and Lee said: "This is the shortest visit to a foreign port on record."

"It has bucked me up," said Westerholm. "If I can do anything more for you, cable me from Ponta Delgada tomorrow."

NEXT MORNING, at the time of the captain's inspection, the island of Sao Miguel was close aboard; wicked-looking, scarred, brown cliffs, green shoulders, and a great central mass mounting until it was lost in cloud.

Captain Gonçalves entered the de luxe cabin with a scowl. "What should I do about Franklin today?" he asked. "We'll be here six hours. I can't very well keep all the passengers aboard. I've a good mind simply to forbid Franklin to go ashore, and the hell with him. After all, I'm the captain of this ship. I don't have to give my reasons."

Lee shook his head. "Better not, Captain; it would be showing too much of our hand. After all, it makes little difference. As soon as we land in Lisbon he'll convey the news of my arrival to his friends. Let him send a cable from Ponta Delgada if he wants. It would be worth something to me to find out who he cables to."

"Very well, sir," said the captain, "if that is your wish."

However, when the ship dropped anchor before that dazzling white town, when the lordly stairway was let down on the starboard side and the launches gathered around the foot of it, Ronald Franklin did not press forward with the other passengers. He remained leaning his elbows on the rail of the promenade, looking down with a superior smile.

"Not going ashore?" said Lee as he passed.

"What's the use?" said Franklin nonchalantly. "Stuffy little burg! I've seen it all a dozen times."

From the launch on the way ashore, Franklin could still be seen leaning negligently on the wall. William said softly to Lee:

"What's he up to, anyhow? I didn't like the look on his face."

Lee answered calmly: "Thinks it will be more profitable to search our cabin while everybody is out of the way."

William started. "Good God! I locked the door."

"Surely. But don't you reckon, after all his voyages on this ship, that he has collected a set of passkeys? Three master keys will open every stateroom door."

"I'll go back!" said William grimly.

Lee shook his head. "I want him to search the cabin. He will find nothing that he ought not to see."

"Do you carry your papers about with you?" said William. "That's dangerous, too."

Lee smiled. "They're not on my person, either . . . Have you any papers on you?" he asked.

"I possess no incriminating papers," growled William.

"Good!"

"Gott! how I hate him!" muttered William under his breath. Unconsciously his big fist clenched. William in his pink and white-ness was apt to impress the beholder as soft, but it was a false impression. "When he comes close to me my bristles rise!" he went on. "A Judas! Some day, some day there will have to be a show-down between him and me."

"That would be fatal to our work . . . now!" suggested Lee dryly.

William gritted his teeth. "I know! I know!"

They were seated alongside the engine trunk while the other passengers stood or sat towards the bow of the heavy, broad-beamed launch. Among them, Miss Kate McDonald, the pseudo-Scotswoman, turned her handsome face.

"Oh look, Mr. Brown! We are entering a little inner harbor. It looks as old as time itself. And see the quaint arcades all around it!"

Lee moved forward to join her. In her well-fitting suit of Lincoln green with a beret to match, she was charming. She owed little to make-up; the pallor of her smooth cheeks was seductive, and her great dark eyes were full of mystery. But she was uneasy, too; the handsome eyes were never still.

In going up the stone steps of the quay she was immediately in front of Lee. She paused and wavered slightly. Lee quickly put a hand under her elbow.

"Silly of me!" she said with a laugh. "The thought of toppling into the water occurred to me, and right away I began to stagger!"

This bit of clinging-vine business did not sit very well on Miss McDonald, who was obviously well able to take care of herself. But Lee supported her to the top of the steps.

On the quay the passengers were surrounded by native men and boys, who with more or less English were recommending themselves as guides to the town. Miss McDonald pressed a little closer to Lee.

"Let's not have a guide," she murmured. "It's so much more fun to mooch around by ourselves."

"Surely!" said Lee, drawing her hand under his arm and making for the street. Today Lee and William had no cares beyond seeing the sights. William followed the couple, looking grim. Life had borne hard on William, and the springs of joy were dried up in him; women had little appeal.

"They say the Madeira work is better here than in Madeira itself," the girl was saying. "I'd like to get some, but I expect it will turn out to be dearer than in New York."

"It will be while the ship's in harbor," said Lee.

The girl intrigued him. In the midst of her chatter, he noticed how her eyes were painfully drawn aside by the sight of a long-lashed little girl staggering under the weight of an adorable dirty baby. "Like babies?" he asked idly.

She quickly recovered herself. "Dear me, no!" she said with a tight laugh. "I'm not the mother type! It's a crime to bring babies into a world like this!"

Up and down the main street of Ponta Delgada the old houses had broken out in a rash of modern store fronts with show windows displaying all the attractions of the A. & P. or Woolworth's at home. Lee found it rather depressing.

"Let's strike uphill," he said, "and see some gardens. This town is famous for its gardens, I've heard."

"Let me do a little shopping first," pleaded Miss McDonald. "Just half an hour for shopping and the rest of the afternoon is yours."

She paused at the door of a shop that sold embroideries and women's wear. "Better let me go in here alone," she said archly. "I've got to look at all kinds of unmentionables."

"Old-fashioned?" said Lee, affecting to be astonished.

"No, Scotch," she answered with a smile. "Come back in half an hour and pick me up?"

"Surely."

The two men walked on. A group of boys followed, running out in the street, or darting ahead under their feet to get a look back at them. Some dropped away when their curiosity was satisfied, but others took their places.

"Damn the woman!" grumbled Lee. "I know I'm not attractive to the sex. I know she's playing me for a sucker. But God forgive me! I like her!"

"You're not obliged to come back in half an hour," said tight-lipped William.

"Of course not."

They turned up one of the sun-drenched streets accompanied by their admirers and presently came to a pretty little *praça*. One side of it was filled by a magnificent building, and through an open gateway they glimpsed a garden with old trees of strange shapes. They turned in, hoping to lose their attendants, but the boys came, too.

Inside, the wealth of verdure was like nothing they had ever seen. Beyond the first garden there was a lovely sunken garden, and beyond that actually a playing field with nobody playing in it. The whole was surrounded by a lavishly decorated stone wall. They sat down on a bench and all the boys stood and stared unwinkingly.

"Look," said William, "do any of you understand English?"

There was a chorus of replies: "Yes, gentleman! . . . *Si, senhor!* . . . Sure!"

"Then get the hell away from here!"

Nobody moved.

By and by, a boy they had not noticed before approached Lee timidly, offering him a rumpled pink card. Lee took it. It bore the address of an antique shop which, among other things, advertised old silver and Portuguese ship models.

"Sounds interesting," said Lee, handing the card to William.

"*Qual é a distância?*" William asked the boy suspiciously. "Five minute, gentleman," he answered eagerly. He was a handsome boy, straight and slim, with shadowed black eyes.

"Let's go," said Lee, rising. "It will be more fun than mooching with McDonald."

The other boys accompanied them out of the garden. In the street their young conductor turned on them with a torrent of invective, and they slunk away.

"I don't know what he's saying," said William. "Talks too fast and uses slang words I never heard before."

Having got rid of their hangers-on, the boy led them through one narrow, close-ranked street after another. Window sashes and doors seemed to be unnecessary in Ponta Delgada, and they had intimate glimpses of domestic life as they went. Often they were hailed in English in friendly fashion. It was surprising to find how many of these islanders claimed to have worked in Brooklyn or Pittsoborgo or New Bedford. To all of William's questions, their young conductor only answered, "Five minute, gentleman."

Several times five minutes passed, and William finally halted. "We're getting too far from our base," he said. "Any reputable shop ought to be in the center of town."

The boy pleaded piteously with William. There were actually tears in his big brown eyes.

"What's he saying?" asked Lee.

"Oh, the usual stuff about his poor father and mother and his sick sister," said William. "He says they haven't made a sale in the shop since the last ship called."

"Let's go on," said Lee. "We have all afternoon."

They were now in the poorest and most ancient quarter, where the houses appeared to be on the point of collapsing and the gutters were full of trash. Upon turning a corner they came upon several rough-looking men leaning against the wall on both sides, with arms folded and hats pulled over their eyes. They had not seen so many men in one spot before. The women and children of this corner had disappeared. Lee glimpsed frightened faces peeping around the upper window openings.

William stopped. "I don't like this," he muttered. "Where's the boy?"

They discovered that he had disappeared as if swallowed by the pavement.

Upon turning to retrace their steps, they found that several of the men had slipped behind them, cutting off their retreat. Additional men were silently edging out of doorways, perhaps a dozen in all. None spoke; out of dead-pan faces, the stare of bright, inhuman, black eyes never wavered.

A hairy individual with villainous blank features blocked Lee's way. Lee demanded boldly: "What do you want?"

By way of answer, another man silently leaped on his back, bearing him to the ground. Some of the women at the windows whimpered. Lee made no struggle. It would do him no good, he knew, and he'd only get hurt. Out of the tail of his eye he saw that it was taking four or five men to get William down. Then a hand-kerchief was thrown over his eyes and tied. His arms were expertly pinioned to his sides, and a gag forced between his teeth. He could still hear William cursing furiously and thrashing about. After a while it stopped. Have they killed him? thought Lee. No sound came from any of the Portuguese except their heavy panting.

He heard a motor car draw up and stop. He was unceremoni-ously picked up and dropped in the rear compartment on top of William. A tarpaulin was thrown over them. Lee was overjoyed to find that William was still able to struggle in his bonds. He nudged him urgently to persuade him to be still, but William continued to strain at his bonds.

The car sped through the streets, honking continuously, turn-ing the corners on screaming brakes. In a few minutes they slowed down and sped along a smooth, straight road. A breath of flower perfume reached Lee's nostrils. Out in the country, he thought. Turning out of the smooth road they began to climb a stony track in first gear. Then the engine was thrown out of gear and they bumped slowly down a long descent and stopped. What now? thought Lee.

They were lifted out and dropped in grass. The rope was un-wound from Lee's body and while a man sat on each limb, another started frisking him. The thought flitted through Lee's mind: Fancy! four men to hold down little me! He could hear nothing from Wil-liam. Lee's snuffbox, his wallet, and his loose change were taken, besides what other trifles they found in his pockets. Every inch of his clothes was felt between thumb and finger for concealed papers. They took off his shoes and socks to examine them. When they put them back on, Lee's heart leaped in joy. They are going to take us back, then!

Sure enough, they were loaded back in the car and the return journey began. It took longer than on the way out, and Lee guessed they were entering a different part of the town. He heard the scuff of rope soles on the pavement, and many voices. These townspeople never stopped talking!

The car turned into a quieter street and stopped. Lee and William were quickly lifted out, and dropped on the pavement. The car sped away. For a moment there was silence, then little shuffling sounds as people stole up; they whispered excitedly. Lee heard exclamations of pity. He twisted in his bonds and groaned under the gag. If they're honest, why the hell don't they release us? he thought. He heard the word *policia* repeated.

Finally the police arrived. The bandage was thrown off Lee's eyes, the gag removed, his limbs unwound. A second policeman was questioning the bystanders. All insisted on talking at once. A roar of talk now filled the narrow street. When William was freed he added to it with his mighty cursing.

"In broad daylight! In broad daylight!" he shouted. "What the hell kind of a town do you call this!"

Lee and William were led to the police station in the nearby main street, followed by an ever-increasing crowd. Lee had no doubt that the kidnapers formed part of it, but how could he identify them? He noticed that William was limping.

"Badly hurt?" he asked.

William shook his head. "Only bruised."

"You shouldn't have struggled so hard."

"Couldn't help it . . . In broad daylight! We might as well have been in Chicago!"

"It is possible our efficient friends were trained in our country," said Lee.

"They were after more than our wallets," growled William. "A fat lot of good it's going to do us to tell our story to the police."

"Sure! But we must act the part of good citizens. The police must be allowed to believe that it was just a common robbery."

In the police station they found partial quiet at last. William told their story to a soldierly and courteous inspector. As it proceeded, the officer lost his calm, pounded his desk, and burst into grieved protests. William translated.

"He says such an outrage has never before been perpetrated on this island. Says they have no serious crime here. Says it is all due to the war."

"He's nearer the truth than he suspects," murmured Lee.

The officer broke out afresh when William ended. William translated impassively. "Says they will leave no stone unturned to apprehend the miscreants. Says they can promise us they'll have them in custody within twenty-four hours."

"Police talk the same way in any language," murmured Lee.

William continued: "But how can they convict the scoundrels, he wants to know, if we are not here to identify them?"

"Explain that that would be impossible," said Lee, "but suggest that if they arrest the kidnapers and get evidence against them, we might come back. That may spur the police to greater efforts."

They left a minute description of the stolen property. All this took time, and when they issued from the police station it was near the hour for the launch to return to the ship. The crowd in the street gaped at them as if they had been circus freaks. Out of the crowd appeared Miss Kate McDonald, who clung to Lee's arm, almost weeping.

"Oh, Mr. Brown, what happened? I searched for you everywhere and when I saw you and Mr. Miller led through the streets by the police I nearly fainted!"

Lee suspected that the tearful girl knew exactly what had happened, but consoled himself with the thought that, after all, she hadn't got what she was after. "We weren't the criminals but only the victims," he said dryly.

"How dreadful! How dreadful!" she mourned.

On the launch, and on the ship when they boarded her, Lee and William had to run the gauntlet of incessant questions from the passengers. Lee, fearful of an outbreak from the grim William, answered all as politely as he could. Franklin was on the promenade. He had already heard something of the story and was full of sympathy. Lee noted how eagerly his eyes ran over their persons, looking for evidences of the struggle they had been through.

Later, after Kate McDonald presumably had reported to him, his eyes were glum enough.

Lee was thankful when he got William down to their cabin. A glance around the little room revealed signs that it had had a thorough going-over while they were ashore. Lee did not mention this to the fuming William. Captain Gonçalves presently came to them. He, likewise, was seething with indignation, and it was up to Lee to soothe them both. He told Gonçalves the whole story.

"How could Franklin have engineered such a thing when he never left the ship or sent any radiograms?" said the captain.

"Kate McDonald."

Gonçalves' eyes opened wide. "What makes you think that those two . . ."

"Simply because they have never been seen to speak to each other aboard ship. Young, personable, and unattached, it's not natural."

"Of course!"

"I fancy they're both well known in Ponta Delgada," said Lee, "and McDonald would know exactly whom to approach. She carried Franklin's instructions ashore and the money for the job."

Gonçalves sadly shook his head at the venality of his countrymen.

"It could happen anywhere," said Lee. "These poor fishermen and laborers want us to win, but they cannot resist the temptation of turning a German dollar."

"Well, by God!" cried Gonçalves, striking his fist into his palm; "I'm going to take a chance on it and put Franklin in irons for the balance of the voyage."

Lee laid a hand on his arm. "No, my friend. What would be the result? Franklin would be released in Lisbon, and you censured. We have no evidence."

"Very well! Very well! But that fool of a steward put Franklin at my table simply because he has traveled on this vessel before, and I have to look at his smug face at every meal!"

"No harm to let him see that you don't like his face," said Lee mildly.

CHAPTER THREE

EARLY ON THE MORNING of the ninth day, the *Dom João III* steamed grandly past the noble tower of Belem on the Tagus. An enormous huddle of palaces, churches, convents, and hovels followed, rising from the river as on steps and crowned by a hoary old Moorish fort with square towers. Along the quays at the water's edge spread the markets of the town, and moored to the quays, bow foremost, stretched an endless rank of picturesque fishing boats with lateen sails. In front of the city the narrow river spread out in a wide, placid lake with ferryboats crossing to and fro.

"So this is Lisbon!" murmured Lee. "What's it going to do to us, William?"

"Whatever it does, we can take it," growled William.

The ship was moored to her dock. After the formalities of the customhouse had been concluded, Lee and William taxied to the hotel with their luggage. They crossed fine squares, each with its noble monument in the center, and each surrounded by handsome buildings. Since this part of the city was leveled by an earthquake in 1755, it all bore the formal stamp of the eighteenth century.

The Lisboa Palace was an immense and too-ornamental pile, typical of the European de luxe hotel. Since it was half a century old, its magnificence had become a little old-fashioned and faded, but it still had an air. Like others of its kind, the entrance was deceitfully modest; a revolving door, a small room with four chairs, the "bureau" on one side and the head porter's desk beyond; stairway and lift on the other. All the magnificent public rooms, lounge, restaurant, etc., were above.

"The restaurant is said to be the best in Lisbon," said Lee. "That's why I came here. I am told they serve salt codfish in forty-one styles, all delicious."

"They can keep it," grumbled William.

Lee registered under his own name, and secured a corner suite on the third floor. The door was opened with a big brass key. On one side their windows gave them an oblique view of the Rocío, the principal center of Lisbon, and on the other side they glimpsed a corner of the huge Central Railway Station. The furniture of the suite was upholstered in red velvet with antimacassars over the backs of the chairs and sofas; old-fashioned lace curtains hung at the windows; but the service was such as we have not attained to in America. The smiles of the porter in his striped vest, and the buxom chambermaid, suggested that they had known and loved these *Americanos* for years. Lee knew how to make these smiles permanent.

William immediately set out to find a couple of rooms from which they could conduct their affairs inconspicuously.

"Must be central," suggested Lee, "yet a little retired . . . Try to find a place that has a way out at the back," be added dryly.

William had also to set lines in motion towards finding a trustworthy Portuguese messenger or servant. He had a couple of addresses furnished by Westerholm. "Offer good pay," the consul had suggested, "but not too good or the Portuguese will make up his mind that you are wicked fellows. Almost any Portuguese will serve you faithfully—unless the enemy gets at him with a bigger offer."

Lee taxied to the United States Legation in the western Part of Lisbon to pay a courtesy call. His driver, like the previous one, tore through the streets, sounding his horn continuously. All the other taxis were doing the same. He could speak English after a fashion, and he explained to Lee that if there was an accident, unless he could prove that he had blown his horn he was liable to be convicted of manslaughter. So to be on the safe side he blew it all the time.

At the Legation, Lee, who appeared to be expected, was shown directly into the Minister's private office. He was received by a tall, lanky gentleman, gray-haired, handsome, whose slightly derisive American grin instantly recommended him to Lee's affections. What a satisfaction, after all the Latin faces in the streets! He said:

"Welcome to Lisbon, Mr. Brown! I have been advised of your coming. I know who you are, of course. In fact, I have read one of your books."

"That didn't improve your mind any," said Lee. "Better address me as Mappin, and have done with it."

"But I might when others were present make a slip."

"It wouldn't matter. My presence in Lisbon is already known to the enemy, and I decided to register under my own name. It's more dignified and not a bit more dangerous."

"But how will you account for your trip to Lisbon and your stay here?"

"Amos Lee Mappin has come to Lisbon to gather material for a book. I won't get far with that, of course, but it do for a talking point."

The Minister looked at Lee ruefully. "I suppose it has not occurred to you that your stay here adds to my difficulties."

"How come?" asked Lee.

"Well, I've been advised that the Legation must not under any circumstances give countenance to your activities in Lisbon. I haven't been told what those activities are, but I can guess."

"I'll tell you . . ." began Lee.

The Minister quickly held up his hand. "Don't! If you get into trouble with the Portuguese authorities I will have to go on the stand and swear I know nothing about it. It's a game we all have to play, this neutrality."

"I knew that before I came," said Lee, "but what . . . ?"

"Here's the nib; a broad hint has been conveyed to me that your person is dear to the State Department and to the Administration generally, and that if anything should happen to you in Lisbon, it will be the worse for me."

Lee laughed. "You're a good fellow!"

"Same to you," said the Minister.

"I know quite well," said Lee, "that in Lisbon I am, so to speak, a man without a country. If I get in a jam I shall not call on you. On the other hand, I intend to keep out of jams if it is humanly possible."

"Does the enemy know the nature of your business here?" asked the Minister.

"Not yet. But of course they will know as soon as I get busy."

"You will be in grave danger, Mappin."

"Let's not talk about that."

"You will need a bodyguard. I employ several Portuguese agents. Let me lend you a couple of them."

Lee shook his head. "Better not," he said. "I've already learned that working as a secret agent for one of the powers is a leading industry in Lisbon. Your agents must be known to all the other agents, and if they followed me around, the trail would lead direct to you. Let me find my own bodyguard."

"Lose no time about it," said the Minister earnestly.

"Here's a thing you can do for me," said Lee. "Advise the British Ambassador of my presence in Lisbon, and say what you can in my favor. You might suggest to him that he recommend me to the British consular agents throughout Portugal. They have so many and we have so few."

"I'll do that," said the Minister.

Lee stood up. "One question before I go. Is it proper for you to tell me if you have received any instructions respecting Friedrich Erbelding and his family?"

"No, Mappin. There's no reason why I shouldn't tell you if I had."

"You know who he is, of course?"

"The famous author, certainly."

"The admirers of his books are making a concerted effort to get him out of Germany," said Lee.

"Difficult, Mappin; he makes no secret of his scorn for the government."

"All the more difficult because he has a wife and several small children. He can't leave them behind."

"I had heard he was in a concentration camp."

"He was. Where he is now I don't know. I have to find out."

"Even if he has escaped from Germany," said the Minister, "he would have to cross occupied France and Franco's Spain in order to reach neutral Portugal. And encumbered with a family. I should say it was a sheer impossibility, Mappin."

"Suppose, just for the sake of argument, that he does reach Lisbon," said Lee. "What would you do for him?"

"I'd issue him a temporary United States passport," said the Minister promptly. "A man like that is a citizen of the world."

"Well, wouldn't that be enough?"

The Minister shook his head. "Before he could board a ship or a plane, he would have to have a Portuguese exit visa."

"Any difficulty about that?"

"It depends. Suppose Germany represented to Portugal, as a friendly nation, that Erbelding was a dangerous criminal and asked for his detention?"

"What would Portugal do?"

"Frankly, I don't know. But I know what they would like."

"What is that?"

"They would like to have the Erbeldings smuggled out of the country without their knowledge."

"I see," said Lee. "Thanks for the tip."

"But, Mappin," the Minister continued, "it is useless to talk about diplomatic usage and passports and visas in this case. The Germans will be panic-stricken if Erbelding escapes them. They have good reason to fear what he would write in a free country. If he should reach Lisbon he will never get as far as my office. The Gestapo is here in force. They have had the nerve to hire a hotel."

Lee took out his notebook. "I'd better have that address."

"Hotel Excelsior, Rua Azorrague, 38."

Lee turned towards the door.

"What are your plans?" asked the Minister anxiously.

"I don't know . . . yet," said Lee. "But I have promised not to drag you into it. If you hear anything I suppose you'll let me know."

"Surely! And good luck, Mappin!"

"Thanks. Reckon I'll need every bit of it."

THE DAYS THAT FOLLOWED were busy ones. The *Dom João III*, having discharged her cargo, sailed for New York. William found two rooms in the Rua Cachimbo, 23, that seemed to suit their purpose. It was a street of no special character on the edge of the business district, lined with third-class hotels, small business offices, cheap apartments, and neighborhood stores at the street level. Number 23 was supposed to be a business building; consequently it had no concierge, and the street door was always unlocked. One could enter or leave at all hours without observation.

"That has its disadvantages as well as its advantages," remarked Lee.

"I shan't leave you alone in that building," said William.

"Nonsense! You can't play nursemaid all the time. You have other work to do."

William set his lips obstinately. "The back door of the house opens on a narrow passage or alley," he went on, "that finds its way out to another street."

"Good! That may prove useful."

"Only for a short time," William pointed out. "As soon as they discover that this house is our hangout, they'll watch both entrances."

"We must have other hangouts or hideouts in reserve," said Lee. "What about the house of Pedro Chavez, the fisherman that Westerholm recommended to us?"

"That address is in the Alfama," said William, "the ancient Moorish quarter, a sort of rabbit warren on the slopes that lead up to the castle. I'll visit it tomorrow."

William reported next day that Pedro Chavez' house seemed ideal for their purposes. Teresa Chavez, the wife, lived there alone when her husband and son were away fishing; a woman of character, William said, who enjoyed the respect of her neighbors. A tiny house in an out-of-the-way lane, it contained only three rooms, but Teresa was glad to rent a room to William. Her son could sleep in the kitchen when he came home, she said. There was a secret way out through the garden. The fishermen were expected to return in two days. Lee subsequently visited the house, and approved of the arrangements.

William rounded up a Portuguese youth named Manoel to be
their messenger and general utility man. He was a student of the
university of Coimbra, but assured his new employers that he had
plenty of time on his hands. A typical, happy-go-lucky product of
Lisbon, with a black cape slung over his shoulder, he was forever
singing, whistling or dancing.

"I hope his head is not as empty as it sounds," said Lee.

They determined to keep Master Manoel under observation for
a few days before entrusting him with any confidential work.

To receive their mail and telegrams, Lee engaged a lock box in
the general post office. "I do not believe," he said, "that the enemy
has succeeded in getting his tentacles into the Portuguese post office. If our letters get as far as Lisbon, they will get to us."

In due time William found Pedro Chavez aboard his boat, the
Enguia, moored to the Cais do Sodre. His report was favorable. "A
simple, honest fisherman, strong as an ox, ignorant, but shrewd;
looks on our enemies as his. By paying him something in advance,
I have persuaded him to lie in port for a week while he overhauls
his engine and mends his nets. He will sleep at home and we can
get in touch with him at any time. His boy, Carlos, is eighteen years
old and cast in the same mold as his father."

So far, neither Lee nor William had been followed in the streets.
They were prepared for it as soon as the enemy became organized.
They used taxicabs when they had anything to conceal. It is difficult
to trail a taxi through traffic, and in a taxi you can find out at once if
you are being trailed by another taxi. They wanted to keep the secret of the Rua Cachimbo as long as possible, and it was absolutely
essential to keep their connection with the Chavez family a secret.

For several days now Lee had been established in his "office."
William had put in a desk, a few plain chairs, and a cheap couch.
The previous tenant's telephone was still connected. Otherwise the
rooms were bare. The entrance door was at the head of the first
flight of stairs. From the stair hall you entered an inside room without windows, through which you had to pass in order to reach the
front room, which had two windows looking down on the noisy
street.

Here Lee, by interview, by wire, and by post, had started gathering together the threads of an organization that stretched across Spain and central France to neutral Switzerland—and beyond. Here he received oddly contrasting visitors; a fisherman in a stocking cap, a banker in a silk topper, a railway guard, a Portuguese waterfront bum, and others. There was no sign on the door of the office, only a number.

Lee's first great task was to instruct his agents in the new code, and to make sure that it was passed from one to another. It was not to be written down. His predecessor in this job, in traveling between two stations of the underground, had simply disappeared and been heard of no more. Lee therefore had been instructed by his employers not to leave Lisbon, but to let others do the traveling.

So far the enemy had made no overt move, but Lee and William neglected no precautions. At the Lisboa Palace they had a sitting room and a bedroom beyond, which could be entered only through the sitting room. William insisted on sleeping on a day bed in the outer room, though there were two beds in the bedroom.

"Surely they would never dare to stage a show in this flossy joint," said Lee.

"I don't know," said William. "This old hotel has so many corridors, so many pairs of stairs, so many entrances, so many servants who might be bribed, I wouldn't put it past them."

Finally they discovered that they were followed whenever they left the hotel. It was not far to the office, but they always used a taxi for the journey. When they were followed they went somewhere else, and after a while started out again.

Ronald Franklin and Kate McDonald had both booked at the Lisboa Palace—separately. From time to time they ran into Franklin around the hotel. He was always polite, but betrayed no interest in their movements. After a few days Miss McDonald checked out. She had taken the plane for England, a clerk told them. On the sixth day after their arrival in Lisbon, Franklin ostentatiously bade them good-by. He was flying to Switzerland, he said; would be back in time to catch the next ship for New York. Manoel, sent to the airfield to watch, reported that Franklin had actually boarded the Swiss plane.

Meanwhile, Lee had found a little restaurant on the Largo do Socorro that suited him to a T. It was called the Macaco Branco, a modest place where the proprietor was a Cook, as Lee put it, the greatest prize a stranger could stumble on in a foreign land. They saw the same people there every night, and soon cultivated a bowing acquaintance with all. Stout, middle-class Portuguese, it was by observing them through the windows that Lee had first been led into the place.

Every night, alter returning to the hotel by taxi, they walked to the restaurant, indifferent as to whether they were followed. Lee sampled the Portuguese dishes, one after another, and fell in love with the native *vinho verde*, which is not green at all, but red and sparkling. It had a bouquet, Lee said, as delicious as spring flowers. Afterwards they would go to some little café to hear the *fado* singers.

In spite of all precautions, Lee discovered after a week that their hangout in the Rua Cachimbo had been spotted. From the front windows all day he could see men walking up and down the other side of the street, watching the door. They frequently relieved each other. "Well," said Lee with a shrug, "sooner or later it was inevitable." Next morning, for an experiment, he and William entered from the back street. So far, that door was not watched.

Disquieting news arrived from underground sources. News had leaked out in Germany that Friedrich Erbelding and his family had escaped the country, and Gestapo circles were violently aroused. For a week nothing had been heard from the Erbeldings. Lee's Swiss agents were silent.

"I wish you could fly to Basle and make your way across the border as you have done before," Lee said to William. "We have good friends in Munich. Perhaps you could trace the Erbeldings from there."

"My first duty is to you," said William, scowling. "I couldn't leave you here alone without a guard, without even an interpreter."

"Manoel will do till you get back," said Lee.

"A boy of eighteen!" said William scornfully.

Next morning there was a message from the agent in Grenoble, France, that the Erbeldings had arrived safely and had been passed on to the south.

"Crossing the Spanish border is the greatest risk," said William. "The Gestapo is watching every road."

Four days later, more news came, and it was the worst that could be. Lee's agent in Barcelona reported that, at the request of the German authorities, Friedrich Erbelding had been arrested. The charge was traveling on a forged passport.

Lee carried this to the United States Minister, who promptly telegraphed to the consul in Barcelona, asking him to investigate. In due course there was a reply saying that the Spanish authorities in Barcelona asserted Friedrich Erbelding had escaped from prison, and that his present whereabouts and that of his family were unknown. Nothing further from Lee's agent.

"A likely story!" said Lee bitterly.

"Probably led out by the Gestapo and shot," said the Minister.

Lee flung up his hands and let them fall. "Those little children!"

LEE HAD NO SOONER got back to the office than the telephone rang. He heard the cautious voice of the American Minister asking: "Is that you?" Both men had in mind the danger that the wire might be tapped.

"It's me," said Lee.

"I want to see you."

"Okay, I'll be right over."

As a matter of precaution, Lee and William went out the back way. Consequently they were not followed to the Legation. Lee had recognized from the tone of the Minister's voice that they were not going to hear good news. They found him pacing the floor of his study.

"Thank God I was able to find you!" he said. "The Gestapo has it all fixed to do away with you tonight."

"So soon?" said Lee in an even voice.

The Minister stopped and stared. "Is that all you have to say?"

Lee smiled crookedly. "Well, maybe I'm not so cold-blooded as I'm trying to make out." He dropped in a chair and wiped his face.

"It was only by the merest accident that I learned of it," the Minister went on; "that's what makes me tremble Do you eat at a restaurant called the Macaco Branco?"

Lee nodded.

"I thought so! Two agents of the Gestapo who look like Portuguese, but God knows what their real nationality may be, will be dining there tonight. They plan to pick a quarrel with you in the course of which you'll be knifed. In the confusion they expect to escape through the kitchen."

Lee had recovered himself. "Fancy that!" he said. "How did you hear of it?"

"These agents are a pretty worthless lot," said the Minister. "Many of them, including my own, congregate in a bar near the Cais do Sodre. One of my men happened to hear a whispered conversation in English there. No doubt the thugs thought they were safe in speaking English. You weren't named, but if you eat at the Macaco Branco, of course you're the one they referred to. Keep away from that place as you value your life!"

"But it's an excellent restaurant," protested Lee. "The sole with mussels is as good as it ever was in Paris. In all Lisbon, I doubt if I could find a restaurant that would suit me so well."

The Minister stared. "Surely you're not in earnest, Mappin!"

Lee considered the situation. "If we stop going to that restaurant, they'll find us somewhere else. We'll never know when to expect an attack. But if we beard them there, it will demoralize them. They'll never dare attack us in that place again, and I can at least continue to eat well."

"Consider the risk!"

"William and I will be armed," said Lee in his mild way, "and guns are quicker and more deadly than knives."

"Well, you know your own business best," said the Minister, with many shakes of the head.

"Lee turned to William. "Am I not right?"

"Yes, sir," said William promptly. "If we let them get us on the run we're done for."

AN HOUR LATER, Lee and William were entering the Macaco Branco. There was a long, narrow room with a double line of tables, each set for four. The walls were decorated with tropical scenes, and down at the end wall, looking down the lines of tables, a handsome white monkey sat in an ilex tree. A long time ago these pictures had been painted by a poor artist in payment for his meals. With the passage of years they had become rather dingy, but the worn table linen was snowy and the thick glasses shone like crystal.

It was early, and the tables were not all filled. Lee and William bowed to all the regulars and paused to pass the time of day with the *Senhora* at the counter. Her broad face was wreathed in smiles. These were the only *Americanos* among her guests. She approved of them highly, and hoped they might be the first of many. The table they usually occupied was close to the kitchen door.

"This would be just in line with the plans of our friends," remarked William.

"Let us hope that they will not get to carry out their plans," said Lee.

Lee, keeping the tail of an eye on the street door, studied the *lista de comida*. He ordered a *galhina branca* for the main dish, and with it chose to drink *Colares*, another fragrant local wine that he favored. He and William were sipping it when two burly men entered the restaurant.

"Here they come," said Lee, putting down his glass.

The *Senhora*, seeing new customers, bustled out from behind her counter. She offered them a table near the door, but they ignored it, and came slowly back, looking from side to side as if to choose the places that were most to their liking.

"It's a mistake to suppose that assassins give themselves away in their faces," Lee said to William softly. "Look at these two, with their smooth mugs and their neat and sober, clothes. If you didn't know better, you would swear that they were respectable tradesmen or minor professional men. They are, however, just a little too unself-conscious; they are taking too much pains not to look at us."

William's eyes behind the thick glasses were like points of ice.

The newcomers, having chosen the table next to the Americans, seated themselves and ostentatiously shook out their *guardanapos*. One asked for the *lista*.

Lee took another sip of wine. "Well," he said, "let's get it over with," and pushed his chair back. Facing the two at the next table, he said with slightly exaggerated politeness: "Good evening, gentlemen. I understand that you speak English."

The two men gaped at him like clowns. This was out of line with their well-rehearsed program. Their yellow faces turned slightly greenish. Their team play was broken up. One tried to make believe that he was insulted; the other stammered:

"No, sare! No Angleez! No Angleez!"

The tall William with his glittering blue eyes stood close beside Lee, with his right hand thrust significantly in the pocket of his jacket.

Lee continued in his pleasant voice: "I am told that it is your intention to provoke a quarrel here and in the end to stick a knife in me. I only want to warn you that we are ready for you."

Their mouths fell open; their two faces made a picture of comic dismay. They leaped up so suddenly that their chairs crashed over backward. Snatching their hats, they charged blindly for the door, knocking against the tables, colliding with the waiters. In a flash they were gone. Lee and William looked at each other and laughed.

"*Qué há? Qué há?*" demanded the distressed *Senhora*, clasping her hands.

"Scoundrels! Assassins! Malefactors!" said Lee with gestures.

She got it. A new flood of Portuguese poured from her lips.

"What's she saying?" asked Lee.

"Just thanking you for running them out of the place," said William.

"Tell her the pleasure's mine!"

They resumed their seats and the *galhina branca* appeared from the kitchen, lovely under its blanket of snowy sauce. "Now we can enjoy our dinner," said Lee. "They won't bother us again in this place."

ON THE FOLLOWING MORNING at the office there was a letter from Manoel in the mail. Freely rendered into English, the boy said "with a thousand regrets" that they would not see him any more. He had been warned that it would be extremely unhealthy to work for "O Senhor Mappin." He was young, he said, and he wanted to have some fun before he was liquidated.

"Well, we must try again," said Lee.

CHAPTER FOUR

ONE NIGHT, upon returning to the hotel after listening to the *fado* singers, Lee and William saw an incongruous figure loitering outside the entrance. It was a middle-aged man who looked like a peasant laborer. His hair and beard were matted and soiled, his clothes torn, his hat a wreck. But there was something in the nobility of his glance that made them look a second time.

"This person wants to see you, sir," said the commissionaire, with a contemptuous jerk of his head.

When Lee turned around, a wild eagerness broke in the man's face. "Mr. Mappin?" he stammered. "You are Mr. Mappin?" He spoke English with a strong German accent.

Lee seized his dirty hand in both of his and pressed it.

"Erbelding!" he murmured, completely shaken out of his affectation of calmness. "Thank God! Thank God! We had given you up for lost!"

"You know me?" stammered the man.

"From your pictures . . . Your family?"

"They are safe, too," said the other, ". . . at least they were an hour ago when I left them."

"Where?"

"In the railway station. The most public place seemed to be the safest for them."

"That's right."

"But what an agony of terror they are enduring!"

"Let's go! Let's go!" cried Lee.

"Who is this?" asked Erbelding suspiciously.

"William Miller; a German like yourself who fights for freedom."

They shook hands.

The Central Station was almost next door. As they hastened along the pavement, tears were making channels down Erbelding's grimy cheeks. Lee caught up his hand and pressed it.

"Don't notice me!" Erbelding murmured, "It is the relief! . . . We have been through so much! . . . And such a slender hope of finding help here! . . . The blessed face of a friend . . ."

"Don't talk," said Lee. "There'll be time later."

At the foot of the stairs leading up to the station, Erbelding held back. "What if the police have laid a trap for me here?" he said nervously. "I have no papers. Anybody is privileged to arrest me!"

Lee thought fast. "Look, William, engage a taxi, and have it wait here at the foot of the stairs. Let Mr. Erbelding sit inside it where he can't be seen, and you stand on the curb with your hand on the door so I'll know which is the right cab when I come back."

Erbelding wrung his hands. "She won't come with you. I have instructed her not to move under any circumstances."

Lee pulled out his notebook. "She is familiar with your hand. Write her a note on a page of my book. Write: 'This is our friend, Mr. Mappin. Come!' And sign it 'Friedrich.'"

It was done, and, slipping the book in his pocket, Lee scampered up the stairs. In the big waiting room there was no chance of mistaking the group he was looking for. There they sat, a young flaxen-haired German woman, with three little towheads pressing against her. All four faces, frozen with terror, were still turned towards the archway through which their man had disappeared. They were miserably unwashed and uncombed, and they had not even so much as a lunch box to carry.

Also, across the room, Lee saw two cagey-looking, well-dressed men—obviously somebody's secret agents, how well he knew the type by now!—watching the Erbeldings.

Lee went quickly to the mother and her babes, and the two watching men became alert. Lee said: "I am Mr. Mappin. Your husband is waiting outside in a cab. Was afraid of running into a trap. Come with me and you'll be safe."

All four pairs of clear blue eyes studied Lee's round face with a heartbreaking look of doubt. Even the youngest, who could not have been more than three. Lee thought with a kind of fury: There are men in the world who could betray such innocence! Slipping the notebook out of his pocket, be showed the young woman her husband's message in such a way that the watchers across the room could not see what he was doing. The two men were edging nearer.

She made up her mind.

"Come, children," she said in German. "This is our friend."

Lee picked up the youngest, the mother took the other two by the hand, and they started for the stairs. The two men followed. The children's lips were pressed together; none made any sound. The little one in Lee's arms leaned away from him a little, still piteously searching his face as if she dared not let herself believe that help had come.

At the foot of the broad stairs a taxi was waiting beside the walk, with William Miller holding the door open. The father spoke quietly to them from inside and, suddenly coming alive, the children scrambled in, followed by their mother. Lee said to the driver:

"Rua Cachimbo, 23."

William squeezed in last. "Those men were near enough to hear you," he murmured to Lee.

"Okay," said Lee. "That's part of the scheme."

They drove away. Looking through the back window, Lee saw the two men enter another cab and follow. Inside, the children were distributed on their parents' laps. There was much clinging and soft weeping, but an enormous relief could be felt in the air.

"*Ich hab' Hunger! Ich hab' Hunger*," whimpered the little one.

"They haven't had anything since morning," explained the mother apologetically.

"I'll take care of that," growled William.

The ride was a short one. As they turned into the Rua Cachimbo, Lee said to William:

"You run upstairs and turn on the lights in the front room, and leave them burning. We'll go right on through the back and get another cab for the Alfama. Follow us as fast as you can."

"Right;" said William. "I'll buy food on the way."

"Get plenty."

They drew up at number 23 and piled out on the walk. As he shepherded his charges through the door, Lee, out of the tail of his eye, saw the following car stop some yards behind them. One man stood beside it, watching, while the other darted into a shop. To telephone! thought Lee.

Leaving William to pay the taxi, the others by-passed the stairs and went on out through the back door into a narrow passage which led them into a wider lane and thence into an unfrequented street. Throughout this little journey the children were as quiet as mice. Lee thought: They've learned to take whatever comes!

The little street brought them to a thoroughfare where stores were still open and traffic passing. Here they climbed into another cab and Lee gave a new address; he now had enough Portuguese to get around with.

"Calcado Burro at the end of Rua dos Bacalhoeiros."

They sped away with the usual squawking of the horn. Lee looked out of the back window until he was certain no other cab was following.

"You can relax now," he said. "The danger is past."

This was a longer drive, and Friedrich Erbelding had time to tell part of his story. "It was in Grenoble," he began, "that I first heard the name of Amos Lee Mappin as one who had come to Lisbon to help us and others like us. It remained in my memory. In occupied France we found friends. We were traveling on a false German passport. There was no difficulty until the fact of our escape from Germany became known; then the Gestapo began searching for us everywhere."

"How did you get across the Spanish border?" asked Lee.

"I engaged a fishing vessel to bring us from Perpignan in France to a point on the coast of Spain near Barcelona. It cost me dear, but it was the only way. In Barcelona I was arrested and thrown into prison, and my family detained in another place. My passport, my money and credits, everything I possessed, was taken from me. I shall arrive in my new home a pauper!"

"Don't worry about that part," said Lee. "You'll be taken care of."

"Charity!" said Erbelding bitterly.

"Not at all! Your books sell widely in America. There will be royalties waiting for you, lecture dates if you want them; and you can write more books . . . Go on with your story."

"When I was thrown into prison," Erbelding continued in a low voice, "I thought it was the end. You can imagine my feelings in respect to these helpless beings who depend on me. I cannot tell you exactly what happened; I have no Spanish. In Barcelona there are many brave Republicans. I suppose bribes were paid. In the night I was led out of prison and brought to my family by unknown friends. We were given tickets on the express to Madrid, some money to buy food, and the address of another Republican in Madrid. By a miracle we found him.

"The Gestapo is very strong in Madrid, and I was advised that it would be impossible to travel further by railway. A cart and a driver were secured for us, and we were driven by unfrequented roads to the Portuguese border. We slept in farmhouses. The people were kind. Poor people everywhere are kind. The driver put me over the border by a smugglers' path. Then he had to leave us. We walked the rest of the way to Lisbon, sleeping where we could. That is why you find us in such a state."

"Good God!" murmured Lee. "These little kids!"

"In Lisbon," Erbelding continued simply, "I didn't know where to go. I knew the Gestapo was here, too. All I had was a name I had heard in Grenoble; Amos Lee Mappin. I inquired the way to the leading hotel and I learned that you were living there. So I waited and you came!"

"America will try to make it up to these children for what they have been through," said Lee.

"It is my dream!" murmured their father.

They left the taxi at the opening to a steep and narrow street that presently broke into steps continuing up. This was the Alfama,

a maze of narrow alleys running up and down in every direction,
breaking into steps, diving under archways, crossing bridges over
alleys below. Here and there, on an angle that was not covered with
buildings, grew a tree.

"No wheeled traffic in this part of town," said Lee. "Only donkeys!'

Late as it was, there was plenty of life in the quarter. From
within the houses came the sound of guitars and singing; endless
conversation. Cloaked figures loitered in the doorways or gossiped
companionably from balcony to balcony overhead. Lee, counting
the corners, turned to the left and presently knocked on a heavy
oaken door. This alley ended in a cul-de-sac.

"Looks like a trap," said Lee, "but there's a way out in the rear."

The door was opened by a neatly dressed Portuguese woman,
old before her time. This was Teresa Chavez. She started to frown
at the soiled and bedraggled travelers. Lee, she knew. Lee pushed
forward the little children and her face melted. She murmured compassionately and led the way through a tiled passage to the room
at the back that William had engaged for such an emergency. It
was a good-sized room and contained two big beds. The German
woman's harassed face lighted up at the sight as at a glimpse of
heaven.

Lee, indicating the children to the landlady, said:

"*Banho!*"

The Portuguese woman's voluble answer floored him. He could
only shake his head and pull at his ears. However, it was clear she
agreed that baths were desirable. Never ceasing to talk, she
dropped to her knees beside the littlest one and unfastened its
jacket. The child, staring with round eyes, made no objection.

The mother understood the other woman better than Lee did.
Pointing to the baby, she said: "Katti," to the little boy "Hansi,"
and to the bigger girl "Trud'l."

Flinging her arms around Katti, Teresa administered a whole
fusillade of kisses. The alarmed child looked imploringly at her
mother, but said nothing.

William presently arrived laden with bottles of milk, loaves of
bread, butter, cheese, cooked meat, and oranges. How the

children's eyes glistened! Their mother said firmly: "They must be washed before they eat," and the three small faces fell.

"Have a heart!" said Lee. "They'll have to be washed afterwards anyhow."

The mother relented. The food was spread on the table and the children fell to. Lee watched them with delight. "Me, I'm fond of my food, too," he said, "so I have a fellow-feeling." When the edge of their appetite was taken off, they began to chatter quietly together in German between bites.

Meanwhile, William had gone downstairs to the kitchen with Teresa to consult about baths. The little house had two rooms on the street level and a kitchen below, that looked out on a tiny garden. William reported that there was no plumbing in the ancient house, but Teresa was already fetching water from the fountain, and there was plenty of fuel in the house to heat it.

"We will leave you now," said Lee at last. "You are safe here, so have a good sleep. Teresa is provided with funds to purchase new clothes and whatever else you may need."

Erbelding started to protest.

"I'm not paying for this," said Lee, waving his hands. "The money is put up by the admirers of your books in America . . . We'll be back tomorrow," he went on. "You mustn't be anxious if it is late before we get here. We'll be closely watched and we must take no unnecessary risk of leading them here."

Lee and William backed out of the room, embarrassed by the travelers' expressions of gratitude. Little Katti slipped out of her chair and, running to Lee, held up her arms to be lifted so she could kiss him with a bread-and-buttery mouth.

CHAPTER FIVE

NEXT MORNING, Lee was eating breakfast in his sitting room at the hotel when William came in. William had gone out earlier to see what arrangements he could make.

"Had good luck," he said briefly. "The fishing smack *Enguia* is still lying at the Cais do Sodre and Pedro was aboard her. He is willing to make the voyage to the island of Fayal." William named a sum of money.

"Not too much," said Lee.

"He asked double," said William, "and according to instructions I bargained with him. He expected it."

"When can he sail?"

"Tonight."

"Good!"

"It is customary for the fishing boats to sail at night," William explained, "so it won't attract any attention. The *Enguia* has a small cabin. The crew will sleep outside. I don't suppose our friends will object to the hardships, after what they have been through."

"Not likely," said Lee. "Wouldn't it be dangerous, though, to embark the Germans in a public place like the Cais do Sodre?"

"We talked about that. Chavez suggested that we carry them to Belem by car. At ten o'clock tonight he will come ashore in a small boat to pick them up at a point on the beach a hundred yards west of the big tower. No one will be hanging around there at such a time, he said, unless we are followed."

"We'll take care of that," said Lee.

"I gave him some more money on account," William went on, "to lay in provisions for the passengers, including tinned milk, fruit, and so on for the children. Also clean bedding, towels, soap, and other things. Chavez is to receive the balance from Westerholm upon the delivery of his passengers at Fayal."

"Good!" said Lee. "You thought of everything."

"I called at Teresa's house," said William. "Everything okay there. Our friends were still sleeping. I left word for them to be ready to start at nine tonight."

After William had eaten something, Lee proposed that they visit the Rua Cachimbo. "We must make it appear to those who are watching us that we are keeping to our usual routine."

They took a taxi from the hotel and were followed by another. One of their trailers took up his post opposite number 23, while the other went to telephone. Lee found the outer door to their offices broken in. It bore only a flimsy lock and the damage was not great. Inside, the electric light was still burning. The place bore signs of having been ransacked, but that troubled them little, because all compromising letters and telegrams were destroyed as soon as read and digested.

Five minutes after their arrival, a dandy young officer of police entered the office, complete with cocked hat, sword, and white gloves. Saluting smartly, he said: "I am sent by the Minister of Police to request the Senhor Mappeen to accompany me to the Ministry."

Lee's eyebrows ran up.

"With pleasure," he said, rising.

When William also rose, the officer said: "The presence of this gentleman is not necessary."

"He's *got* to come," said Lee firmly. "He's my secretary and interpreter."

The officer acquiesced with a shrug.

In an official car they sped through the streets, attended by outriders on motorcycles. Driving into the courtyard of a palatial building, they were conducted through corridors and a waiting room into a private office. An important-looking young officer in uniform arose with a bow and introduced himself as "Inspector da Gama." He spoke English.

"A distinguished name in Portugal," said Lee, bowing.

To the right of the inspector's desk sat a magnificent personage, elderly, tall, and slender, in impeccable morning dress. He did not rise. The cropped head and dangling monocle, the scarred cheek, proclaimed his nationality. Beside him sat a little stooge, whose anxious eyes were continually searching his master's face. On the other side of the inspector at a smaller desk sat a secretary-interpreter, who took down Lee's answers. There was nobody else in the room.

The personage screwed his monocle into his face and looked Lee over arrogantly.

"And who is this gentleman?" Lee asked very politely.

"He attends on behalf of a nation friendly to my country," said the inspector. There was a hint of dryness in his voice.

Lee bowed ironically to the personage. "Charmed!" he murmured.

The personage allowed the glass to fall out of his eye and looked straight ahead.

Lee introduced William, and they seated themselves facing the inspector. The latter said:

"Senhor Mappin, I have to ask you a few questions."

"By all means!" said Lee with careful politeness. "May I inquire if it is on behalf of the Portuguese government or of the government of this gentleman? This gentleman's government may be friendly to the government of Portugal, but I doubt its friendliness to *my* government."

The inspector bit his lip. "It is the Portuguese government that desires information," he said.

"Then, if I may ask," said Lee, "why does this gentleman honor us with his presence during the interrogation?"

"Patience, senhor. That will presently appear."

Lee was heartened by a certain brightness that had appeared in the officer's eye. The personage must have sensed it, too, but it was nothing he could object to. He became stiffer than ever. His little attendant looked terrified.

"Mr. Mappin, what is your business in Lisbon?" asked the inspector.

"By profession I am an author," said Lee. "I am about to write a book about your beautiful city and I am here to gather material for it."

"We are honored," said the inspector, bowing. "Why, if you are only an author, was it necessary for you to rent an office on the Rua Cachimbo?"

"I have to know the people of Lisbon," said Lee. "I walk about and make the acquaintance of fishermen, porters, newsboys, all kinds. I could not talk to such people in the Lisboa Palace, so I ask them to come to this humble office where I can question them about their lives."

A sound like a snort escaped the personage, but the inspector of police was pleased with this answer, which let him out.

He took a new tack. "Mr. Mappin, I am informed that you met a woman with three children at the Central Station last night and carried them to the Rua Cachimbo."

"That is correct, Senhor Inspector."

"Who were these people?"

"I forget the name," said Lee blandly; "some common German name like Schmidt."

"Senhor," protested the inspector, "how could you so soon forget the name of people you were appointed to meet?"

"There was no appointment, senhor. The meeting was accidental. When my secretary and I returned to the hotel last night, a wretched man accosted me at the door. He had brought his wife and children to Lisbon, he said, and here they were without money or food. I had never seen the man before, but my heart was touched by his story. I hastened back to the station with him and picked up his family. I gave them money for food. They said they had friends in Oporto and I supplied them with money for the tickets. That's where they've gone, I suppose."

"There were no more trains to Oporto last night, senhor."

"Well, they had money enough for a night's lodging. They took the morning train, no doubt."

"Senhor, why did you find it necessary to leave the house on Rua Cachimbo by the back door?"

"Because we had been followed to the front door," said Lee quickly. "It appears that I am followed in Lisbon wherever I go."

"Not by my men," said the inspector.

"I didn't think it was," said Lee.

"Senhor," said the inspector, "this man you assisted is described to us as a dangerous criminal seeking to escape justice."

"Really!" said Lee, opening his eyes wide. "Of course I knew nothing about this. One does not think of hungry little children as criminals."

"You are right, senhor. Where did you feed them?"

"I could not take them to a restaurant," said Lee. "They were, well, too dirty, senhor. We stopped at a shop and my secretary went in to buy food. They fed themselves in the taxi, while we took another cab and returned to our hotel."

"The address of the food shop?"

William gave it.

The personage rose abruptly. A rusty flush was creeping up over his withered neck and into his cheeks. "Enough!" he said harshly. "This man is lying, as you are well aware, Inspector. It makes a farce of your neutrality! Senhor Salazar shall hear of this!" He marched out of the room with the little stooge creeping at his heels and casting terrified glances behind him.

Lee and the inspector exchanged a glance—not entirely neutral. "Senhor," said the latter gravely, "believe me, you are in the most extreme danger. Unless you can satisfy me that there is nothing in this gentleman's charge, I can't give you the protection of the police."

"I don't want it," said Lee guardedly. "If you will let me have a car, I'll drive directly to the United States Legation and ask the protection of our Minister."

The inspector looked relieved. "That would be much the better plan. The car you came in is waiting in the courtyard." Coming out from behind the desk, he offered his hand. "How do you say it? Good lok, senhor."

They drove to the Legation with their hooting escort. At the door Lee said to the police chauffeur: "Do not wait for me. It may be some time before I can obtain an audience with His Excellency, the Minister. I will take a taxi back to my hotel."

The moment the Minister caught sight of Lee he said: "You have brought important news?"

"Bless me!" said Lee. "Do I give everything away in my face."

"Only to a friend."

"Well, it's true. The friends whom we gave up for lost have turned up in Lisbon."

"What are you saying?" cried the Minister, staring. "Is it true? . . . Well, thank God! Where are they?"

"For your own sake, you'd better not know," said Lee. "Safe for the present."

"Right! The next thing is to get them out of Lisbon."

"It's all arranged," said Lee. "For tonight."

Striding across the room, the Minister clapped Lee on the shoulder. "Mappin, you're a wonder!"

"I almost think I am!" said Lee, grinning.

"Can I help?"

"Yes. I suspect the Gestapo may force the Lisbon police to send out a general alarm for the little family. Three little towheaded kids, fatally easy to identify in this dark-haired city! Therefore, I dare not transport them in taxicabs. Have you a car in the establishment that doesn't show the United States coat of arms that I could borrow for tonight?"

"They all have to carry the official license plates, but I have private plates for an emergency."

"And a chauffeur you can trust? The Gestapo knows that our family is in Lisbon."

"I think I can trust him, but he's not an American . . . No, by God! If you need a chauffeur I'll drive the car myself!"

Lee shook his head decisively. "If you were discovered it would provoke a diplomatic crisis. William can be the chauffeur. It's only that I don't want him to have to come here to get the car."

"Very well, I'll have my chauffeur park the car on the east side of the Praça do Carmo—you know where that is? North of the Rua Garrett."

Lee nodded.

"He will lock the car," the Minister went on, "and bring me the key. I'll send the key by another servant to you at your hotel."

"Good!" said Lee. "William will pick up the car at the Praça do Carmo about 7:15."

"Mr. Mappin," put in William agitatedly, "I can't leave your side on a day like this."

Lee wagged his hand soothingly. "Now, William, don't begin that again. We're in the same danger, alone or together, the same for me, and a greater danger for you."

William frowned. "But Mr. Mappin . . ."

"We'll discuss that later," said Lee. To the Minister he went on: "Could you furnish Erbelding a United States passport just on my say-so?"

"Not the customary passport. But I can give him a letter that will carry him past all United States officials. And of course I'll cable the State Department that he's on the way." He sat down to write the letter on the spot. "What's the wife's name?"

"Gertrude."

"And the children?"

"Trud'l, aged seven, Hansi five, and Katti three."

The seal of the United States was affixed to this document, and the Minister handed it over. As Lee and William were leaving, he said longingly:

"I wish I could go all the way in this with you two men."

"You have trouble enough," said Lee.

AT HALF-PAST SIX Lee set out for the Macaco Branco as usual. William was to take a different course and have the legation car waiting in the Rua dos Bacalhoeiros at the mouth of Calcado Peixe at nine o'clock. The keys of the car had been received. William was still reluctant to divide forces.

"It gives us two chances," said Lee. "If you should be stopped I can chance taking the Erbeldings to Belem by taxi, and if I am stopped you can run up the back way and fetch them to your car. Do not be anxious about me. I will not be liquidated as long as they think I may lead them to the Erbeldings. After they find out that their prey has escaped them, then look out!"

Lee was followed to the restaurant by two men. These men—not the same two that he had put to rout on a former occasion—watched from the little square opposite the restaurant. Lee ate his dinner with his customary deliberation. When he paid his shot he said to the *Senhora*: "I want to pay my compliments to the cook." Maybe she understood him, maybe not. At any rate, he went back into the kitchen. It was a tidy place with rows of copper pots hanging from above. There was a door with glass panes giving on an alley, but—alas for Lee's plans!—one of the watchers had come around and was loafing in the alley.

Lee had no intention of trusting himself alone with the man in a dark alley; he returned through the restaurant and asked the *Senhora* to phone for a cab. When it came, he climbed in and had himself driven to the Central Station. On the night before, he had unconsciously noted the layout of the station. It had two broad stairways, one on each side. Lee scampered up one side, ran across the concourse as fast as his short legs would carry him and down the other stairway. The sight of a running man in a railway station attracted no particular attention. At the foot of the stairs he dived into the first taxi in the rank.

"Take me to Black Horse Square," he said.

The ruse was successful. He was not followed. After waiting about at the square for a minute or two to make certain, he took another cab to the Rua dos Bacalhoeiros. No other cab tailed him; he let out a long breath of relief and relaxed.

At Teresa's house he found the Erbelding family all dressed in their new clothes and ready to go. After twenty-four hours of rest and good feeding, Trud'l, Hansi, and Katti looked as good as new. Each member of the family now had a little satchel to carry, and the father a small tin trunk ready to hoist on his shoulder. Lee glanced at these objects with some anxiety; another means of ready identification. However, if William kept the appointment, they would only be exposed to the public view for a few seconds.

Lee explained the plans that had been made for them. The mother paled a little at the thought of an ocean voyage in a fishing smack, but said nothing; the father was dumb with gratitude. Afterwards, all sat in a strained silence waiting for the zero hour. Teresa kept offering the children more food until they turned away their heads. She stuffed their pockets with bananas.

At five minutes to nine, Lee, with a final glance at his watch, said: "Well, let's go!"

Teresa burst into noisy weeping and embraced the children one after another. She led them out the back door of the house and across a tiny garden to a door in the garden wall. Here they left her, wiping her eyes on her apron.

Turning to the right in a narrow passage between walls, they went down a flight of steps, passed under a building through a sort of tunnel, and found themselves in a narrow, winding street. This was the Calcado Peixe, which ran steeply down to the Rua dos Bacalhoeiros. The passage of Lee's little party attracted a good deal of notice from the loiterers in the doorways; however, there were no policemen in this out-of-the-way lane. What Lee feared was the brightly lighted street below. Big in his mind loomed the question: Will William be there?

At the last turn in the Calcado, Lee halted his convoy in the shadow while he looked around. His heart gave a leap of joy when he saw the big black Legation car resting squarely across the opening below, with William sitting at the wheel. A slight puffing at the rear told him that the engine was running.

They hastened down the last few yards. William saw them coming, and, leaning out, opened the rear door. They scrambled in, the door slammed, and the car started westward. The three children sat on the floor so that no telltale white heads should show through the windows.

Keeping to the level streets close to the river, William drove at customary Portuguese breakneck speed. At such a speed there was little danger of a chance recognition through the windows. Westward to Black Horse Square, across the Cais das Columnas, the Praça do Municipio, past the long Marine Arsenal, and back to the quays again. To reach Belem they had to cross the whole of Lisbon. There was no conversation. The little children crouched in the bottom of the limousine without making a sound.

So speedy was their passage that they reached Belem almost half an hour too soon. Lee had William drive on to the west for several miles at a more moderate speed and back again. Nobody took any interest in their progress. Finally William drew up at the corner of a quiet street in Belem. He had been over the whole route earlier in the evening.

"This is the nearest we can drive to the beach," he said.

Off to the right the great medieval fortress rose against the stars, with its battlemented tower like a gigantic pepper shaker. Turning to the left, they silently proceeded through a lane between garden walls, meeting nobody. Another sharp turn brought them out on a shingly beach. The black river lapped it softly and, stretching away, lost itself in the night. Far away, pin-point lights sparkled.

Glancing at the shadowy tower, William said: "This is about a hundred yards east."

"He might not land at this exact spot," said Lee. "Better walk up and down."

William vanished in the darkness. The others sat against an overturned boat to wait. Soon William reappeared, saying:

"Pedro is coming."

A heavy boat pulled by two men grounded on the shingle. The oarsmen got out and joined the waiting group.

"This is Pedro," said William, "and this is Carlos."

In the dark, Lee had to take them on trust; however, there was something in their tall, lean figures, in the way they kept their heads up, in the firm clasp of their hard hands, and in their deep, male voices that inspired confidence.

The final arrangements were quickly made. It appeared they had made other voyages to the western islands; they had worked for Mr. Westerholm; they knew his place; there was a little beach immediately below his house where the passengers could be put ashore in secrecy and safety.

"How about petrol?" asked Lee.

"We have sufficient for the outward journey, senhor. Senhor Westerholm will provide for the return."

"He will be expecting you," said Lee. "I'll cable."

"Make your mind at ease, senhor," said Pedro in his deep, slow voice. "The accommodations are rough, but we have carried a lady before and she did not complain. There is plenty to eat and drink. Your friends will be in good hands!"

"Good luck to you all!" said Lee.

He squatted down to give each of the children a hug. At a word from their father, the stoical little beings allowed the fishermen to lift them into the boat. The father and mother clung to Lee's and to William's hand, struggling to find speech to thank them.

"Not a word!" protested Lee. "We'll meet again in happier days and talk our heads off!"

The father and mother followed their children and the fishermen pushed off. Lee and William followed the boat with their eyes until darkness swallowed it. They returned to the car.

CHAPTER SIX

THE LOCK ON THE OFFICE DOOR in the Rua Cachimbo was repaired. Lee and William continued to spend a while there every day as a feint. Meanwhile, William found another room where they could carry on their business over one of the jewelry shops in the Rua Augusta. This was near the post office where they had to go every day. By the reckless use of taxicabs, with many changes en route, they kept the secret of their new address from those who continually watched and followed them.

Lee grew weary of the continual espionage. The spies were often changed. One night, walking from the restaurant to the hotel, they found themselves trailed by two new men. These looked like Portuguese, and therefore less formidable than the usual hard-faced men without a country. Lee said to William:

"Let's brace them, just for fun."

Turning around, they walked up to their sleuthhounds, who became extremely self-conscious and tried to pass. Lee planted himself squarely in their path. They were in front of a motion picture theater.

"Good evening, gentlemen," said Lee pleasantly. "Wouldn't you enjoy seeing this show?" At the same time he showed them the corner of a fifty-escuda bill, which represented a couple of dollars American.

These were simple fellows and, being found out, they couldn't think of anything else to do but accept Lee's offer. They nodded and grinned. Lee gave them each one of the bills, bought them tickets at the bureau, and saw them inside the swinging doors. After lingering a minute to make sure they didn't come out again, Lee and William walked on.

"Now I feel as light as air," said Lee. "We can mooch about a while and see the sights."

Crossing the Rocío, the principal square where the *electricos* start, they were accosted by a newsboy whose post was on an island between two streams of traffic. He was about seventeen years old. Half boy, half man, he wore his ragged clothes with a gallant air, cap cocked on one side of his head, and a damaged carnation in his buttonhole. The expression of good-humored impudence in his bright eyes appealed to Lee.

Sizing up Lee from head to foot in a lightning glance, the youth drew a paper from his bundle, saying: "Americano gentleman. I spik Americano; hokay; out of this world!" He thrust the paper under Lee's nose. "Here you are, gentleman; *New York Times!*"

Lee, having a mind to draw him out, affected to scowl and shake his head angrily. "*Nein! Nein! Deutscher!*"

The youth turned his head and spat on the pavement with inimitable contempt.

Lee was delighted. "Here, give me that paper!" he said. "I was fooling you. So you don't like Germans."

In untranslatable Portuguese, the young man voiced his opinion of the race.

"Walk along beside me a little," said Lee. "I've got a proposition to make you . . . William, how the hell do you say proposition?"

"He's got the idea," said William dryly.

Lee passed the young fellow a folded fifty-escudas note. "What's your name?"

"Bosco, gentleman." He executed a few dance steps.

"Listen, Bosco. The Gestapo hangs out at a hotel in the Rua Azorrague, 38. I'll pay well for any important information you can bring me from there. Get me?"

Bosco nodded.

"I don't expect you to get inside the building, but I know they employ Portuguese servants. You can pal up with them."

An enthusiastic nod from Bosco. Obviously he was charmed by the opportunity of doing a little secret service.

"Is this your regular stand?" asked Lee.

"Yes, gentleman."

"Go on selling your papers here each night," Lee continued. "My friend and I will be passing by. Always offer us a paper before you say anything, because we are usually followed. I'll tip you off where we can meet. And listen, Bosco. My name is Mappin. Say it."

"Senhor Mappeen."

"Right. What I specially want to know is anything the Germans say about me. Savvy?"

"Hokay, gentleman."

After they had passed on, Lee said to William: "Of course, I'm taking a chance on the boy; but if he does sell us out to the Germans, they can't hate us any worse than they do already. At the same time, I have a hunch that this boy is going to serve us."

"When he does have something to report to us," said William, "how will you arrange to receive it? We can't shake off our trailers every night."

"He can telephone to the hotel."

"The Germans may have got at the switchboard operators."

"We'll test that out when we get back."

In the hotel, they paused in the lounge before going upstairs. The effulgent Miss Kate McDonald came swimming to greet them. In a black dinner dress with rhinestones, she looked dazzling.

"Mr. Brown!" she cried. "I'm so glad to find you! I just got back. I asked for you at the bureau, but they said there was no such person stopping here."

"I'll tell you a secret," said Lee. "My name is not Brown, but Mappin; Amos Lee Mappin."

"Ohh! Then you're the famous author!"

"Not too famous," said Lee.

"I have always wanted to know a famous author!" she gushed. "I would so like to be able to write myself . . . I'm just going in for a late dinner. Won't you join me?"

"Sorry," said Lee, "we have just eaten. We're full to the neck."

"Too bad!" said Miss McDonald. "I have a holiday for a few days. Can't we see a little of this town together?"

"Delightful!"

"How about tomorrow?"

"Sorry! Tomorrow my secretary and I are booked up all day."

"Well, I'll be seeing you again." She sailed away.

As Lee made for the lift he growled to William: "Is it possible the fool woman still thinks I'm not on to her? . . . She's very handsome," he added regretfully. "I'll call up the Legation now."

William returned downstairs to watch the switchboard.

From his sitting room above, Lee called up the Legation. Getting the Minister on the wire, he said:

"I have a little piece of news for you. My fellow traveler, Miss Kate McDonald, is back. You remember what I told you about her."

"Surely. The British Embassy will be interested. And in return for your piece of news, here is one for you. I have a dispatch from Basle saying that your other fellow traveler, Ronald Franklin, has booked a place on the plane for Lisbon tomorrow."

"Really! What a coincidence!"

"I'll have him met at the airport in the afternoon, and report further."

"Many thanks," said Lee.

In a few minutes William came upstairs. He said: "I had my eye on the switchboard girl while you were talking. She didn't know I was watching her."

"Did she make notes of the conversation?" asked Lee.

William shook his head. "Didn't even listen. She was gossiping with a friend on another wire."

"Good!" said Lee. "Then that means of communication is open."

BEFORE STARTING OUT for dinner next day, Lee called up the Legation again. "What about our traveler from Basle?" he asked.

"Sorry," said the Minister ruefully. "My friends, after seeing him descend from the plane, lost him on the way into town."

After dinner, as Lee and William returned across the Rocío trailed at a distance of fifty yards by a couple of men who were certainly not Portuguese, they saw Bosco again. He thrust a paper at Lee. The young fellow's speaking eyes proclaimed that he already had something to report. To gain a moment, Lee dropped the paper and, as Bosco picked it up, murmured: "Wait a while and phone me at the Lisboa Palace." With the change for the paper, he passed Bosco a bill folded small. Bosco palmed it as expertly as a magician.

Later, in their suite, William took down Bosco's communication over the phone, since the young fellow was more fluent in Portuguese. Lee, listening with some impatience, was surprised at the length of it.

"Smart lad, that," said William when he hung up. "Apparently you were not mistaken in him." William read from his notes, translating as he went: "Bosco hung around the Rua Azorrague all morning. All the people in that neighborhood spend their time gossiping about the Germans. They are well hated, Bosco says. With his bundle of papers under his arm, he can go anywhere without attracting attention. He scraped acquaintance with a Portuguese fellow who is employed by the Germans as a porter and messenger.

"The porter couldn't tell him anything, but he had a friend, also Portuguese, who operates the lift in the hotel and does various inside jobs. This man has picked up quite a little German while working there, and as the Germans don't realize it, they sometimes give themselves away in his hearing. He said he had heard your name but couldn't connect it with anything. Bosco, the porter, and the lift operator met in a *leiteria* at lunch time. Bosco said he didn't get much from them then, but he divided the fifty escudos, and so laid the foundation of a beautiful friendship.

"At six-thirty," William continued, "when the porter and the lift operator came off work, the three met again at the same place. The lift operator said a new German had arrived during the afternoon. He understood this man had come from the airport. He carried a suitcase. He was a tall, blond fellow, maybe thirty years old, wearing American-style clothes. He Heil-Hitlered with all the other Germans. This would be Franklin, of course."

Lee smiled. "We'll have him if he tries to travel on that American passport again!"

"As Franklin went into a room with the other Germans," William continued, "the lift operator heard your name spoken. Then the door closed and he could hear no more. Shortly after five, Franklin left the hotel. The lift operator carried his suitcase out to the curb and heard him tell the taxi driver to take him to the Victoria. That's all."

"Excellent!" said Lee. "Tomorrow night I'll give Bosco a hundred escudos."

With a smile, Lee then called up the Legation. When he got the Minister on the wire, he said, not without malice:

"I can add a little to your news of our friend from Basle."

"What's that?"

"Upon leaving the airport he drove direct to the hotel of our acquaintances in the Rua Azorrague. After spending a couple of hours in consultation with them, he was driven to the Hotel Victoria."

"Ha!" said the Minister sorely. "You enjoy better service than I do!"

WHEN THEY RETURNED to their suite after dinner on the following night, a note in a plain envelope was brought to their door.

"Where did this come from?" asked Lee.

"Delivered just now by a private messenger, senhor. He said there would be no answer."

On a plain sheet of paper inside appeared two lines of typewriting; no superscription; no signature:

> The Hotel Excelsior has discovered that Herr E. and
> family have escaped the country. A word to the wise.

"This was inspired by Inspector da Gama," said Lee. "He's a good fellow."

Soon after, there was a call from Bosco. William, after taking down his communication, reported to Lee.

"This afternoon about three a gray sedan stopped before the door of the Hotel Excelsior in the Rua Azorrague. This was a private car, not a taxicab. It was driven by a tall young man with a wicked-looking face; has a scar down one side. A short, heavy-built man got out and went in. Had a face so ugly you would never forget it, Bosco said, like a *Cão de fila*, he means bulldog. The grey car drove away. After a little while the young man with the scarred face came back on foot and went into the hotel. So Bosco assumed he had put the car in a garage and that these two are going to stop at the Excelsior. The car carried a French license plate."

"Good observation," put in Lee. "That boy's all right."

"At quarter past six," William resumed, "Bosco met his two friends at the *leiteria*. The lift operator had not yet learned the name of the Bulldog visitor, but he's evidently a big shot. Has all the others scared speechless. He closeted himself in a room with the local leaders. He pounded the table and shouted so loud he could be heard all the way to the elevator. But not what he said. The lift operator could not go any closer because some of the Gestapo men were listening outside the door.

"When the Bulldog came out of the room he was still in a rage. Cursed everybody who got in his way. The local leader of the Gestapo is a tall, skinny man with a prominent Adam's apple and a long nose. Bosco calls him the Stork, but his name is really Schoënhut. Schoënhut, it seems, is an amorous fellow, and as such is an object of ridicule to the Portuguese in the Rua Azorrague. He was sweet on the cigar-naker's daughter. She led him on. One night she invited him into the room back of the store where her boy friends were waiting. They gave Schoënhut's jacket a terrible dusting. The whole street is laughing over the story.

"The Bulldog happened to meet Schoënhut in a corridor and gave him a terrible dressing-down before all the others. He slapped his face so hard that Schoënhut staggered against the wall. Yet he took it without a word. They are all ready to crawl on their bellies before the Bulldog. The telephone was going all afternoon. Men were continually coming in and being sent out in different directions. The slick fellow who looks like an American was one of the busiest. In the scraps of conversation that reached the lift operator's ears, two names kept recurring. One sounded like Urbaldino, the other was Mappin."

"Something cooking," said William as he concluded.

"Obviously," said Lee, "and it promises us no good."

"I suggest we stay in our rooms tomorrow," said William. "We have Bosco to report what our enemies are doing, and we can telephone the Legation."

"Okay," said Lee. "But we're not going to ask the Legation for help except in the direst necessity . . . Let's go downstairs and buy some reading matter before we retire from the world."

Outside the lounge, as Lee turned away from the newsstand with an armful of magazines, he came face to face with Ronald Franklin. The young man's face lighted up; his glance was apparently as open as the sky. "What a pleasure!" he cried, offering his hand.

Lee took it. William watched Franklin, stiffening. Lee did not feel that any harm could come to himself there in the lounge of the Lisboa Palace; moreover, he felt a professional interest in such a perfect specimen of effrontery. Franklin's busy eyes took everything in and gave nothing away. Lee lingered to draw him out a little. William was disgusted.

"I got back yesterday," said Franklin enthusiastically. "I'm registered at the Victoria. This old dump is a little too rich for my blood."

"How's business?" asked Lee.

"Not too good. The demand exceeds the supply. I've been combing Switzerland for fine watch movements. No dice."

"When do you sail for America?"

"I'll travel by plane if I can get a place. A mere civilian like me doesn't stand much of a chance against the brass hats."

Franklin detained Lee for several minutes longer by describing his alleged experiences on the recent journey to Switzerland. Lee listened with a half-smile, mentally adding the young man to his gallery of specimens for future use.

When he and William finally made their way to the lift, Lee said: "He's wasted as a spy—and a second-string spy at that. He has the makings of a great actor."

William growled: "If I had his smooth throat under my thumbs, how I would enjoy squeezing it! . . . I wonder what brought him here tonight?"

Lee had no answer to that.

Ever afterwards, he was to remember a little talk he had with William that night before they turned in. They were seated in the red velvet chairs with the antimacassars, smoking a last pipe. William's face, as always, was as blank as a sheet of note paper that has not been written on. The thick lenses guarded the secrets of his eyes. Yet every now and then Lee received an intimation that William at heart was one of the simple, kind-hearted Germans that typified the race in happier times. It was the experience of unspeakable wickedness and injury that had driven him in on himself and made him hard. Lee had become strongly attached to William.

"William," he said, "do you sometimes become weary of the everlasting strain of danger we are under?"

Even the thick lenses could not conceal William's startled glance then. "Why . . . why, I don't think of it," he said. "I accept it as my fate."

"But you remember a time when a man could take his ease and let himself go?"

"Please," said William in a distressed voice, "I would rather not talk about those days."

Lee spared him. Later he said: "This Bulldog that Bosco tells us about sounds like a pretty important guy. You know the Gestapo better than I do. Have you any idea who he is?"

William nodded. "The French license plate gave me a clue. It will be Albrecht Stengel. He is chief of the Gestapo in the occupied countries."

"Stengel!" cried Lee. "The Butcher of Paris! My God, William, we must be big men in their eyes if they send Stengel after us!" Lee jumped up and paced the room. "Stengel is an adversary worth having! If we could put an end to Stengel's foul career it would be as good as winning a battle, William!"

"Sure!" said William grimly. "If he doesn't put an end to us first!"

LEE AWOKE IN HIS BED feeling giddy and sick. Some moments passed before his brain cleared sufficiently for him to realize where he

was. Then he saw by the square of brightness on the carpet that
the sun was high in the sky. Focusing his eyes with difficulty, he
glanced at his watch. Nearly noon! He sat up abruptly and such a wave
of giddiness came over him, he had to press his knuckles against
his eyes and wait for it to pass. When he felt better, he put out his
hand towards the water bottle on the night table—and quickly drew it
back again. There's something the matter with me, he thought. I
never oversleep like this. I've been drugged. Maybe it's in the water.

He put his feet to the floor and, holding his head between his
hands, staggered to the door leading to the sitting room. He got it
open; he looked into the room beyond, and his heart sank like a
stone. William's bed was tumbled and empty. Lee was aware of a
sickening sense of loss. The quiet William, who said so little and
who felt so much!

With a great effort of his will, Lee cleared his foggy brain and
searched the room foot by foot with trained eyes. William's clothes
were gone; a couple of small coins lay on the carpet; his clothes,
then, had been snatched up in a hurry. The bedclothes were not
thrown back, as they are when a man rises, but tumbled in a heap.
An extra blanket which William was accustomed to throw over the
back of a chair was gone. There was another bottle of water on a
stand beside the bed, half empty like his own. Both he and William were great water drinkers. Had somebody counted on that?

Finally, lying on the carpet near the door to the corridor Lee
saw a significant clue, the key to their suite. Yet he remembered
how William had always taken care to turn the key sideways in the
lock so it could not be pushed through. They must have had a thin
instrument to turn the key from the outside. When Lee tried the
door it was locked. So they had a passkey! Why William instead of
me? Lee asked himself.

Upon examining the necks of the two water bottles under a
strong glass, Lee found strange fingerprints. Unfortunately, his
prints and William's covered them. But by piecing bits of the
strange prints together he was able to secure and preserve a complete set, fingers and thumb of a right hand.

When Lee considered how to meet the situation, despair seized
on him. William was his sole prop. He could speak but a few words

of the language of the country. What was he to do first? A blankness faced him. Lee shook his head violently to rid himself of such unnerving thoughts and started for the telephone. Before he reached it, the bell sounded.

He heard a male voice, unknown to him, ask in slow, careful English: "Is this Mr. Mappin?"

"Yes," said Lee. "To whom am I speaking?"

"Are you looking for your secretary?" The sleek voice seemed to writhe with malevolence like a snake.

"Who are you?" Lee asked again.

He heard a short laugh. "A friend . . . Your secretary is waiting for you at Rua Cachimbo, 23." Click. The connection was broken.

Lee immediately called the number of his office on the Rua Cachimbo. There was no answer.

He called the Ministry of Police and asked to be connected with Inspector da Gama.

While he waited with the receiver at his ear, William's question of the night before came into his mind: "I wonder what brought Franklin here tonight?" An answer suggested itself: While Franklin kept me in talk downstairs, the woman slipped into our suite—I know they had a passkey—and doctored the water bottles!

When he heard the inspector's voice, he said: "This is Mappin speaking."

"Yes, Senhor Mappin."

"My secretary, William Miller, has disappeared from the hotel. He would not leave me voluntarily at such a time. I fear that an ugly crime has been committed. Can you come?"

"Immediately, senhor!"

"Bring a sufficient escort," said Lee dryly.

He ordered coffee from the restaurant and dressed himself. His nerves had quieted now and his hand was steady. Before he finished drinking the coffee, Inspector da Gama arrived with two plain-clothesmen. The anxious resident director of the hotel followed at his heels, but this elegant gentleman was requested to wait in the corridor for the present.

Lee told his story briefly. On hearing it, the inspector said:

"We will proceed to the Rua Cachimbo."

"It may be a trap," warned Lee.

"Possibly," said the inspector, "but I do not think so. It is too obvious. In any case, the police are prepared for traps . . . I'll leave men in the hotel to start an investigation—unless you wish to be present."

Lee shook his head. "I don't understand the language. I would only delay matters. But leave a man who can make an intelligent report."

Leaving the detectives in the suite, they descended in the lift and picked up two more men in the foyer. Lee, expecting the worst, carried the little satchel in which he kept his aids to detection. The police car waited in the street with its motorcycle escort. During the drive, Lee was aware of nothing in the streets; his eyes were turned inward. The same question was still plaguing him, and he put it to the inspector:

"Why did they choose him instead of me?"

"Because he was German," said da Gama. "They hated him worse than you. It suited them to call him a traitor."

Their arrival in the Rua Cachimbo created a sensation. People came running from the little stores and out of hallways. Lee glanced around the circle of gaping faces, asking himself: Which of these are agents of the Gestapo?

They proceeded into the house and up the dark stairs. The uniformed officers went first, gun in hand, then the detectives. Lee and the inspector brought up the rear. The door from the hallway was not locked; the room inside it was empty. It had no hiding places. An officer opened the door to the front room and drew his breath sharply. The inspector put out a restraining hand.

"Don't go in, Senhor Mappin."

Lee pressed forward. "Nonsense!" he said. "I am no stranger to death."

William had been flung across Lee's desk on his back. He was still wearing pajamas, now drenched with blood. His clothes were scattered about the floor; also on the floor lay the hotel blanket and some lengths of rope, indicating how he had been brought through the city. The marks of a gag showed around his mouth.

Lee looked down at his dead friend with a face of stone. Ugly burns on his breast showed how he had been tortured before he was killed. His sufferings had been ended by a knife thrust in the heart.

Lee, calling on all the strength of his will, started his examination of the room and the body. There was no lack of fingerprints. No less than five men had taken part in the torturing and murder of William—possibly six, because there was one bloody print on the dead man's breast of gloved fingers, a left hand. Lee showed the Portuguese officers the modern method of lifting fingerprints and preserving them on his films of rubber.

Though they were six to one, William at one moment had succeeded in partly freeing himself, and had put up a desperate struggle. The room was wrecked. In the course of the fight, a man had had his glasses knocked off. They had been stepped on and broken; the two little ovals of broken glass lay separated on the floor. Lee, with a hard smile, carefully gathered them up in two separate envelopes. This was priceless evidence.

In the end, William had died almost instantly. There was not a great deal of blood. He had been stabbed by a knife with a thin blade ten inches long, driven to the hilt. Only a powerful young arm could have delivered that blow.

Forcing open one of the dead man's clenched hands, Lee recovered several coarse, crinkly hairs, black interspersed with white. These went into another envelope; more valuable evidence. William's strong white teeth were clamped together in the throes of death. Forcing them apart, Lee found between them a torn scrap of a brown cotton material with a seam in it. Was it the end of a glove finger? Finally he picked up some small lumps of charcoal. Others had been stepped on and ground into the floor. Such was the sum of the evidence yielded by the scene of the murder.

Inquiries by the police among the neighbors in the Rua Cachimbo brought forward one man who had something to contribute. This man lived across the way from number 23. About half-past two in the night, aroused by some activity in the quiet street, he had looked out of the window and had seen a small black truck of elegant design standing in front of number 23. It was the sort of vehicle, he said, that is used by undertakers to transport bodies from place to place. Such trucks usually have plates affixed to the sides bearing the name of the undertaking establishment, but this had none. It drove off almost immediately. The driver was outside his range of vision. The license plate on the rear had been smeared with mud or some such substance and was illegible.

On his return to the hotel, Lee received the report of the detectives who had been left there. It gave him very little additional to go on. Afterwards he made an examination of the courtyard on his own account. Just beyond the service door he found a thin film of mud on the asphalt paving which had dried since night. During the night it had taken the tracks of a car which had turned around in the courtyard and waited there for a space. This car was shod with four new tires, all of the same popular make. Such treads gave him little ground for hope, until he found that the right-hand rear tire had a cut in it which left a distinctive mark. He carefully sketched the imprint of the treads and the cut in his notebook.

Without saying anything to the police, Lee engaged a certain M. Gade, who had been recommended to him at the Legation, to search for the car, possibly an elegant little black truck. M. Gade was a French refugee who had set up for himself in Lisbon as a private investigator. So far as Lee could learn, he had no political affiliations.

CHAPTER SEVEN

THAT NIGHT, as the solitary figure of Lee crossed the busy Rocío, Bosco was selling his papers as usual on the island between two streams of squawking taxis and clanging *electricos*. It was the busiest hour of the evening. About fifty yards behind Lee followed a pair of secret agents with their hard eyes fixed on every movement of the plump little figure in the expensive Panama hat. In Lisbon, Lee carried a Malacca stick.

As he bought a paper, he exchanged a look with Bosco. Lee could see in Bosco's expressive eyes that the youth knew what had happened. Turning aside his head, Lee murmured:

"Call me at nine o'clock."

The extra half hour was to give him time to procure an interpreter. From the hotel he called the Legation and the Minister said he would send over his own private secretary, a Miss Whiteley.

Soon afterwards she arrived, and Lee was relieved to find that she was of the efficient type of secretary instead of the merely ornamental. He had no heart tonight to flatter a pretty woman. Miss Whiteley declined refreshment, and they got down to business. She was aware of what had happened.

"I have a Portuguese agent," said Lee, "who calls me up every night about this time. He has only a few words of English and I need you to take down what he says and translate it for me. You will find him a pretty rough character."

"I am accustomed to all kinds," said Miss Whiteley demurely.

When the telephone rang, Lee answered it. "This is Senhor Mappin, Bosco. Get me?"

"Yes, gentleman. My heart, he is sad tonight."

"Mine too, Bosco. I have a lady here who will take down what you have to say and translate it for me. You can talk to her just as you would to me. Understand?"

"Yes, gentleman."

"Hold the wire."

As Miss Whiteley took the instrument, Lee said to her: "After he has finished talking, tell him to wait half an hour and call up again for instructions."

Miss Whiteley took down what Bosco had to say in shorthand, so he was able to talk as fast as he liked. After she had finally hung up, she read Lee what she had written, translating as she went:

"From nine o'clock this morning, I was selling my papers in Rua A." Miss Whiteley raised her eyes inquiringly.

"Go ahead," said Lee. "I know the street."

"Several men came to the Hotel E.," she resumed, "and others went away. They were not all the same men I had seen before. About eleven o'clock my friend the porter came out and went into a restaurant on the same side of the street. They do no cooking in the hotel. I waited in the doorway until he came out carrying a tray. He could only stop to tell me that the Bulldog had slept in the hotel and the food was for him.

"Half an hour later the blond American, F., drove up to the hotel in a taxi. He was pleased with himself. After he went in, his taxi drove on a little way and stopped, and the driver went in to get a drink, so I followed him in and made up to him and offered to buy him a second glass of wine. All we Portuguese stand together when our country is full of foreigners. What I was after was to find out where he had picked F. up. He said at the Lisboa Palace, and he got a good tip out of him.

"When we came out of the wine shop there was another taxi standing in front of the Hotel E. The Bulldog came out. He had been drinking. His ugly face was red. He felt good. He got in the taxi, so I got in the other taxi and followed. Bulldog was driven to the Central Station and took the noon express for Madrid . . ."

"At that moment I was just coming to my senses!" muttered Lee.

"I drove back to the *leiteria* in the same cab," Miss Whiteley resumed from her notes, "and joined my friends who were eating their lunch there. The lift operator said there was a big change around the hotel this morning. Everybody happy. Bulldog slept in the hotel. He didn't wake up until eleven and sent out for his break-fast. They were all drinking and slapping each other on the back. When the young blond fellow came, they all went into a room and shut the door. The news he brought them made them laugh like hyenas . . ."

Lee, pacing up and down the sitting room, drove his fist into his palm. "I'll make them laugh! I'll make them laugh!" he mut-tered.

Miss Whiteley went on reading from her notes. "They were very cautious in their talk. As they came and went through the corri-dors, my friend was listening with long ears to find out what made them feel so good, but he got no clue. When he was telling me this I didn't know what had happened. In the afternoon, when I went for my evening papers, I heard the story. Then I knew what made the Germans laugh. I was sorry I hadn't known it in the morning. I met my friends at suppertime and I told them. I told the lift opera-tor he must find out more, more. What time did Bulldog return to the hotel this morning? Was he seen? Was there anybody with him? What did his room look like?—he could get this from the chamber-maid; she's Portuguese. Was there blood on him? I told him you would pay well for any information, and they said they'd find out what they could."

Miss Whiteley closed her notebook. "That's all."

Lee, pacing the room, muttered: "The boy's got eyes in his head. But he tries to do too much. They'll catch him!" After taking a minute or two to digest what he had heard, he went on: "When Bosco calls again, tell him this . . ."

Miss Whiteley wrote as Lee dictated:

"After this I won't stop and buy a paper from you every night. The men who trail me have sharp eyes. It's too risky to pass you money the way I've been doing. Give me your address, and I'll send it by mail. If I need to see you I'll come to your house. Call me up every night about eight-thirty whether you see me in the street or not. And also call me up in the mornings at eight so I can give you instructions. Always use a different pay station when you call.

"Don't try to sell your papers in the Rua A. any more. There's not enough business in that little street to justify it, and the Germans would soon get on to you. Nor should you undertake to watch the Hotel B. yourself. No matter how clever you are, if they see you hanging around day after day they will smell a rat. You're doing good work. I don't want to lose you. Get your wide-awake friends to watch the hotel and report to you. Change them often. And make certain that the porter and the lift operator are not followed to the *leiteria*. Remember Germans are suspicious of everybody. Tell me over the phone each day how much you spend, and how much you need. *Don't display your money or tell anybody how much you're making.*"

When Bosco called again, Miss Whiteley gave him all this in his own language.

After she had hung up she said to Lee: "Bosco says he understands everything. He lives at Calcado Poço, 7." Lee entered it in his notebook. "He says," she went on, "that he will continue to sell his papers every evening at the same spot on the Rocío because people are accustomed to seeing him there. If you want to use him at that hour, he can get another fellow to take his place. He says, do him the favor to pass there when you can, whether you speak or not, so he'll know you're safe."

CHAPTER EIGHT

EARLY NEXT MORNING, Lee visited an optician and handed him the two broken lenses. The man put the pieces together without too much trouble and pasted them with transparent gummed paper. Measuring the refraction of light with his instruments, he wrote out the prescription from which they had been made.

Later, Lee and his friend the Minister were sitting in the study of the United States Legation. Their faces were heavy. Lee said:

"The police seem to be active in the case. Inspector da Gama is a first-rate fellow—up to a point. I have the feeling, however, that word has come down from above that it would be better for the state to hush up this crime rather than to solve it. No Portuguese wants it to be known that Lisbon is a place where such an outrageous crime could be committed."

"Sure," said the Minister, "and Portugal's neutrality is precious to them. The death of an individual weighs nothing beside reasons of state."

"A man without a country at that," murmured Lee. "Right. That's why I can't come forward and demand a complete investigation. He was not an American citizen."

"I suppose you noticed," said Lee, "that the Lisbon morning papers did not carry a word about it."

"Sure. But it's being gossiped about freely. The American correspondents have been to me to ask if they should cable the story home. I put them off until I could consult you."

Lee shook his head. "If they tried to send it, it would be censored. In this case I agree with the censors. If the story were published in America, it would set up a reaction against Portugal that might have unfortunate results. Sooner or later, Portugal will be forced to abandon neutrality. When that happens we want her to come in on our side. That's a reason of state, too."

"Then we must allow this crime to be hushed up?" said the Minister gloomily.

"Not necessarily," said Lee. "It certainly originated in the Hotel Excelsior, but we have as yet no legal evidence. If we can bring it home to the real murderers, the shoe will be on the other foot. It will give Portugal a shove in our direction."

"But if the Lisbon police won't solve this crime . . . ?"

"I will," said Lee quietly.

The Minister sprang up from his desk. "What are you saying?"

"I mean of course, unless the Gestapo gets me first," amended Lee.

The Minister strode agitatedly back and forth. "Impossible!" he said. "I can't allow you to remain in Lisbon after what has happened."

Lee merely smiled.

"You would simply be inviting the Gestapo to shoot you!"

"My position is no more dangerous today than it was day before yesterday," said Lee. "Of course they'll get me—if they can."

"Your life is too valuable to be sacrificed in such a fashion, Mappin!"

Lee raised his eyebrows. "Valuable? Why? Hundreds of Americans are giving their lives daily. This is the best way I can serve."

"But your hands are tied! What can you do?"

"Frankly, I don't know yet. But I've had a certain experience in solving murders." As the Minister prepared to bring up further reasons, Lee raised his hand. "William Miller gave his life," he said. "A man without a country, without a family or a friend, so far as we know; a solitary patriot. There is nobody in the world to avenge him but me . . . Besides, I'm not going to let the Gestapo put a stop to all my other work, too."

The Minister threw up his hands. "Well, if you won't leave Lisbon, at least come and live in the Legation."

Lee shook his head. "Many thanks, but if I had to sit in the Legation all day doing nothing, I'd go off my nut. Let me go my own way, Mr. Minister. Our country mustn't be dragged into this affair—in case I fail."

The Minister dropped in his chair. "If they get you, that can't be hushed up," he said gloomily, "and I'll be blamed for it."

"Not if the full facts are published," said Lee.

"You're an obstinate man, Mappin!"

"I don't think I am," protested Lee. "I often change my mind. But once or twice in every man's life a situation arises where only one course is possible. In such cases, argument is futile."

"You must have a proper guard . . ."

"I will find him."

"More than one."

"Too obvious a guard would hamper me . . . Please see that the British Embassy is informed of the true facts."

"I will . . . How does the case stand today?"

"Inspector da Gama expresses himself as baffled. Upon analysis, the drinking water was found to be drugged with Duotol, a tasteless anodyne that can be purchased anywhere. Two guests at the Lisboa Palace who have rooms on the same corridor as mine heard the kidnapers as they passed in the night. From one we got the exact hour, 2:18. The other man was awake. He actually opened his door and looked out. He saw a group of men disappearing around a corner carrying a body on a stretcher. They were dressed like undertakers' assistants. This man knew it was customary, when death occurs in a de luxe hotel, to remove the body at night without the knowledge of other guests. He therefore went back to his bed and thought no more about it."

"Could he describe the kidnapers?"

"No. Couldn't even swear to the number. However, I know there were four to carry the stretcher and another to lead the way."

"How could they get out of the hotel?"

"Quite easily, it seems. They carried William down a service stairs, two flights. At the bottom there was a watchman stationed between stairway and service entrance. This man presumably went off duty at seven o'clock in the morning. When the police searched for him at noon, he had vanished; he had not been home."

"Perhaps they got him, too."

"Perhaps, but it is more likely he received a bribe—a bribe that would look princely to a watchman. Anyhow, he has disappeared."

"Is that all?"

"That is all the police have to tell me," said Lee. "I have a report from my agent." He described what Bosco had told him.

"I'll ask Madrid for information about the Bulldog," said the Minister.

"Also Paris," suggested Lee. "Paris is their headquarters. I suspect that the Bulldog is no other than the infamous Albrecht Stengel, the Butcher of Paris."

"What about the body, Mappin?" asked the Minister. "Let that be my care. What are your instructions?"

"The English cemetery is a pretty spot," said Lee softly. "Bury him there and put a simple stone on his grave. If he had a family or friends in Germany, he concealed it for their sakes. Perhaps when the war is over I'll be able to find those who were close to him. I don't even know his true name."

When they shook hands the Minister said: "I shall be anxious about you every moment of the day, Mappin."

"Forget me! Forget me!" said Lee. "You have plenty more important things on your mind."

As he crossed the Minister's anteroom, Lee's eyes fell upon a tall, young American standing there, who nodded and smiled. Clearly he wanted to speak, but was waiting for the older man to speak first. Lee, taking him for one of the correspondents, had no heart for speech. He answered his greeting and passed on out.

As he arrived at the door of the hotel, another taxi dashed up behind his. Lee, who carried his gun in the side pocket of his jacket, instinctively put his hand on it. But the man who tumbled out of the second taxi was the same one he had seen at the Legation.

"Mr. Mappin," he said, a little breathless in his eagerness, "can I speak to you a moment? I'm not after a story. It's a personal matter. I *must* speak to you."

"Why, of course," said Lee. "A fellow countryman. Come into the hotel."

Lee led him to the lounge. "Will it take long?" he asked.

"I hope so," said the young man, half modest, half bold.

Lee laughed, almost won already. They found seats. "Shoot!" said Lee.

"My name is Luke Tremaine," said the young man. "I'm a free-lance correspondent over here. Not much to it. I'm not a very good reporter, I guess. But I couldn't stay home. I've been turned down by all the medical boards I could get to. On account of what they call a heart murmur. It doesn't interfere with me. I can keep going as long as anybody . . ."

Lee saw what was coming and frowned. "Why are you telling me all this?"

"I want to work with you, Mr. Mappin. This opportunity is like the answer to a prayer!"

"Good God!" said the startled Lee. "You know what happened to my last assistant?"

"Sure, I know. That's why I'm asking you. Don't shake your head. You've got to have somebody. You can't go around alone. I speak Portuguese—colloquially. Picked it up here in the streets this past year. I knew Lisbon like a book . . ."

"There's no story in this—for the present," warned Lee.

The young man looked hurt. "The hell with a story! I'm asking to be your man."

Lee studied him with a fresh interest; brown hair, steady blue eyes set far apart, a nondescript nose, a mouth wide but not loose, and inclined to turn up at the corners. The general effect was of a warmhearted, laughter-loving fellow who was nobody's fool. Well-cut American tweeds hung on his big frame carelessly.

Nice lad to have around, thought Lee, warming towards him; however, he continued to shake his head. "You've got your whole life before you," Lee said. "Are you married?"

"No. No close ties . . . Don't turn me down because it's too dangerous," Luke went on, at once laughing and beseeching. "It would break my heart!"

"Wait here until I come back," said Lee.

He telephoned to the Legation. The Minister gave Luke Tremaine a first-rate recommendation. Knew the boy well; knew his people at home. Good heart; good head. Luke had been trying for a year to get some newspaper to send him to the front. The Minister had offered him a job in the Legation. Luke wouldn't take it because he said an official job was too soft in wartime. Such was the gist of it.

Lee returned. Luke's eyes sought his face with a painful eagerness. Lee said offhandedly:

"Well, let's play along for a while until we see how we get along together."

Luke let out a subdued whoop that made all the correct Continentals within hearing stare. "When do I start?" he asked.

"Now," said Lee. He named a figure.

"Too much," said Luke promptly.

Lee waved that objection aside.

A SERVANT CAME to Lee to say that Senhor the Resident-Director craved a word with Mr. Mappin in his office.

"You come along, too," said Lee to Luke.

In the director's office, that finished gentleman sprang up from his desk and projected a series of jackknife bows in Lee's direction. Lee said:

"This is my new secretary, Mr. Tremaine."

The director arrested his bowing to stare incredulously at Luke. Another secretary already! Turning back to Lee with hand on heart and tears in his voice, he expressed his horror and grief at the dreadful thing that had occurred. Lee had nothing against the man, but this excessive sorrow annoyed him and he cut it short. The director was implying that after what had happened he could no longer expect Mr. Mappin to stay in his hotel, and Lee said clearly:

"I shall keep my rooms."

This took the wind out of the director's sails. Obviously he wanted to get rid of a guest who might bring down another such catastrophe on his house. "But you must have other rooms," he protested. "There are several suites available . . ."

"The same rooms," said Lee firmly. "They suit me."

The director raised his hands and let them fall in a gesture of resignation. These *Americanos!*

"There is only one thing I must ask of you," Lee continued, fixing him with a stem eye. "I wish to have a strong bolt fixed to the inside of the entrance door to the suite this afternoon. I want the old-fashioned kind of bolt." He illustrated with his hands. "When you shove it across, it turns and locks in its place."

The director started to object, but Lee's eye was too strong for him. "Very well, senhor, it shall be done," he said humbly.

Over lunch in the hotel, Lee said to Luke: "Your first job must be to find buildings around town that have two or more entrances. Hotels, arcades, theaters, and the like. As we can use such a place only once, we must have several in reserve."

"I already know of some such places," said Luke.

"Secondly," Lee went on, "you must understand that we will have to descend to the level of our enemies and snoop and spy and use all kinds of dirty, underhand tricks."

"Okay by me, if they are enemies," said Luke cheerfully.

"I have one spy," said Lee, "who has been very successful. You'll meet him. We must have others."

"Look for them among the poor people of Lisbon," said Luke. "They're good people."

Later, in talking over the case, Lee said, "There were five men in the kidnapping party."

"Why five?"

"Not more than four can carry a stretcher swiftly and silently without getting in each other's way. William was a big man, and they must have been fairly husky. The fifth man was to spy out the way and open doors. Some were Portuguese, I take it. Well, spies have no country. They were dressed in the style of undertakers' assistants. In the Rua Cachimbo, I know they were joined by others, for it was certainly Germans who questioned William and tortured him. Yet it seems to have been a Portuguese who killed him."

"How do you know that?"

"The autopsy revealed that the murder weapon was a slim blade ten inches long. It was plunged to the hilt with one sure stroke. In other words, a stiletto. That's a weapon unfamiliar to Germans and Americans."

"Americans?" said Luke, opening his eyes.

"One of the principals is an American of German descent . . . At first I believed that the water bottles were drugged by a woman," Lee went on, "but now I doubt it. The woman I had in mind is one of them, but I don't believe they'd trust her as far as murder."

Luke's eyes brightened at the mention of the word "woman." "Who is she?" he asked.

"She's lunching at the fourth table behind you. Wait a minute before you look."

Luke presently took a fleeting glance behind him. "Gosh! What a smooth piece of dress goods! What is she?"

"Calls herself a Scotswoman," said Lee.

"Scotch! That's a new thing in camouflage."

"She's already full of curiosity about you. When she starts making up to you, don't discourage her. You might learn something."

Luke took another glance. "Discourage anything like *that!* No fear!"

When they had finished eating, Lee said: "Now run along and find some buildings that have a way out behind. We must be prepared with as many tricks as a fox to throw our trailers off the scent."

A look of concern came into young Luke's face. "Should I leave you alone?" he said.

The words brought a memory of the lost William winging back. Lee touched the young man's arm. "Good fellow!" he said warmly. ". . . They won't attack me today. As I figure it, they don't want to liquidate me if it can be avoided. My death would make a noise that couldn't be silenced. They are hoping that the murder of William will send me skedaddling back to my own country. When they find that I mean to stick, it will be different."

Luke was not entirely convinced. "My main job is to stay with you."

"This afternoon," Lee went on, "I have some work to do in the hotel. I am developing a new theory as to the drugged water bottles. I know they possessed a passkey to our suite."

"How do you know that?"

"Because when I entered the sitting room our key was lying on the poor, yet the door was locked . . . I promise not to go out until you return."

Luke's face cleared.

"Bring your clothes when you come," said Lee. "Are you armed?"

"Always," said Luke, touching his hip pocket.

"If your gun is not too big, I suggest you carry it in the right-hand pocket of your jacket. Then you don't have to draw."

"I'll change it as soon as I'm alone," said Luke.

CHAPTER NINE

WHEN LUKE RETURNED to the Lisboa Palace with his suitcases, Lee said: "I need your help. I've been trying to talk to Natalia, our chambermaid. She has as much English as I have Portuguese but our words don't match. So we bogged down."

He rang, and Natalia presently entered, bobbing and smoothing her apron. She was ample and good-natured, and her expressive eyes had a gallant roll. It was evident from her smile that Lee had laid a foundation for good will. He said:

"This is my secretary. He speaks Portuguese."

Without waiting for questions, Natalia burst into a flood of passionate oratory. She shook her fists, she held out her arms, she crossed herself repeatedly and pointed to heaven.

"Wait a minute! Wait a minute!" interrupted Lee. "What's she trying to tell me?"

Said Luke: "She says the police accused her yesterday of poisoning the water bottles. And she swears by Mary and all the saints that it is false!"

"Tell her to make her mind easy," said Lee. "It never occurred to me that she could have done it, or I wouldn't be making friends with her now."

This was repeated to Natalia and she smiled again. Lee went on:

"I want to ask her some questions about the gentleman who occupied the adjoining room, number 218. His name, as I got it from her, sounded like 'All go down.' What is it exactly?"

Luke spelled it out after Natalia: "Algodão—with a little jigger over the last *a*."

"When did he take that room?"

"The day after you came."

"When did he leave?"

"Day before yesterday; eight o'clock in the morning."

"Ha!" said Lee. "Before the crime was discovered! We appear to be getting warm! Ask her if she knows where he went from here."

Luke repeated Natalia's answer. "He said he was going to Madrid."

"Madrid again!"

"But he bought a ticket to Torres Pretos. The porter told me. The porter carried his bag to the station and heard him ask for a ticket."

"Where is that place?"

"It's a small port on the ocean about two hours by the railway."

Lee shifted his line of approach. Pointing to the brass key which hung on a chain from Natalia's waist, he asked: "Does that key open all the doors on this corridor?"

The answer was "Yes." Natalia explained that each corridor in the hotel had its own master key; that nobody was authorized to carry this particular key but herself; that there was a duplicate kept in the office.

"Natalia," asked Lee, "did you ever lose your key for a while? Did you ever lend it to anybody? Was it ever out of your possession?"

She answered with a whole series of denials.

"Now think well before you answer this one: If you can help me, Natalia, I'll double what I gave you before. Did Senhor Algodão ever have that key in his hand?"

As Natalia cast back in her mind, her eyes widened, and suddenly a whole fusillade of "*Si, senhors*" broke from her.

"Under what circumstances?" asked Lee.

Natalia's story, as translated by Luke, was as follows. Four or five mornings previously, while she was doing up Lee's room, the door to the corridor was open and Senhor Algodão came in. She remonstrated with him, saying what would the *Americano* gentleman think if he came back, Algodão did not leave immediately, but took time to look around and open the bedroom door and look in. He remarked what a handsome suite it was. Then he told Natalia he had forgotten to ask for his key at the office, and to lend him hers to open his door. Natalia, thinking no harm, unhooked her key and handed it to him. He unlocked his door and brought it back to her.

"Right away?" asked Lee. "Think before you answer."

"He unlocked his door; he went into his room; he came out right away again and brought me the key."

"Time enough to take an impression of it," Lee murmured to Luke.

Natalia had more to say: "He stayed in his room a little while, then he went away. When I brought clean towels to his room the door was locked. So he had his key all the time."

"How did you explain this to yourself?"

Natalia shrugged and looked self-conscious. "Well, senhor, old as I am and the mother of four . . . well, gentlemen will be gentlemen! When the senhor came in this room he threw his arm around my waist and gave me a kiss. I thought he asked for the key just to save his face."

"Did you tell the police about the key?"

"No, senhor. It seemed of no importance. It did not come to my mind."

"Natalia," said Lee, "I never happened to see this senhor entering or leaving his room. Describe him to me." As much with graphic pantomime as with words, Natalia pictured a man of about forty-five, average height, with a moderate protuberance in front. He had what she described as a greedy expression, a long nose, shifty black eyes, and lank black hair. He dressed like a lawyer, meaning that he wore a black cutaway coat, striped trousers, and a black, soft hat with the brim turned down in front like an American. She mimicked the flat-footed, pompous walk of the man.

"Excellent!" said Lee. "By the way, Natalia, who is occupying that room now? I hear somebody moving around."

"Two Portuguese gentlemen, senhor."

"Two of them, eh? This hotel is not patronized much by Portuguese. I doubt if these two mean any good to us."

He gave Natalia what he had promised her and she disappeared.

On their way out to dinner, Lee remarked to the clerk in the bureau of the hotel that he had broken the key to one of his cases, and where could he have another made? He was given an address just around the corner from the hotel. As Lee did not want to risk giving a premature alarm, he and Luke drove halfway across town and shook off their trailers before returning to the locksmith's shop.

To the workman Lee said: "Could you make a key from an impression in wax or some other soft plastic?"

"Certainly, senhor . . . As it happens, I did such a job for a senhor less than a week ago."

Lee and Luke looked at each other. This was better luck than they expected.

"A key like this?" asked Lee, exhibiting their hotel key.

"Of that same size, senhor."

"Would you know that man again?"

"Si, senhor."

"But you have many customers. How could you be sure of knowing this one?"

"This was such an unusual order, I took a good look at this man. A man of forty-five, senhor, with the beginning of a nice belly. He was dressed like an advocate and he walked like this." The locksmith illustrated.

Luke let out a soft whoop and clapped Lee on the back. The locksmith looked suspiciously from one to another. However, the gift of a twenty-five-escudo note satisfied him that these were right men.

"Say nothing about this to anybody," warned Lee, "and there will be more in it for you."

As Lee and Luke strolled on to the Macaco Branco, the former said: "What say we take a little trip to Torres Pretos tomorrow? If we can shake off our sleuthhounds, a day in the country would be charming."

"Suits me all right," said Luke.

THE SALIENT PART of Bosco's report that night, when they returned
to the hotel, had to do with Schoënhut. Schoënhut was described
by Bosco as the local chief of the Gestapo. He was a tall, skinny
fellow with a prominent Adam's apple, a long nose and tousled gray
hair. Bosco had christened him "the Stork." During the morning
the Stork had sent the lift operator to an optician (not the same
one that Lee had consulted) to order a pair of glasses. The lift operator was given a prescription from a German oculist to have
filled. He had had the wit to copy down the figures of the prescription and had given them to Bosco. Bosco repeated the figures over
the phone, and Lee took them down.

Lee and Luke compared the two sets of figures in mounting
excitement.

"Glory be, they match!" cried Luke.

"That ought to settle the hash of number one when the time
comes!" said Lee.

THE PORTUGUESE LOCAL RAILWAYS do not go in for speed; however,
Luke and Lee did not find the next day journey tedious. They had
succeeded in evading their trackers before going to the station;
consequently they were free from espionage until they chose to
return to Lisbon, and they felt like schoolboys on holiday. The scen-
ery was magnificent, and at each little station they were intrigued by
the human scene. Between stations, Lee took lessons in Portuguese
from Luke, assisted by fellow passengers amidst great laughter.

Torres Pretos was a hoary little seaport on the estuary of a small
river. It had a look of having been forgotten by the world. Colum-
bus could have sailed into the river in his caravels without being
surprised by anything new, for the railway station was out of sight.
There was a fort, a castle on a nearby hill, a tiny cobbled *praça*
facing the quay, and a huddle of tall houses separated by dark lanes.
An old stone hotel, the Grande, faced the *praça*, and along the other
side was moored a rank of picturesque fishing smacks with their
bowsprits pointing ashore.

During the afternoon a British destroyer steamed into the river
and dropped anchor, making a strikingly incongruous note amidst

all the antiquity. A boat came ashore to purchase fruits and fresh vegetables. The hearty English voices echoed oddly in the dim lanes.

Lee and Luke were the first guests to enter the restaurant of the Grande for dinner. They had registered at the hotel, since there were no more return trains. It was not difficult to establish the fact that a Senhor "Gomez" had arrived three days before and was assigned to room four. He was the only recent arrival. They had not identified him yet, but felt pretty sure he would come to dinner since there was no other respectable eating place visible in town.

Other guests were entering the restaurant singly and in couples. The door was thrown open with a bang, and a party from the English destroyer barged in; the handsome young commander, his navigating officer, a couple of blond juniors, a young engineer officer, and a little gray man in civvies whom Lee guessed to be the local British consul. A couple of tables were pushed together at the back of the room and the Britishers seated themselves with loud talk and great laughter. Their conversation was even freer than might have been expected from man-o-war's-men, since they supposed there were no other English-speaking persons within hearing.

"It would be nice to join up with those babies," said Luke enviously.

"Later, perhaps," said Lee. "I have an idea."

They were in the middle of their dinner when Lee, who faced the front, looked down in his plate, saying: "Here comes Senhor All-go-down. Don't look right away."

The newcomer seated himself at a table opposite theirs on the other side of the room. Luke, after giving him a glance, said:

"He answers to the general description, but how can you be sure?"

Lee said: "(a) it is a man I have seen in the public rooms of the Lisboa Palace. (b) He knew me the moment he saw me, and it has upset him horribly. He can't make up his mind what to do."

"If he knows he's discovered, he may make a break for it."

"In that case, break after him. Luckily for us, he's a stranger in this town. He won't be missed."

Luke grinned.

The man across the room decided that if he did make a break, the long-legged one would certainly nab him; he might as well have his dinner.

Lee's eyeglasses glittered. He said to Luke: "Did you notice there was no key to the door of our room? In these village hotels the keys are always mislaid. Maybe there's no key to All-go-down's room either. Have you the nerve to go up and try the door of number four? If the door is open, go through his things. You know what we would like to find. I'll be keeping an eye on him."

"I've got the nerve," said Luke, rising to suit the words, and putting down his napkin. He strode out.

The man across the room was missing nothing. At Luke's departure he became even more nervous than before. However, he continued to eat his way doggedly through his dinner.

Luke was gone about ten minutes. He came striding back with a perfectly dead pan and seated himself. "Okay," he said. "I found a bottle half-full of Duotol tablets. It is in my pocket."

"Not the passkey?"

Luke shook his head.

"Well, I suppose he has turned that over to one of the others for future use."

"What are you going to do with him?" asked Luke. "Turn him over to the police?"

"That was my original idea . . . I don't know. Finish your dinner and watch him. If he leaves, follow him. Don't let him out of your sight. If necessary, seize him and hang on to him."

Lee strolled towards the hilarious party at the back of the room. "Gentlemen," he said to the officers, "when I heard your English voices . . ."

"An Englishman!" they shouted.

"Well, not exactly . . ."

"American!" they cried, leaping up, and all trying to take his hand at once. When it had been well shaken, a chair was drawn up and Lee pushed into it. A glass was filled and refilled for him. They toasted him and Lee toasted them. Lee ordered more wine. Amidst the confused conversation he learned that the destroyer was the *Egret*, and that they were sailing at ten o'clock Out of the tail of his eye he saw Algodão leave the restaurant and Luke follow him.

The handsome young commander introduced himself as Esme Harrington-Long. "He's an Honorable," added the little gray man in Lee's ear. "Son of Lord Fausley." The other officers were introduced; the grey man was Mr. Daw, and, as Lee had supposed, he was the British consul in Torres Pretos.

Lee said to the company: "I am an American, as you have guessed. My name is Amos Lee Mappin, I am hoping that Mr. Daw here may know something about me."

The little man stared. "Amos Lee Mappin!" he repeated solemnly. "Of course! Of course! I have had advices from Lisbon concerning you." He got to his feet. "Gentlemen," he said, leaning across the table impressively, "I am not at liberty to divulge just what my advices were, but I can say this: Mr. Mappin is a famous man in his own country, and at present he is engaged in an important and merciful work on behalf of the United Nations."

Cheers and felicitations from all around the table. Lee had to drink with each of the Britishers in turn. He merely touched his lips to the glass. He took his passport from his pocket and offered it to the consul. There were loud protests.

"No! No! . . . Not necessary between friends and allies. We can see what you are!"

"Please," insisted Lee. "This is wartime and I would like to show my credentials. Read it to the gentlemen, Mr. Daw."

The consul read: "Amos Lee Mappin; occupation, author; height, 5 feet, 6 inches; weight, 170; eyes, gray; hair, brown . . ."

"What there is of it," put in Lee.

"Distinguishing marks: mole on left shoulder . . ."

Lee glanced down the restaurant. "If there were not ladies present, I would take off my shirt."

Much laughter around the table.

"Hold up the photograph so all can see it," said Lee.

"Hardly does you justice," said Mr. Daw.

"Looks like my idiot cousin," said Lee, "if I had one."

The passport was returned to Lee's pocket. More wine was brought and toasts drunk. All this took a lot of time. The absence of Algodão and Luke caused Lee a keen anxiety, but it would have been fatal to try to rush matters. When he saw his chance, he got to his feet again.

"You fellows will make me tight if I don't look out," he said. "I mustn't get tight tonight. I didn't come to this God-forsaken town for the beauty of the architecture. I have business here. As a matter of fact, I am faced by a certain difficulty, and I'm going to ask you fellows to help me out, as one ally to another."

There were loud cries of approbation and agreement around the table. The sailors were delighted by the suggestion of an adventure ashore. They begged Lee to go on. Only the young skipper maintained a certain reserve; his was the responsibility.

"Perhaps I ought to speak to your commander in private," said Lee.

Lieutenant Harrington-Long shook his head. "Tell all of us," he said.

This was what Lee wanted. "Well, it must be off the record, as we say. In strictest confidence, gentlemen."

The restaurant had emptied when Lee began his story. While he talked, he watched the faces of the two waiters covertly. They were not listening. He told briefly of the murder of William Miller— but not too briefly, because he wanted to enlist their feelings. The Britishers' jaws hardened when he spoke of the Gestapo. Lee laid before them what he had learned of the circumstances leading to the murder. He described the net he had succeeded in weaving about the man he knew as Algodão, and how he had found him in Torres Pretos.

"He is number two on my list," said Lee.

It was not difficult to win sailors warmed with wine. Long before Lee got to the end of his story, they were raring to go. "Where is he? Where is he?" they demanded. Only their commander was still silent.

"Wait a minute," said Lee. "I haven't yet told you what I want you to do . . . I meant to turn this fellow over to the local police until you blew in. Nothing else I could do. Here's my difficulty.

I've had evidence that the Portuguese would rather have this case hushed up than solved. They feel it is dynamite for them. You can hardly blame them. It would be useless to try this fellow until I have rounded up his confederates. Some time may elapse. And I have a fear that when Algodão is wanted for trial, he will turn up missing . . ." Lee paused and looked around at his eager hearers with a fatherly smile.

"Well? . . . Well?" they asked.

Lee said softly: "I want the *Egret* to carry him to some spot on British territory where he can be detained until he is wanted."

It created a sensation around the table. They were hot to do what Lee wanted and said so—still they kept glancing at their commander, who did not commit himself.

"He's a stranger in this town," said Lee. "If we can carry him off without raising an alarm, he'll never be missed."

Lieutenant Harrington-Long still looked down at his plate, considering.

"I suggest," added Lee, "that we ask Mr. Daw to call up the British Ambassador in Lisbon and ask for instructions. His Excellency knows all the circumstances."

It turned the scale. The skipper looked up with a broad grin. "That would take too long," he said. "Besides, it's two to one His Excellency is dining out and couldn't be reached. I'll take a chance on carrying him to our next port. That's Gibraltar."

There was tremendous enthusiasm around the table.

"I will see that a full account of the circumstances is in the hands of the authorities before you reach Gibraltar," promised Lee, "so the burden of explaining it won't fall on you."

"Where is he? Where is he?" demanded the younger officers.

"He left the restaurant about half an hour ago," said Lee. "My secretary is shadowing him. We shall have word directly. In the meantime, another glass of wine to Hands Across the Sea!"

A little later a rough-looking fisherman entered the restaurant from the street. The waiters glided to prevent him from annoying the gentlemen. He raised his voice indignantly, and those at the table heard the words: "Senhor Mappeen."

"Bring him here!" said Lee.

The fisherman offered Lee a scrap of paper torn from Luke's notebook. On it was scribbled: "I have A. cornered in a wine shop. The man will show you the way."

"Well, gentlemen, let's go," said Lee.

After an amiable wrangle about the bill, Lee got his way and paid for the wine, and they departed.

The wine shop was in a dingy basement at the westerly edge of town. It had a forbidding aspect, and Lieutenant Harrington-Long said:

"You mustn't go into such a place, sir. The white waistcoat would start a riot."

"I expect you're right," said Lee. He scribbled: "Bring him out," on the bottom of Luke's note and sent the fisherman in with it.

The lieutenant meanwhile had sent Mr. Daw back to the town quay for the *Egret's* boat. To Lee he said: "We don't want a fracas here. Would attract too much attention. We'll walk on down the road and you follow. If you need help, you have only to sing out."

"We won't need any help," said Lee, smiling.

The officers disappeared in the darkness.

Out of the wine shop came the miserable figure of Algodão, Luke close behind him with his hand held significantly in his pocket. As Algodão stumbled up the steps, Lee wondered to see him carrying his suitcase, and chuckled. All fixed for the journey, he thought.

"Let's take a little walk," said Lee pleasantly. He indicated the road out of town.

Algodão hesitated, looking around him desperately. Luke poked the gun in his ribs. "Get going," he said.

The prisoner started off briskly enough, but soon faltered and began to whine pitifully.

"Wants to know what we're going to do with him?" said Luke.

"He's not going to be harmed," said Lee.

As they left the town behind them, the prisoner's knees began to give under him and they had to support him on either side. When his legs failed him altogether, Luke stopped and said harshly:

"I'm getting good and God-damned tired of this. Walk, you swine, or your walking days will end here and now!"

Algodão recovered the use of his legs.

As they proceeded, Luke told Lee his side of the story. "He left the restaurant and went up to his room. When I was in there before, I saw a little balcony overhanging the lane at the side, and I thought he might try to get out that way. So I posted myself at the corner of the hotel, where I could watch both the front door and the side lane. Sure enough, All-go-down came out on the balcony, dropped his suitcase over, and then let himself drop. It was only about nine feet or so.

"He went through several lanes, thinking he had shaken me off. I believe he was making for the railway station, but he met some natives who told him there were no more trains, and he turned back. I ducked into a doorway until he passed me. He made a detour to keep away from the praça and went to a garage. There was a fellow, working there, and All-go-down tried to hire a car. I was afraid he might be successful, so I went in and said to the mechanic:

"'This so-an-so is an agent for the Gestapo.'

"Gosh! All-go-down almost passed out when I materialized out of the night. The mechanic didn't need any proof of what I said. All-go-down's face convicted him on sight. I suppose the mechanic thought I was some sort of British secret agent. Anyhow, he held All-go-down while I frisked him and took his gun. Then I marched him out of there, pronto. The mechanic was a wise guy; he wasn't mixing in anything that didn't concern him.

"Outside, this fellow whined and begged for mercy. Offered a thousand escudos to let him go. When he raised it to two thousand, I made out I was interested and we went into the wine shop to talk it over. I had him covered under the table with one hand while I wrote the note to you with the other. He knew it was all up with him then, but there was nothing he could do. If I had raised the cry of Gestapo in that tough joint, they would have taken him apart . . . Where are we going now?"

"The British officers are just ahead of us," said Lee.

When the five waiting figures loomed out of the dark, Algodão stopped short and caught his breath to let out a yell. Flinging an arm around the man's head, Luke held him until one of the

Britishers had him firmly gagged, and his hands knotted behind him. Nothing more than a grunt or two escaped the prisoner.

"Well, Lieutenant, here's where we part," said Lee. "Where's your boat?"

"Coming down the river, sir. Well signal her from the beach with a flashlight. . .I wish I could ask you and your friend aboard, but we must sail at once."

"That's all right," said Lee. "Our acquaintance has been brief but intimate. Good-by, but not forever."

Hands were shaken all around. Lee and Luke turned back.

"That accounts for number two," said Lee.

UPON GETTING BACK to Lisbon next afternoon, Lee's first act was to drive to the Legation to report. The Minister laughed at the story of what had happened in Torres Pretos.

"I will lay the matter before the British Ambassador at once," he said.

"If he cuts up rough," said Lee, "if the young lieutenant is likely to be reprimanded, better make an appointment for me to see His Excellency."

"Make your mind easy," said the Minister. "His Excellency's a good fellow. If the Portuguese don't make an issue of it, why should the British worry?"

"Algodão will never become an issue," said Lee. "He has disappeared into thin air with his suitcase!"

"By the way," said the Minister, "I have a cable from Westerholm. The Erbeldings have arrived safely."

"Good news," said Lee.

Lee and Luke then drove to pick up their letters and telegrams at the central post office on Black Horse Square. Lee always had in mind the danger of being jostled upon leaving the post office and the letters snatched. Today, however, they were still free of their trailers. From the post office they went on without fear to their room in the Rue Augusta, where the mail was read, answered, and destroyed. Other fugitives from Germany were to be expected.

At six they returned to the Lisboa Palace for baths and clean clothes. Here, of course, the secret agents were waiting. One, a flashy-looking fellow, was in the little foyer of the hotel, and Lee went up to him.

"Glad to see you again," he said affably. "Have a cigar?"

"Many thanks," said the man, taking it without cracking a smile.

As they went up in the lift, Lee said to Luke: "Silly game, isn't it? They know that I'm on to them, and now they know that I know they know."

They had not been long in their rooms, when the telephone rang. It was Bosco. As this was not his usual hour, Lee knew that the message must be an important one, and stood beside Luke while he took it.

Luke repeated: "Bosco says the Bulldog has returned to Lisbon."

"Ha!" exclaimed Lee. "Ask him how he found that out."

The answer came: "Bosco has just met his friends at the *leiteria* and the lift operator told him. He thought you ought to know immediately."

"Very good. What were the circumstances of the Bulldog's return?"

"He arrived at the Hotel Excelsior about an hour ago. He was evidently expected, because the Germans were all as nervous as cats. Bulldog came into the hotel in a black rage, and they cringed before him. He met Schoënhut in the foyer. In the lift-operator's hearing, the Bulldog asked him if he had picked up the little pig. Schoënhut said no, and there was a terrible scene. The Bulldog stamped and cursed like a madman. He dragged Schoënhut into a room and slammed the door, and the lift operator couldn't hear any more."

Lee glanced ruefully in a wall mirror. "I suppose I could be called a little pig," he murmured.

"Bosco says," Luke continued, "that the lift operator seems to be scared half out of his wits, and says he's not going back to the Hotel Excelsior to work any more."

"That would be very inconvenient for me," said Lee. "Ask Bosco if he has a hundred escudos on him."

"He say's he's got two hundred."

"Tell him to pass it to the lift operator and say there's a thousand a week in it for him as long as he sticks to his job and reports on what goes on in the Excelsior.

"Bosco says that will keep the lift operator going for a while longer."

"All right. Tell Bosco to try and establish another connection inside the hotel. Ask him how about the chambermaid?"

"Bosco says he'll look into the chambermaid."

"And tell Bosco to have the Bulldog followed, if possible, but not to expose himself."

"Bosco says okay."

CHAPTER TEN

AT NOON NEXT DAY Lee and Luke set out for the Macaco Branco for the meal that the Portuguese termed *almoço*, meaning breakfast, which, however, was a tolerably sustaining meal. Two racks of glass trays containing hors d'oeuvres would be followed by a fish course, that by an entree, and that by a chateaubriand, say, which they took it was the generic name for steak in Lisbon. The *Senhora* was always disappointed when they declined to order wine for breakfast like everybody else.

They followed their usual course across the Rocío and through the Rua do Arco de Graça. In this street they came upon an arresting figure. It was a tiny old woman walking along uncertainly, while she searched the faces of the passers-by with a dreadful expression of anxiety in her faded eyes.

She looked like a print out of an old-fashioned book of fashions, with her dress reaching almost to the ground, a wrap of the sort that used to be called a dolman, and a little bonnet trimmed with jet. She was lugging a satchel. It wasn't very big, but it was too heavy for her. In her other hand she carried an umbrella. Her clothes were not shabby, but looked as if they had been kept for years in a press with lavender, only to be brought out on rare occasions. Lost, strange, distressed persons were so common a sight in Lisbon, nobody was paying any attention to her. Lee and Luke paused instinctively.

"Speak to her," said Lee.

Luke addressed her in Portuguese. "Can we help you, madam?"

She looked at him searchingly, like a child, and sadly shook her head.

"Try her in English."

English had no better success. "*Sprechen Sie Deutsch?*" she whispered.

Lee came forward. "I speak a little German," he said in that tongue. "How can we help you, madam?"

Her face brightened. But Lee and Luke were a little stunned by her answer. "Can you direct me to the Hotel Excelsior in the Rua Azorrague?"

Lee's expression hardened. "Sorry, I do not know that street."

The little old lady drooped. Lee understood her to murmur: "*Ich hab' hunger.*" Pity revived.

Lee said quickly: "My friend and I are on the way to eat. If Madame would do us the honor of accompanying us. There is a restaurant on the little square yonder."

She thanked him prettily. "I have money," she explained, "but I cannot speak the Portuguese. I was afraid to enter one of the restaurants alone."

Luke took the satchel and they walked on. Lee and Luke exchanged a wondering glance over the bonnet of their little companion. Who or what was she?

"Are you gentlemen English?" she asked in her deprecating way.

"American," said Lee. "But though our two countries are at war that is no reason why we . . ."

She quickly interrupted him. "I am not at war with America. America loves liberty."

Once again Lee gasped for breath, so to speak. "Then why are you looking for the Hotel Excelsior?" he asked.

"They told me it was the headquarters for German people," she said simply.

"Not your kind of Germans," said Lee grimly.

"I do not understand you, sir."

"Wait until we get to the restaurant," said Lee. "It is right before us. There we can talk at our ease . . . By the way, my name is Amos Lee Mappin and this is my secretary, Luke Tremaine."

"I am Frau Anna Mahler."

Her fears departed. She settled herself at the table like an obedient child. Lee translated the *lista de pratos* for her and she expressed herself as pleased with everything. "But I could not eat all that!" she protested.

"Neither can we," said Lee.

Lee and Luke were charmed with her old-fashioned, ladylike manners.

"What is wrong with the Hotel Excelsior, Herr Mappin?" she asked anxiously. "You looked so strange when I mentioned the name."

Lee said bluntly: "it's the headquarters in Lisbon for the Gestapo."

She fell back in her chair with a look of pure terror. "Gestapo!" she whispered. "Are you sure? How do you know that?"

"It is something everybody in Lisbon knows."

"Mein Gott! What a narrow escape!" she whispered.

"Where did you get the name of that hotel?" asked Lee.

"I came by railway last night," said Frau Mahler. "On the street I saw a sign 'Hotel' and it was late, so I looked no further. They gave me a room. There was no restaurant in that hotel. This morning I ask them if there is a hotel for German people and they tell me Hotel Excelsior. It was not far, they said. I could have taken a cab, but the drivers looked so fierce, they drove so fast, I was afraid."

"It was a lucky escape," said Lee. "If you're a free German, you are one of us and you can be quite open. Tell us how we can help you, *gnädige Frau*. Where did you come from, and where are you going?"

"I want to go to Amerika," she said unhesitatingly. "I have a son there."

Luke heard the word "Amerika" and blurted out: "Well, you certainly came to the right shop, lady!"

Lee sent him a warning glance. "Does your son know you're on the way?"

"No! No!" she said. "How could I let him know? I would have been stopped."

"You can let him know safely from here," said Lee. "That's the first thing to be done." He took out his notebook and she obediently gave him a name, "Ludvig Mahler," and a street and number in Chicago. "It is long since I had a letter," she said sadly.

"You have a passport?" asked Lee.

She made haste to open the satchel and produce it. "It's a good German passport," she explained, "from before the war. With my name and photograph and all. Only the exit visa is false. There are men in Germany who will do that for you for money."

"Didn't these same men tell you where you could find friends on the way?"

She shook her head. "I had no friends on the way."

"In Germany didn't you hear about the Underground?" Another shake of the head.

"An innocent abroad!" murmured Lee. "Tell us about the journey, *gnädige Frau*."

"No trouble," she said. "My passport was good in Switzerland, in France, in Spain, there are many Germans. In the railway station I write 'Lyons, third class,' or Madrid, or Lisbon, on a paper and shove it in the ticket office. Nobody questioned me."

"Well, you're all right now," said Lee, ". . . if you can keep out of the hands of the Gestapo. All you need is an American visa, and you can walk on a ship and walk off in New York. You would have to wait a long time for a seat in a plane."

"No plane!" she said, looking scared again. "How would I get an American visa?"

"You will have to tell the American Minister all about yourself and let him investigate."

"There is little to tell," she said sadly. "I will tell you . . . I was born Anna Ehrlich. My husband, Hans Mahler, was a clerk in the municipality of Muenchen. He never rose very high, and we were poor but contented enough until the war. We had one child, our son Ludvig. He was a Social-Democrat and he went to America when Hitler rose to power. Since then things have gone from bad to worse in the Fatherland. We were little people; we didn't mix in politics. We suffered and kept our mouths shut. Nobody bothered us. Six months ago my husband died. We had our savings. I thought and thought. Ludvig could never return to Germany again, and I wanted to see him before I died. I made long plans. Little by little, I turned everything we had into money. I was such a little person, nobody noticed me. So at last I set out. That is all, *Mein Herr*."

"It's enough," said Lee. "Life will begin again for you now."

"Where can I stay in Lisbon while I'm waiting?" she asked timidly.

"We'll find you a place," said Lee. "Unfortunately, the Gestapo witnessed our meeting."

The little woman's hand went to her breast. "The Gestapo!" she echoed.

"Follow us everywhere," said Lee cheerfully.

"In a neutral land!"

"They take advantage of neutrality."

"Where are they now?" she faltered.

"Watching the restaurant from the little square outside."

Frau Mahler seemed to lose her appetite.

"For that reason, you cannot live in our hotel," Lee went on. "If you were watched all the time it would be like a prison."

"It should be a modest place, Mein Herr," she said timidly. "I haven't much . . ."

"You don't have to consider money," said Lee. "There is a fund subscribed by loyal German-Americans to enable others to escape from the Nazis."

"How wonderful!" she murmured.

"I know the very place for you," said Lee. "It is not a hotel, but an humble Lisbon home kept by a kindhearted woman. I'll take you there after lunch."

"But if the Gestapo follows us, I will still be watched!"

Lee laughed. "My friend and I have ways of shaking them off when we have need to."

"You are so kind, Mein Herr," she whispered. "And to a stranger!"

"Not kind at all!" said Lee gruffly. "It's my job to help people like you."

When they had finished their lunch, they asked the *Senhora* to telephone for a taxi. They waited for it just inside the door of the restaurant, and the moment it drew up hastened across the sidewalk and got in. There was no other cab instantly available, and in this manner they got the jump on their trailers. After turning half a dozen corners and making certain they were not followed, Lee could safely tell the driver to take them to the Calcado Burro at the end of the Rua Bacalhoeiros—Street of the Codfish-sellers.

The little old lady's fears were relieved now, and as they drove along she chattered about the scenes she saw through the window.

"All these women seem to spend their time gossiping in the street. Their homes must be a sight! . . . Many women are carrying baskets of fish on their heads . . . The men have caps hanging down their backs like children. Fish, fish everywhere."

"This is the quarter of the sailors and the fishermen," Lee explained.

"Fish was always expensive in Muenchen," she ran on innocently. "We were so far from the sea." She touched her handkerchief to her eyes. "Ach! that dear Muenchen! I am old to start a new life, Mein Herr! How can I live without music?"

"There is plenty of music in Lisbon," said Lee.

"Music!" She held up her tiny gloved hands in scorn. "Not German music!"

Soon they were knocking at the great oaken door of Teresa's little house in the heart of the swarming Alfama district. Teresa's wrinkles spread with gladness at the sight of them. Teresa never understood why Lee took so much trouble to save the enemies of his country, but every visit he made always meant perquisites, in addition to the rent, and he was therefore very welcome.

"What about the little white-haired children?" she asked.

"They are safe," said Lee. Luke translated for him.

"Where is the pink-faced young man?" she asked.

Lee, not wanting to provoke an emotional display, merely said: "He has gone home."

Teresa led them into the big bedroom at the back. It overlooked a little pocket-handkerchief of a garden with gay flowers and a miniature ilex tree.

"How pretty!" said the German woman. "Where does that little door in the wall go?"

"To a back lane," said Lee. "We can get out that way if the front door is blocked."

Teresa was studying Mrs. Mahler with strong curiosity. The two women presented a striking contrast. With her deeply seamed face and glowing dark eyes, Teresa looked like a witch beside the dainty little German lady.

"Teresa, this is Senhora Mahler," said Lee. "She has had much trouble. Take good care of her for me."

"*Si! Si! senhor*," said Teresa dutifully. It was clear from her expression, however, that an old woman did not appeal to her sympathies like the German children had. She was noting how sharply Mrs. Mahler's eyes searched the corners. The room was clean by Portuguese standards, but not German clean.

To Mrs. Mahler, Lee said: "You are to ask Teresa for anything you may need. Unfortunately, she does not speak your language, but I am sure, with a woman's wit, you can make each other understand. I will get you a German-Portuguese phrase book."

"Must I stay in my room all the time?" Mrs. Mahler asked wistfully.

"No. You are safe in this district. Ask Teresa to write her name and address on a piece of paper, so you'll be sure of getting back here."

"I shan't go far," she said.

"Better not let anybody know you are German," Lee warned.

"Why?" she asked, with widening eyes.

"Germans are not popular in Lisbon just now," he said grimly.

She touched her handkerchief to her eyes, "Ah, my poor country!"

She recovered her spirits before Lee left. "It is like a beautiful dream," she said, "to find friends in a strange country! . . . What about my business here in Lisbon, Herr Mappin?"

"I will take care of that," said Lee.

"When shall I see you again?" she asked wistfully.

"Tomorrow at this same time, Frau Mahler."

"I shall be waiting for you."

On his return to town, Lee told Mrs. Mahler's story to his friend the Minister, and a cable was immediately dispatched from the Legation to Ludvig Mahler in Chicago.

Later, in the hotel, Lee asked the ample, soiling-eyed Natalia what she had observed of the movements of the two men in number 218 adjoining during the last couple of days. Natalia now had the air of a fellow conspirator with them; she was enjoying the situation.

"Name of Rosado," said Natalia; "old man, young man; they give out they are father and son, but it is not so. The young man when nobody is around calls the other Luiz. Old Man big and hairy like a bear; young man sly and naughty, always after women."

Lee said: "I've seen those two in the lift. I gave the young one a cigar. Go on, Natalia."

"The old man goes out a great deal, the young man hangs around the room doing nothing. I am always finding him there. He makes love all the time. He has had much experience—but so have I! It is very amusing." At this point Natalia gave them an imitation in pantomime of Casanova's frank advances, and how she rebuffed them. Luke rocked with laughter.

"Understand, senhor, he is not doing this because he likes me; it is because he has been told to do it. A woman always knows. He is after something else. I do not know what it is."

"I know," said Lee. "It's what they've been after from the first. All-go-down didn't get it, so they've put the Bear on the job. He sounds like a tougher proposition. The young one, I take it, is just a stooge."

Natalia, through the medium of Luke, continued: "The young man is always asking me what hour do I get my lunch or my dinner, when I go home, and so on. I think maybe they enter this room, senhor, when I am out of the way."

"I don't doubt it," said Lee. "One may assume that they have inherited All-go-down's passkey."

Natalia said: "The senhor takes it calmly!"

"They'll never find what they're looking for in here while we're out," said Lee. "While we're in the room, the door is bolted. When we shoot that bolt we turn it in its sheath. You can't do anything with a bolt like that short of breaking down the door."

Natalia pointed significantly to the water bottle.

"They won't catch us that way twice," said Lee. "We drink bottled water from the bar."

Luke put in: "They have a nerve coming into our rooms. Suppose we were to return and catch them here?"

"Not much danger of that," said Lee. "The men who trail us about can keep them informed by telephone."

Natalia said dramatically: "Look, senhor! Here is something else." She was pointing to the keyhole of the communicating door between their sitting room and number 218. "It was stuffed with paper, senhor, and they have pulled it out!"

Lee laughed. "Childish!" he said. The communicating door was bolted on his side. Shoving back the bolt, he tried the door, and found it bolted on the other side as well.

"I will stuff the keyhole with paper again," said Natalia.

Lee shook his head. "Let them peep and listen. We're on our guard. Let them think we haven't discovered their trick."

WHEN THEY RETURNED to the hotel after dinner, Bosco called up. Bosco, it appeared, had made progress in organizing his forces. He was spending money like a lord on Lee's behalf. Since Lee had told him not to loiter in the Rua Azorrague, he had hired a room across the street from the Hotel Excelsior, with a window commanding the windows of the hotel and the entrance. By keeping a certain distance back from his window, he could see all who entered and left the hotel without showing himself. Bosco had also hired two sharp Lisbon newsboys who knew the city like a book, and he knew where to lay his hands on more if required. They hated Germans, he said.

Senhor Mappin had instructed him to follow the Bulldog without showing himself, he went on. Very well, he had engaged a taxi to wait in the street a hundred yards beyond the hotel, with one of his boys inside, watching through the rear window. Meanwhile, he was at his window opposite the hotel. About ten o'clock a taxi drove up and the Bulldog came out and was driven away. Bosco opened his window and shook out a white cloth like a dusting rag. This was the signal to the boy in the taxi.

Unfortunately Bosco had to report a failure then. The Bulldog soon discovered that his cab was being trailed by another, and he drove around until he succeeded in shaking it off. He returned to the hotel in a couple of hours and remained there all afternoon. Evidently there was something doing, because men were coming and going all day.

Bosco further reported that the lift operator had brought the chambermaid to the *leiteria*. She was an ugly girl, Bosco said, and very pleased to get a little attention. He had a date to take her out on her first night off. Finally, Bosco wanted to know if he could hire a taxi by the week so that he could always have it handy. He would need more money for that, he said. He knew just the man.

"A clever fellow," said Lee dryly, "but he's likely to ruin us with too much cleverness. Tell him this: He is not to hire a taxi. The Germans would instantly get on to it and his friend the driver would be found floating in the river one morning. The public taxis are safer. Change them often. Tell him he is to stay away from that room in the Rua Azorrague. How often does he think he could use that trick with the dust rag before the Germans spot it? It was just dumb luck that he got away with it today. The Bulldog must be already investigating how it happened that he was followed away from the hotel. Let Bosco's boys watch the hotel in rotation and report to him."

NEXT MORNING the Legation telephoned that no answer had been received from Ludvig Mahler, and Lee requested that the cable company be asked to furnish a report on the message. Such a report came from the Legation just before lunch:

"Party moved. Whereabouts unknown."

This was the unpleasant news that Lee had to carry to the waiting mother.

Lee, with the help of the Minister, enlisted the services of the F.B.I. in starting a search in America for the missing man.

When they went for their lunch, Lee noted that they were followed by the same two men as on the previous day. They had the appearance of Portuguese, but were not the same two that he had once sidetracked into a cinema. These were husky bravos with hard, blue-chinned faces. All they needed were black cloaks and broad-brimmed hats to walk on as brigands in a melodrama. The older of the two sported a pair of ferocious mustaches; the younger was decorated by a livid scar from temple to chin. This one habitually kept his hands in his pockets.

While they were eating their lunch, Lee was called to the telephone. On returning to the table he reported that it was Inspector da Gama. "They told him at the hotel that we were here. He wanted to warn me that Stengel had returned to Lisbon. Very decent of him. I didn't tell him that I knew it already. Da Gama wants me to call him back in half an hour, in case he has further news."

When Luke and Lee issued out of the restaurant, they saw that their trackers had taken the precaution to have a taxi waiting near. The Americans entered the first cruising taxi that came along, and the usual chase through the streets began. Lee had it in mind to use a cinema Luke had found with an emergency exit in the rear, but after all they did not find it necessary to change cabs. They lost their pursuers in the winding streets.

"Odd," said Lee, "that they let themselves be shaken off so easily today. You'd think they'd be hell-bent to discover where we've hidden the little woman."

They drove on to the Alfama. At the opening of the steep Calcado Burro they paid off the taxi and Lee went into a pay station to telephone da Gama. "No further news," he said when he came out.

Above the steps, the crooked little street presented its usual lively appearance. Women with baskets darted in and out of little basement shops or paused to exchange the latest news, speaking at the top of their voices to make themselves heard above the cries of the hucksters. Screeching children darted among the legs of their elders, playing a game of their own. A young man posed gracefully on the corner, twanging a guitar and allowing himself to be admired. Always beneath the loud, near voices one could hear a chorus of chattering as of a flock of birds.

"Gay, isn't it?" said Lee. "But I shouldn't like to live in the thick of it."

The cul-de-sac where Teresa lived was strangely quiet by contrast. All the doors of the little one-story houses with red-tiled eaves were shut and the windows shuttered. The inhabitants, it appeared, had gone off to join the sociable throng in the Calcado.

Lee knocked, and the door was quickly opened by little Frau Mahler herself, her face wreathed in smiles. "Teresa has gone to do her shopping," she said. "I was listening for your knock. I am so glad to see you!" The great door swung to and she shot a bolt across. "Teresa said I must always bolt it," she said.

She preceded them through the short tiled passage. The stairs to the kitchen went down at one side. Opening the door to her room, she went in, saying:

"Enter, *Mein Herren!*"

Lee had a glimpse of men within the room, and stopped short on the threshold. Instantly the door of Teresa's room behind them banged open, there was a rush of feet, and two men charged into Lee and Luke, thrusting them into the rear room. The door slammed to behind them.

The little old woman stood before them transfigured with rage and hate. Her faded eyes were blazing. "*Heil Hitler! Heil Hitler!*" she shrilled, thrusting up her hand in the Nazi salute. "Now you see me for what I am! A faithful servant of *der Fuehrer's* and a hater of all his enemies!"

Lee and Luke stared at her in amazement.

"*Heil Hitler!* You shall say it, too, Yankee pigs! Under the whip you shall say it!"

A man's voice rumbled from behind her: "Quiet, woman!"

She could not stop. For twenty-four hours rage had been accumulating in her until it had reached the point of explosion. "Yankee pigs!" she screeched. "Liars! Murderers! I spit on you!"

"Quiet!" repeated the man. "Or you'll be put out of the room!"

She burst into the loud, toneless weeping of hysteria and sat on the edge of the bed. Lee and Luke looked away from the ugly sight.

From the corner of the room a harsh voice said, in guttural English: "Good afternoon, Mr. Mappin. I am happy to make your acquaintance!"

CHAPTER ELEVEN

IN THE REAR BEDROOM of the little house in the Alfama, Lee Mappin and Luke Tremaine were fronted by five hard grinning faces. Beyond them two pairs of windows stood open to the little balcony and the free air of heaven. They could see a patch of blue sky and the sun gilding the green top of the little ilex tree in the yard, a tormenting sight to trapped men. For a moment or two, while the Gestapo agents savored their triumph, nobody spoke.

Luke muttered to Lee: "Anybody would have been fooled! Anybody! She put on a marvelous show!"

"I ought to have seen through it!" said Lee.

Luke moved closer to Lee. He glanced towards the windows.

Lee shook his head. "Useless," he whispered. "Our best chance is to play for time."

In the right-hand corner of the room alongside the window, a tall man with a prominent Adam's apple, a long nose, and gray hair sticking out in every direction, sat at the same table where one night the Erbelding children had eaten their supper. His long fingers beat an idle tattoo while he grinned evilly at Lee. Judging from Bosco's description, this was Schoënhut, the local chief. The man guessed what was passing through the minds of the prisoners.

"Shut the windows," he said. And when this was done: "Tie them up!"

"We have no intention of trying to escape," said Lee mildly.

"Can't trust you!" said the grinning Schoënhut. "Tie them up!"

The other four men circled around them warily. Two had coils of a light, thin rope. It was the same sort of rope that had bound

119

William Miller. The faces of all four were known to Lee. Two he recognized with a grim start of humor as the two men who had been trailing him earlier in the day. "Mustaches" and "Scarface" he christened them for purposes of identification. No wonder they had allowed him to give them the slip. They knew where he was going and desired to get there first. Scarface was still keeping his hands in his pockets. The remaining two were men he had seen around the hotel; his neighbors in room 218, of course: The Bear and the coarsely handsome Casanova as named by Natalia. They were registered as Luiz and Antonio Rosado.

All four of these men were of the type of brutalized, hired murderers. Possibly Portuguese, or they might have been of any race. Professional murderers have no nationality. Though there were so many of them, they hesitated about starting a mix-up. Schoënhut laid a gun on the table and joined the others.

"For God's sake, what are you waiting for?" demanded Lee. "Tie us up and be done with it!" To Luke he whispered: "Don't struggle! You will need all your strength later."

Finally a rope was thrown over Lee's head and drawn tight about his upper arms. When Scarface went into action, he had to take his hands out of his pockets and Lee saw that he was wearing brown cotton gloves. Lee's eyes burned at the sight. Beside him, Lee saw Luke sweating, grinding his teeth in the effort to hold himself in. Hard as his orders were, Luke obeyed. The ropes were cast round and round their bodies and knotted at every turn from shoulders to ankles. They were relieved of their guns. Mrs. Mahler, sitting on the bed, watched the performance with hateful delight. Lee wondered how the woman could ever have made herself look innocent and gentle.

"Push up chairs for the gentlemen," commanded Schoënhut sarcastically. As Lee and Luke sank on the chairs, he went on: "Search their pockets and the linings of their clothes."

Nothing of any account was found upon them but their wallets. There was a considerable sum of money in Lee's wallet. Young Scarface counted it, and his eyes glistened.

"Put it back!" rasped Schoënhut. "We are not robbers!"

Lee permitted himself to smile.

Schoënhut was disappointed at not finding any papers. "You have not been to the Rua Cachimbo lately," he snarled. "Where's your new office?"

"Rua Ventura, 11," said Lee calmly. "On the fourth floor."

Lee's seeming candor took the other man aback and he scratched his chin to hide it. Luke grinned.

"There's nothing there," added Lee, "but of course, if you want to break into the place and search it, I can't stop you."

"Where do you keep your papers?" demanded Schoënhut.

"There are no papers," said Lee mildly.

"You lie!"

Lee went on: "As soon as it is read and digested, everything is destroyed." He tapped his skull. "Everything is in here."

Schoënhut pounded the table. "And we know how to get it out of there, too!" he cried with an oath.

It galled him that Lee was able to keep cool and smile while he could not. Rising, he walked across the room and back; stood for a moment or two looking out into the sunny yard. When he resumed his seat his face was smooth.

"Well, we have all afternoon," he said with pretended joviality; "Teresa won't disturb us and her husband is at sea."

"Where is Teresa?" Lee demanded boldly.

"Down in the kitchen," said Schoënhut.

"Alive or dead?"

Schoënhut made believe to be grieved. "Why, Mr. Mappin, what do you think we are?"

"I'd hate to say," retorted Lee.

"We have no desire to injure that good woman, but only to keep her out of the way while you and I transact our business."

"What is our business?"

Schoënhut did not answer him directly. "We have no desire to injure you either, but only to remove you as a threat to our work. As an enemy spy, Mappin, I'd be justified in shooting you at sight and throwing your body in the street. But you're such a little fellow, I couldn't bear to do it!"

"You haven't answered my question," said Lee. "What's our business this afternoon?"

As Schoënhut started to speak again, the bearded man whom Natalia had christened the Bear, interrupted him: "Better wait until he comes," he said significantly.

Schoënhut subsided, lit a cigarette, and leaned back in his chair. "You're a pretty cool customer," he said to Lee.

"I see no reason to be otherwise," said Lee.

Lee was presenting a perfectly bland face to his tormentors, but Luke, glancing sideways, could see the fine drops of perspiration springing on his upper lip. By twisting a little in his bonds, Lee was able to glance at his wrist watch. "Quarter to three," he murmured to Luke. Luke wondered what difference time made to them now.

Silence fell in the room. The two beds had been pushed to the back to make more space. Mustaches and Scarface sat down beside Mrs. Mahler and the three of them lit cigarettes. It was odd to see the difference a cigarette hanging from her lips made in the prim old woman. She looked like an old vixen now. Schoënhut leaned back silently, drumming his fingers on the table. The Bear stood against the wall in a state of suspended animation. Casanova opened one of the windows and lounged beside it, breathing in the fresher air. Minutes passed.

Lee smiled at Luke. "Keep your dander up!" he murmured.

"I'm okay," said Luke quickly. "I was prepared for something like this."

More minutes passed. In the distance they could hear the human bustle far off in the Calcado Burro. Luke twisted restlessly in his bonds.

"God! it's hard to wait in silence," he muttered.

"Having to wait is a godsend!" said Lee quickly.

Luke glanced sharply in his face, but Lee volunteered no further explanation.

Lee looked at his watch again. "Seven minutes to three!" Finally there was a double knock at the street door. Mrs. Mahler sprang up from the bed. "Here he is!"

Schoënhut rose. "Listen!" The first double knock was followed after a space by another, then a third. "All right!" said Schoënhut. "Let him in!"

In passing Lee the woman spat and whispered with an ugly, contorted face: "Now you'll get what you deserve!"

They heard her open the street door and close it. The iron bolt scraped across; heavy footsteps sounded on the tiles, and into the room strode the man who had figured in Bosco's reports as the Bulldog. He was of medium height, but the big head and the immense breadth of shoulder seemed to dwarf him. With that broad face, heavy brows, flattened nose, undershot jaw, Bulldog was inevitable. Ordinarily his little pale eyes had a pained roll—such a man is never satisfied—but now they were swimming with venomous pleasure. At the moment everything was going well for him.

Ignoring Luke, he stood in front of Lee. "So we meet at last!"

Lee said nothing.

"I did it! I did it!" shrilled Mrs. Mahler. "I delivered him into your hands!"

He glanced at her contemptuously. "You shall be suitably rewarded. Leave the room now."

"No! No!" she protested, clasping her hands. "Please let me stay! I've earned it!"

"It is no sight for a woman."

"I have no sex! I am a servant of *der Fuehrer! Heil Hitler!*"

Stengel shrugged and forgot her. She resumed her former seat on the edge of the bed, watching and listening, moistening her dry old lips in anticipation.

Stengel said to his men: "I have received information that Pedro Chavez' fishing boat has entered the river. He may be expected home in an hour. We'll deal with him when he comes."

Stengel spoke a medley of tongues; Portuguese or German to his men; English to Lee—all in the same thick, guttural tones. When he spoke Portuguese, Luke softly translated for Lee.

With an arrogant jerk of the head, Stengel ordered the table shoved up closer to Lee, and the chair placed behind it. Schoënhut obsequiously hastened to obey. Stengel sat down, smiling derisively.

"Well, Mappin!"

"Well, Stengel!"

"So you know me!"

"Your name is known all over the world."

"It's pleasant to find oneself famous."

"Well, that depends," said Lee, "upon what one is famous for."

Upon Stengel's entrance, Scarface started to unwrap a cube-shaped package that stood on the floor between the windows along with a paper bag. The package contained a little charcoal brazier, such as plumbers use, together with several irons; the paper bag had charcoal to feed it. Lee grimly took note of the charcoal. Scarface carried the stove out on the balcony, where he proceeded to make a fire in it, blowing the charcoal until it glowed cherry red.

"First of all," said Stengel to Lee briskly, "describe your relations with the United States Minister to Portugal."

Lee sparred for time. "With a view to forcing the Portuguese government to ask for his recall?"

"Never mind why."

"I have had that danger in mind from the beginning," said Lee, "and I have been most careful not to draw the Minister into any unneutral acts on my behalf. It is true, he issued a pass to the Erbelding family, but that cannot be called an unneutral act, because my country has accepted the Erbeldings as citizens."

Stengel's face darkened. "Criminals and traitors!" he cried, rapping the table sharply.

"In that case, why not let us have them, and all others like them," asked Lee mildly.

"Germany punishes traitors!" said Stengel. He commanded his anger. "You would like to draw me into a discussion, wouldn't you? Pardon me if I decline." His stubby forefinger shot out. "Mappin, who supplies you so generously with money?"

"There's no secret about that, Stengel. It's a private organization in America known as the Association for Aiding Anti-Nazis. It's supported by voluntary contributions, principally from German-Americans."

Stengel swallowed this pill with a wry face.

Scarface brought the little brazier into the room. The charcoal was glowing redly. He stuck the irons into the fire and blew on the coals. The irons were long and slender, and had wooden handles. Lee and Luke watched with fascinated faces.

"This is reproducing the scene that was played in the Rua Cachimbo," murmured Lee.

"Now," barked Stengel. "I want the names of your European agents. You have a sort of underground railway, haven't you? Reaching across Spain and France and Switzerland into Germany itself. Give me the names of the agents beginning with those *in-side Germany.*"

"There are agents in Germany, no doubt," said Lee, "but I have no concern with them. I don't know their names. All my communications are cleared in Switzerland."

"How are they passed back and forth across the border?"

"I don't know. By many routes, I assume."

"Whom do you address in Switzerland?"

Lee hesitated. Scarface drew one of the irons out of the fire to look at it. It glowed almost white-hot. He thrust it back.

Stengel rapped on the table. "Answer the question!"

No sound from Lee.

"Schoënhut," said Stengel, in a slow, caressing voice, "take off Mappin's shoes and stockings. He has such dainty little feet I'm sure they must be tender."

The tall German hastened to obey. The sweat ran down Lee's white, masklike face. Luke could bear no more.

"If they hurt you . . . If they hurt you," he cried brokenly, "I can't stand it! I'm going to talk!"

"Go ahead!" said Lee, loud enough for Stengel to hear. "Talk, if it will ease you! Anything you like! Now you know why I have never taken you into my full confidence."

Luke's head dropped on his breast. He gritted his teeth in the effort to regain control.

"For the last time!" Stengel barked to Lee. "The name of the Swiss agent?"

Silence from Lee.

Stengel nodded to Scarface, who approached Lee with the glowing, white-tipped iron in his hand. Scarface had the most villainous face of them all; retreating forehead, bright, glassy, black eyes without a vestige of human expression. He dropped to his knees in front of Lee.

"Stop! Stop!" cried Lee breathlessly, "I'll talk!"

Luke jerked up his head. "No!" he cried, turning a face of horror and dismay. What he read in Lee's face reassured him. His chin dropped on his breast again. He was silent.

"Get up!" said Stengel to Scarface.

The young man rose with an ugly look of disappointment, and thrust his iron back into the coals.

"Proceed!" said Stengel to Lee.

Lee was breathing fast. He spoke a name and an address in Bern, Switzerland. Stengel wrote it down. "Go on!" he said.

Under his questioning, Lee gave other names in Grenoble, in Lyons, in Marseilles, in Nîmes, France; in Barcelona, Madrid, and other towns in Spain. As he proceeded, Stengel's face darkened with suspicion.

"If you're lying, it won't do you any good," he said. "I shan't let you go until I have verified these names." To Schoënhut he went on: "If there is another knock on the door it will be Pedro Chavez and his son. Let the woman open the door, and you men fall on him inside. They can join the woman below. If necessary, we'll spend the night here."

Lee lowered his head so that Stengel could not see into his face.

Taking an envelope from his breast pocket, Stengel removed the letter it contained and spread it on the table. "This will be the test," he said to Lee. "Your next answers will tell me if you are lying."

Lee, who thought he recognized the writing, eyed the letter anxiously.

"This is a letter to you," Stengel went on, "which I intercepted—never mind how. It doesn't make any sense as written, and I want you to decode it. It's postmarked Nîmes, France, and addressed to Monsieur Mappin at the Lisbon post office."

Lee said nothing.

Stengel read from the letter:

Dear Sir:

The news from the front continues to be discouraging. The Americans are still advancing in Italy, but at an enormous cost to themselves in men and materiel. A mere handful of Germans is keeping their whole armies in check.

My aged and respected Aunt Clora Duval passed away last Wednesday at Montpelier at six o'clock in the evening. She did not suffer in the end. Our respected friend, Major Wertheim, the German Commandant for this district, sent a beautiful wreath of wax flowers. His wife and sister were amongst the great throng who attended the last sad obsequies. My good aunt was so long a sufferer, we cannot regret her passing. But our hearts are very sad.

In Russia the German armies continue to retire, contesting every foot of the way. In this manner we shorten our lines, especially our supply lines, while the enemy's lines are always lengthening. As we retire, our matériel rolls up like a snowball. In the spring you will see everything changed. Our leaders are preparing a secret weapon that will annihilate the foe.

Sincerely your friend,
Armand

"Who is Armand of Nîmes?" asked Stengel with an ugly smile.

"I have already given you his real name," said Lee. "Naturally, letters are signed with a pseudonym."

"What is he reporting to you in this letter?"

"Just what you have read," said Lee. "All our letters are not about business. The man's aunt dies. He is my friend. He tells me about it."

Stengel flushed darkly. "Do you take me for a fool?" he snapped, rapping the letter. "This pretense of friendliness to the Germans is only to fool the censors. Would any enemy of Germany write such a letter to another enemy if it was not to deceive?"

Lee was silent.

Stengel changed his line of attack. "Is Walther Niebuhr named in this letter?"

Lee looked innocent. "No," he said. "I do not know that name."

"You lie! It is known that Niebuhr has lately passed through Nîmes!"

"The name means nothing to me," said Lee.

"Then translate this letter," shouted Stengel, "and prove it!"

"The letter tells its own story," persisted Lee.

"Bring the iron!" roared Stengel.

Scarface moved with alacrity to obey. Lee began to sweat again. Luke turned away his tortured face. Scarface, with the glowing iron, dropped to his knees at Lee's feet.

"Wait!" said Stengel suddenly.

Scarface turned a scowling face over his shoulder.

"Mappin may fancy himself in the role of a martyr," Stengel went on with a curling lip. "He's such a humane little man. Perhaps he'll yield quicker to the sight of pain in another." He jerked his head in Luke's direction. "Take off his shirt!"

"No!" cried Lee involuntarily. "He knows nothing!"

Stengel laughed. "Maybe not. But you do . . . I think this is going to work," he went on to his men. "If it doesn't, if the young fellow dies on us, we still have Mappin to work on."

In order to remove Luke's jacket and shirt, they had to throw off the ropes. Scarface thrust his iron back in the coals so he could give a hand. Luke got his arms free and started to fight. Lee had no heart to forbid him now. The chair crashed over and there was a wild confusion of beating fists and threshing legs on the floor. The tall Schoënhut walked around the struggling men looking for a chance to help; Stengel sat back in his chair, laughing; the old woman watched from the bed with a clenched hand pressed against her lips.

Though they were four against one, it took time to subdue Luke.
Lee glanced at his watch again. Finally the chair was planted back
on its legs and Luke dropped on it, bruised and bloody. They had
torn his shirt off him piecemeal, and he was bare to the waist. He
was a little groggy, and his head rolled helplessly on his neck. They
tied his hands behind him to the back of the chair, and his legs to
the chair legs.

"He's a pretty fellow, isn't he?" drawled Stengel in English.
"Hey, you!" he went on to Scarface. "Can you write 'Heil Hitler!'
across his manly chest? I'll spell it out for you."

Scarface laughed and drew the pot of glowing coals up to Luke's
chair.

"Have you anything to say before we begin?" Stengel asked Lee.

Luke, recovering partly from his stupor, cried out: "Don't
weaken! Don't weaken! I can take it! It's better this way than . . ."

Lee slowly shook his head.

Stengel nodded to Scarface. "Go ahead! Make a neat job of it.
First, a capital H."

There was a faint hissing sound, and the stench of burning flesh
filled the room. The sweat poured down Luke's face but he made
no sound. The convulsed face of the man who wielded the iron was
like something seen in a nightmare.

The dreadful silence was broken by a peremptory pounding on
the street door. Scarface held his hand. The woman jumped up from
the bed, but halted irresolutely, looking at Stengel. Stengel rose,
growling:

"That don't sound like a man at his own door. Go with the
woman, some of you. Don't open unless you're sure . . ."

Three of the men ran out. They had no more than reached the
passage when the knocking was renewed and voices were heard,
demanding admittance. Stengel's men came tumbling back.

"The police!" they gasped.

Stengel broke into low, furious cursing. The powerful blows on
the street door convinced him. His face expressed a hellish disappointment. "Out through the yard!" he ordered. The men started
tumbling down the kitchen stairs, the woman with them. "Take that

with you!" Stengel ordered Scarface, indicating the brazier. "Empty the coals in the alley."

Stengel was the last to leave the room. Schoënhut's gun was still on the table. He picked it up, glanced at Lee, hesitated. In that instant, Lee looked squarely into the face of death. But Stengel thought better of it, thrust the gun in his pocket, and hastened after his men. The kitchen door slammed shut, and after a moment, the door in the garden wall.

The police had secured something to serve as a battering-ram, and there were repeated heavy blows on the street door. It yielded with the sound of rending wood and scraping iron, and men poured into the passage. Inspector da Gama came running into the rear room followed by his men.

Luke managed to smile at him with stiff lips. "Just in time!"

Lee was sagging limply in his bonds. Da Gama bent over him. "Are you hurt, Mr. Mappin? Are you hurt?"

Lee shook his head feebly. "A man can stand a strain . . ." he muttered. "Goes to pieces afterwards . . . All right now . . . There's a woman in the kitchen. Take care of her."

"They escaped through the yard," volunteered Luke.

The inspector took three men and went after the fugitives. One was left to free Luke and Lee, another told off to keep the curious neighbors out of the house, and a third to take care of Teresa.

When the ropes were cut away, Lee and Luke stood erect and stretched their cramped limbs, then gravely shook hands.

"My boy!" murmured Lee compassionately when his eyes fell on the ugly wound on the young man's breast.

Luke covered the place with his hand. "I got off easy!" he said.

"If I had decoded the letter," said Lee, "it would have cost the lives of three fugitives!"

"I know! You did right . . . How in hell did the inspector get here?"

"Yesterday," said Lee, "the woman fooled me completely. To-day, when we were allowed to shake off our trackers so easily, I got suspicious. It was just possible, I thought, that she might have been used as a decoy. There were discrepancies in her story. So when I talked to da Gama the second time, I said to him on the chance: 'Inspector, I may be walking into a trap. If I don't call you again in fifteen minutes, come quickly and bring men with you'."

"Too bad you didn't think to tell him about the back way out. Then we'd have them all."

Lee slowly shook his head. "I thought of it. If they were arrested today, what would happen? Stengel would be sent back to Paris and I to New York. All our work would stop . . . We have much to do first, Luke."

CHAPTER TWELVE

TERESA, BROUGHT UPSTAIRS by the policeman, was more frightened than hurt. In the back room she launched into an impassioned story to Luke and a pair of sympathetic policemen. Lee, who could not understand a word of it, paced the little passage, trying to bring his thoughts into some order. Presently Pedro and Carlos came home, amazed to find a gaping crowd before their house and a policeman on guard at the door.

Teresa began from the beginning, and Lee, who wanted action, was ready to tear his hair. He succeeded in getting Pedro out in the passage, with Luke to translate. It was his first sight of the fisherman in the light. Pedro, lean, hard, and weatherbeaten, was a reassuring physical specimen.

"Pedro, where is your boat?"

"At the Cais do Sodre, senhor."

"If it is necessary, could you sail again tonight? Same terms."

A broad smile spread across the fisherman's rugged face. This was more profitable than fishing. "*Si, senhor.*"

"Teresa must not be left alone here while you are gone. Could you take her with you?"

"*Si, senhor.* Teresa is accustomed to the sea."

"I want you and Carlos to come to the hotel with me now. We must act quickly. Get your Sunday clothes on. I suppose you haven't got guns?"

Pedro shook his head. "We have knives, senhor. They are quieter."

"They took our guns, but I have another at the hotel."

Pedro asked only one question: "What are we going to do, senhor?"

Lee answered him indirectly: "Pedro, a man must avenge his own injuries, and not leave it to the police."

This suited Pedro exactly. "Right!" he said, adding an uncomplimentary reference to the police. He called Carlos out, and they disappeared into the front room to change their clothes. Lee kept Teresa going until her men were ready.

In less than a quarter of an hour they started out. Teresa had put a temporary dressing on Luke's wound, and Carlos had lent him a shirt to cover his nakedness. Luke lingered behind for a moment, and overtook them with a paper package under his arm. Teresa was dropped at the house of a sister who lived near. Pleased at the idea of obtaining a new audience, she did not plague the men with many questions. Nothing was said to her as yet about a sea voyage.

Down in the Street of the Codfish-sellers the four men piled into a taxi, and Luke gave the word to drive to the Lisboa Palace. As they started, they passed the police car coming back with its attendant motorcycles and fanfare of sirens. The men exchanged grim smiles.

In the hotel the clerks in the bureau looked askance at the rough fishermen in their ill-fitting Sunday blacks, but by this time Lee was established in the Lisboa Palace as a powerful and mysterious personage whose acts were not to be questioned. They went up in the lift. In the corridor leading to their suite, Lee laid a finger on his lips and they entered their rooms without making a sound. Lee laid an ear to the crack of the door, that communicated with room 218 and turned around, nodding and smiling.

He rang for the chambermaid and opened the door so that she could enter without knocking. Luke unfastened his paper package. It contained various lengths of the light rope that had lately been used to bind Lee and Luke and Teresa. Some of the cut pieces were too short, and Luke coolly proceeded to knot them together. When Natalia entered, Lee received her with finger on lips and pointed next door.

Natalia whispered to Luke, and Luke passed it along to Lee: "She says they came in a few minutes ago and are packing to leave."

Lee said: "These are her instructions: Let her take fresh towels into the room. She had better leave the door open a little so she can make a quick getaway. After arranging the towels, on her way out she is to pull back the bolt on the other side of the communicating door and beat it!"

When this was repeated to her, Natalia was scared but not altogether displeased at the prospect of a row. She nodded her head a great many times and went away to get the towels.

Lee and Luke, listening at the door, heard her come back. She knocked at the door of 218; Lee heard a wary voice ask: "Who is it?" and Natalia's reply: "The chambermaid, senhor." Her voice was steady. A man crossed the room and unlocked the door. He said: "We don't need any more towels." Natalia answered: "Well, since I've brought them let me leave them here." She crossed the room and came back. As she passed the communicating door, the bolt was sharply drawn back. Lee flung the door open just as Natalia's skirts whisked through the other door and it slammed shut.

The four men walked into the adjoining room, Lee first because he was the only one with a gun. "Put your hands up!" he said in his mild way. By the windows the Bear and Casanova presented a comic exhibition of astonishment. Their hands went slowly up. Interrupted in the midst of their packing, they were in their shirt sleeves. Suitcases and jackets lay on the beds. Luke meanwhile had slipped aside to the corridor door, locked it, and dropped the key in his pocket.

While Lee kept the two men covered, Luke came up to frisk them. Pedro and Carlos were pressing up close at either side.

"These boys have knives in case my gun should fail to get you both," Lee said, smiling.

Luke took a gun from each man.

"Now we're better armed," said Lee. "Hand me one and keep the other. The boys will do better with their own weapons . . . I will keep these two covered with both hands, while you search them more carefully."

Luke went back to Casanova. The coarsely handsome, pomaded dandy's eyes glittered poisonously, but Lee stood beside Luke with his two guns, and close by were the two husky fishermen with their hands hovering inside the lapels of their jackets. Casanova's raised arms trembled with rage—but he kept them up.

"The tables are turned, eh?" said Lee.

From his various pockets, Luke drew coins, a penknife, cigarettes, a wallet containing paper money and several misspelled letters from infatuated women, a German passport in the name of Antonio Rosado.

"No good," said Lee. "Put it all back except the passport."

Finally, buttoned in one of Casanova's back pockets, Luke found a brass key and an oddly fashioned pair of tweezers made out of thin metal.

"This looks more promising," said Lee. "Try the key in the door of our room."

Luke reported that it locked and unlocked the door.

"Then this is what we are looking for," said Lee. "The other instrument, obviously, was used to turn the key in the door." Both objects were shown to Pedro and Carlos Chavez. "Examine them well," said Lee. "You will have to identify them later, and testify as to where they were found."

Lee then placed key and tweezers in an envelope, sealed it, and wrote across the flap the circumstances under which they had been found.

As Luke proceeded to search the Bear, the hairy man's little eyes burned and he hissed through his teeth with rage. Luke went through his pockets with an unconcerned air. This man's German passport was in the name of Luiz Rosado. Nothing else of interest to them was found on him.

"Who's got a pair of scissors?" asked Lee.

Luke produced scissors from one of the suitcases. "Cut a little patch from his beard," said Lee.

With an oath, the Bear lunged forward, but Lee raised the gun and he fell back, cursing helplessly. Luke snipped a little patch from his beard. Lee enclosed the hairs in another envelope and endorsed it.

"I have an idea this will prove to be very valuable evidence," he said.

Lee, with a gun in each hand, sat down facing the captives. "Search their bags," he said to Luke.

This operation took a little time. Nothing incriminating was found.

"Now tie them into two chairs," Lee said to the fishermen. He handed one of the guns to Luke. "If either starts to resist, crack him over the head with the butt."

Pedro and Carlos made a seamanlike job of tying up the Rosados. With grunts of satisfaction, they pulled the ropes tight and knotted them. Pedro suggested wetting the ropes to make them contract, but Lee drew the line at that. As they were finishing the job, the telephone rang in Lee's sitting room and he went to answer it.

He presently returned, smiling and twinkling. "It's the police inspector," he said to Luke. "Wants to question us about this afternoon. I told them to bring him up. You had better go and have your wound dressed. There's a doctor in the hotel. Then come back." To the two captives, he went on: "If you holler for help, I'll have to turn you over to the police. So take your choice!"

Lee went into his own sitting room, closing and bolting the communicating door behind him. Inspector da Gama was shown in, followed by his secretary-interpreter and another officer. The smart inspector's face bore rather a hangdog expression.

"Why did you not wait for my return?" he asked reproachfully.

"I had an important engagement at the hotel," said Lee blandly.

"Please do me the favor of describing all the circumstances that led up to the dastardly attack on you and your secretary this afternoon."

"Certainly," said Lee. "Let us sit down, Inspector."

The secretary produced notebook and pencil.

Lee faithfully described his meeting with the woman who called herself Frau Mahler, and how he had placed her in Teresa's house.

He went on to tell how he and Luke had returned there after lunch that day, and how they had been set upon.

"But why?" put in the inspector.

"They were trying to get information about my private business," answered Lee. "They questioned us, and upon our refusal to answer certain questions, they proceeded to torture my secretary."

"Torture?"

"To brand him with hot irons."

"Horrible! . . . Had you ever seen these men before?"

This was a safe question. "There were six of them," said Lee. "Four were unknown to me. The other two I had seen on several occasions as they followed me through the streets."

"Describe all six of these men as precisely as you can."

Lee did so truthfully, leaving the inspector to draw his own conclusions.

Lee answered all questions, but volunteered no information. Since he was not anxious to reveal the whole truth, and the inspector not a bit more desirous of bringing it out, they understood each other pretty well. The Hotel Excelsior in the Rua Azorrague was not mentioned, nor Albrecht Stengel named. In the course of the examination Luke returned to the room.

"Here is my secretary," said Lee. "He will be glad to answer your questions."

"It is not necessary," said the inspector, "since I assume you have told me all."

He finally rose to go. Since he still looked a little ashamed of the part he was playing, Lee said encouragingly: "It's a difficult situation, Inspector. I feel for you."

Da Gama thanked him gratefully. "If you could present me with a case against these scoundrels I could act," he said.

"Perhaps some day the whole truth will come out," said Lee.

"In the meantime I will do all I can, senhor."

When the police left, Lee and Luke returned to the adjoining room. The prisoners still sat bound to their chairs, glaring at their captors in impotent rage. Pedro had found a deck of cards in one of the suitcases, and he and his son, seated on the bed, were playing a game that involved a lot of counting.

"Sociable little scene," said Lee.

Casanova began to curse him thickly in mixed German and Portuguese.

"I'm a merciful man," said Lee mildly. "But if you don't keep quiet, I'll have to order you gagged."

Casanova dried up.

Carlos was given money and dispatched to purchase supplies for a voyage, and to see them carried aboard the *Enguia*. He was then to fetch his mother from the Alfama and put her on the fishing smack. When all this was done he was to report to the hotel by telephone.

Lee consulted again with the buxom Natalia. "Natalia," he said "Is the man who watches at the service door tonight a friend of yours?"

"He could be, senhor," she said, smiling and bridling.

"Can you remain in the hotel later than usual tonight, say until half-past nine?"

"*Si, senhor,*"

"Can I depend on you to tempt the man away from his post for a few minutes at that hour, while our guests are escorted to a taxi?"

Natalia's smile broadened. "*Si, senhor*. It will not be difficult."

"How much money will you need?"

With an inimitable shrug, Natalia said: "Nothing for *him*."

"Very well, then keep it yourself," said Lee, slipping her a bill.

Luke was sent out to buy two of the voluminous black capes worn by the students of Lisbon, and a pair of the broad-brimmed black hats that go with them. Sizes were obtained from the hats worn by the captives. These two looked on and listened with apprehensive scowls.

Luke was further instructed to return to the hotel by way of the Rocío. If he found Bosco selling papers at his usual post, he was to tell the youth to make his way to the hotel by a circuitous route and to ask for Mr. Mappin at the service entrance in the courtyard.

Lee sat down on the bed with Pedro. "Teach me your game," he said.

Luke returned in due course with the capes and hats. When tried on the scowling captives, the hats fitted well enough.

"Where are we going?" growled the Bear.

"We're going to give you a little air later," said Lee. "We want to keep you in good condition."

Luke said that he had found Bosco and that the boy might be expected to follow in a few minutes. Natalia was instructed to watch for Bosco at the service entrance and bring him to Mr. Mappin's suite.

He came with his papers under his arm. A slim, straight youth, seventeen years old and handsome in the dark, Latin fashion, his knowing glance and derisive smile reminded Lee of New York boys he had known. At the moment, Bosco was abashed by the faded magnificence of the Lisboa Palace.

"Let me have a good look at you," said Lee. "This is our first chance to get really acquainted."

Bosco merely grinned.

"Have you anything to report today?" asked Lee.

"Not much," said Bosco. "The Bulldog went out at two o'clock. I didn't try to follow him. I don't know if he has come back. I can find out after six o'clock when I meet my friends."

"You said you knew a taxi driver that we could depend on."

"Yes, gentleman."

"Can you lay your hands on him now?"

Bosco nodded eagerly. "If he has a fare I will have to wait a little."

"That's all right. We won't need him until later. Give him a hundred-escudo note and arrange for him to wait all evening near a telephone. Write down the number and bring it to me. On your way back, stop at the *leiteria* and see if your friends have anything to report, but don't stop to eat there. You can eat here on your return."

Bosco left by the same way he had come, and Lee sat down to resume his game with Pedro.

At six o'clock Carlos called up to report that the *Enguia* was fully stocked and ready to sail and that he had taken his mother aboard. They were not followed through the streets, he said.

Carlos was instructed to cast off after dark and drop down the river to an agreed spot below Belem, where he was to anchor and wait for his father and their passengers. He was to expect them about ten. When he got a signal of five quick flashes from the beach he was to come in for them with a boat and a couple of men.

Lee then ordered a generous dinner served in his suite, including plenty of wine. He ordered covers for four persons only, but took care to include sufficient food for six.

Bosco arrived back about the same time that the dinner came up. He had made a deal with his taxi driver friend, and the man agreed to spend the evening in the garage near the quays where he kept his taxi. Bosco had the telephone number of the garage. They were to ask for José. From the Hotel Excelsior there was nothing to report. The Bulldog had not returned

"He suspects that hotel may be visited by the police," said Lee.

When the waiters had departed, Luke and Pedro carried the dinner table into room 218 so they could keep an eye on their captives while they ate. It was an oddly constituted dinner party and Lee, the connoisseur of humanity, was as much pleased with his guests as with the food. There was firstly his neat little self in a white waistcoat, then big Luke with his bruised face and a livid black eye, the weatherbeaten Pedro in his Sunday blacks, and lastly newsboy Bosco. Bosco's eyes glistened at the sight of the fancy food. But he had never been taught table manners, and he was embarrassed how to begin. Lee said to Luke:

"Tell him to pitch in and the hell with table manners! Tonight we're all men together!"

When the sense of this was conveyed to Bosco in Portuguese, he grinned widely and fell to.

The two captives over by the window looked on at the feast with bitter eyes. Finally Casanova could stand it no longer.

"When do we eat?" he demanded.

"The hell with you," Luke said coolly.

Lee glanced at Luke warningly. "They will be easier to handle if they're fed," he said under his breath.

"All right," said Luke to the captives, "you will get yours after we finish."

When the edge of appetite was dulled, Lee, to draw out his youngest guest, asked: "What are you going to do after the war, Bosco?"

Luke repeated it in Portuguese.

Food and wine had charmed away Bosco's self-consciousness. He said politely: "Do me the favor to spik Angleez, gentleman. I spik Angleez all right. I wish to spik more. After the war I leave Portugal. It is good country but the people are poor. I save my money now. I learn the Angleez more good. I go to America and make moch money. When I have moch money I come back. I live as a gentleman." Bosco looked around the room. "Maybe I live here."

"But everybody in America is not rich," objected Lee.

"All right," said Bosco confidently. "I work hard. The gentleman say I smart fellow. I make good . . . Maybe the gentleman will take me to America to be his servant?" he added with an insinuating smile.

"Servants don't make much money," said Lee.

"All right," said Bosco, "the gentleman will tell me what to do."

"I'm no money-maker," said Lee.

Bosco regarded this as an excellent joke.

"What's Carlos going to do after the war?" asked Lee. Luke translated the discussion into Portuguese.

"Bosco is right," said Pedro in his slow fashion. "Here the people are too poor. I catch fish. So we do not starve. We can buy but little; everything is too dear. Me, I am too old to go to a new country. Maybe the gentleman will take Carlos to America."

"Carlos is a good boy," said Bosco jealously, "but what could a fisherman do in New York?"

"As much as a boy of the streets," retorted Pedro warmly.

To settle this, Lee said: "I will do what I can for both boys after the war."

When they had finished eating, the table was carried close to the captives and Bosco on one side fed the Bear while Pedro did the like for Casanova on the other. It was a remarkable sight to see the two scowling brigands opening their mouths as obediently as baby birds in the nest. Pedro took it as all in the day's work, but Bosco's eyes were dancing. He was warned not to exploit the comic possibilities.

Lee suggested that Luke throw the rest of the men's belongings into their suitcases and close them.

"If we take their baggage along," said Lee, "the hotel management will suppose they have jumped their bill and no alarm will be raised."

Lee, meanwhile, sat down to write the letter that Pedro was to hand John Westerholm on the island of Fayal. Along with his letter, he sealed up a pocketknife in the envelope.

"Keep this on your person at all times," he instructed Pedro, "and if anybody interferes with you, toss it overboard and let it sink."

Bosco called up his friend the taxi driver at the wine shop and told him he was now engaged permanently by Mr. Mappin and should remain on call at the garage at all times. For tonight he was instructed to drive up to the service door in the courtyard of the Lisboa Palace precisely at nine-thirty.

When the time approached, they arrayed their prisoners for the journey. One at a time their bonds were freed and they were required to stand. Their arms were then bound securely behind them. When the capes were adjusted with one end thrown picturesquely over a shoulder in Portuguese fashion, all sign of the rope was hidden. A broad-brimmed black hat cocked at a jaunty angle completed the picture. All being ready, Lee made them a brief speech:

"No harm will come to you now or later if you obey orders and keep quiet. You will be well fed and comfortably lodged. It is not your lives we want, but only your testimony against those who hired you. If you do not obey orders, you will be shot instantly. We are not going to take any chances."

At nine twenty-eight the procession set out from Lee's suite. The communicating door with 218 was bolted on both sides. Lee and Bosco walked ahead; then the two prisoners, draped in their capes, finally Luke and Pedro, each holding a gun concealed inside his jacket. Through the long, softly carpeted corridor they went, making a couple of turns, and then down the service stairs. It was the same route over which William Miller had been carried. They met nobody except a startled waiter on the landing, who stared at the unusual sight and scurried on up. One flight, then another; there was no hitch; the service door was unguarded, and as they reached it, the taxicab drove up in the court.

Not a word was spoken. The Bear and Casanova were placed on the rear seat; Luke and Pedro each with gun in hand faced them; Bosco climbed in beside the driver and the cab drove away. Lee returned up the back stairs to his rooms.

LUKE WAS BACK inside an hour. "All serene," he said. "I waited until I saw them taken aboard the *Enguia* and she started down the river."

"Good!" said Lee. "That accounts for numbers three and four."

"What next, Chief?" asked Lee.

"Do you want to lie up until your wound is healed?"

"No damn it! I want to pay them back for it!"

Lee paced the room. "That letter that Stengel read to me this afternoon told me that the celebrated Walther Niebuhr was on the way. He is bringing his mother and father. Niebuhr is one of the leaders of the Underground movement in Germany. There's a big price on his head."

"How did Stengel get that letter?"

"Intercepted at the post office in Nîmes, I take it. The Germans control there. We must make new arrangements. Luckily, they don't know who wrote it . . . Niebuhr has no papers, consequently his way is full of dangers. The letter was probably written some days ago. They may turn up at any time—they may never arrive. Our job is to help them through."

"Okay, Chief."

CHAPTER THIRTEEN

LEE'S FIRST NECESSITY next morning was to procure his letters and telegrams from the post office. With Luke he set off early in a taxicab, and they soon found themselves, as usual, followed by another cab. Looking through the back window, Lee glimpsed two hard-faced men in the following car in addition to the driver. These were new faces. One man was leaning forward continually urging the driver.

Today their trackers, favored by luck or skill, were not to be shaken off. The Lisbon taxi drivers, sure of a handsome tip, always enjoyed these chases and displayed great skill in navigating the narrow streets. Lee's driver drove east to the edge of the Alfama and back to the west with innumerable tricky turns. It was no use; the following cab clung close behind, and Lee became a little discouraged.

During a brief traffic block in the Rua Garrett, an *electrico* stopped beside them. The view from behind was blocked for the moment by another taxi. Lee looked at Luke and Luke slipped out of the door of the cab and stepped on board the trolley car. When traffic moved again, the car turned one way and Lee's taxi another, and Lee had the satisfaction of seeing the following cab take after him. He led it blithely down one street and up another, finally giving his driver the word to return to the hotel. The other cab was still close at his heels. As he got out, it was pleasant to picture the chagrin of the two men upon discovering that half their quarry had escaped them.

In a few minutes Luke turned up safely with the letters. No telegrams today. The most important communication was a letter postmarked Badajoz, Spain, a city on the border of Portugal. Lee turned it over in his hands before opening it. It had been opened by the Portuguese censor at the border and sealed again.

"It is possible," said Lee, "that this was opened in Spain and put back in the mail. The censor's seal would hide the marks. There are plenty of Germans in Badajoz."

"Read it! Read it!" urged Luke.

The substance of the letter as Lee decoded it was as follows: "I have reached Badajoz after many hardships and dangers. A man here has agreed to put us over the border and to keep us at his house in Portugal for a few days. He is a Republican. Please let me know if it is safe to venture openly into Lisbon. I know where you are stopping, but it would be imprudent for me to show myself there. Please appoint a place of meeting. Address me Juan Barreto, Villa Boim, Alemtejo. That is my host."

"It's not signed," said Lee, "but of course it's from Walther Niebuhr." He began pacing. "This is a dangerous letter," he continued gravely. "He couldn't put the address of his hiding place into code, and there it is for anybody to read."

"What are you going to do?" asked Luke.

"Motor to this address at once."

"All right. Let's go."

"I want you to stay in Lisbon to find a refuge for these people when they get here."

Luke instantly blew up. "No, sir!" he said. "I'm not going to let you go on such a journey alone!"

Lee looked at him, smiled, and gave in. "All right, Fire-eater!"

"Even the two of us is not enough if we're going to run into trouble," said Luke.

"Especially as I'm so little," said Lee.

"You can pull your weight, all right, and then some."

"If we bring them into Lisbon, where can we hide them?" said Lee.

"The *Senhora* at the Macaco Branco has rooms to rent upstairs."

"Telephone and see what she can do for us. Three people; two rooms; it may be very late before we get back."

The report was satisfactory. Luke said: "The rooms will be ready any time we may turn up."

Lee had spread out his road map on the table. "Here's Villa Boim," he said. "It's a hamlet between Elvas and Borba. Four or five hours' journey, allowing for bad roads. The shortest route is from Barreira across the river, but the ferry takes half an hour and what we'd gain in distance, we'd lose in time. Besides more time lost waiting for the ferry. We'll head north and cross the Tagus at Villa Franca de Xira. Call up José at the garage."

"A Lisbon taxi would be pretty conspicuous so far from town," suggested Luke.

"Surely. Ask José if he can hire a car without any markings. Tell him he must bring extra petrol in cans, sufficient for a three-hundred-mile journey and a little to spare. He'll have to buy it in the black market and it will cost like hell, but there's no help for it. Can't depend on getting petrol out in the country. It must be an able car, and the faster the better. If he says okay, ask him how soon he can be waiting for us at the statue of Pombal at the top of the Avenida."

Luke at the phone conveyed all this to José. Turning to Lee, Luke said: "José says yes, he can get the gas and there is a Hispano-Suiza in the garage in perfect order that we can hire for five escudos the mile."

"Good God!" said Lee. "And how much for the gas?"

"Six escudos the liter."

"Robbery! But we've got no choice. Tell him all right."

"He'll be at Pombal's statue in half an hour and wait until we come."

Lee pressed the bell that summoned Natalia. When she presented her blooming self, he said:

"Natalia, you're a sight to cure sore eyes!"

When this was conveyed to her in Portuguese, she bridled and smiled, and smoothed imaginary wrinkles out of her apron.

"The young fellow and I have to go on an expedition into the country today which may prove dangerous," Lee went on. "It might even end in shooting. He's wounded and I'm too little to be much good. We ought to have help. Can you recommend a *man*, Natalia?"

"There is my husband," she said. "He is not afraid of the devil himself. But he has no gun."

"That's easy. We have a spare. Can we get hold of him quickly, Natalia?"

"I can telephone him at his work. He could leave his work if . . ." She concluded with an expressive shrug.

Lee got it. "I'll take care of that," he said.

Natalia went to the telephone. After a spirited exchange with her man, she turned around to say it was all right; he would go with the gentlemen.

"Tell him to meet us at the statue of Pombal in half an hour," said Lee. "He may have to wait a little. Tell him to hold his hat in his hand so we'll know him."

The name of this admirable man was Affonso Fardo.

Lee stuffed his wallet with banknotes and handed Luke another roll. They secreted other money about their persons.

"On an expedition like this we must go well heeled," said Lee.

It was ten o'clock when they set out. Since Lee did not want to waste a lot more time driving around town, they walked to the station and tried the trick of the two stairways again. This time it didn't work; their trackers had been warned, perhaps; but by good fortune there were only two taxis at the foot of the second stairway. Lee took one, Luke the other, and the two spies were left biting their fingers on the curb. Later, Luke and Lee joined forces and dismissed the second cab.

After making a long detour around to the west, they were back at the statue of Pombal within the half hour. José was waiting for them in a sleek Hispano-Suiza limousine, and a moment later they picked up a man carrying his hat in his hand, who introduced himself as Affonso Fardo.

Affonso was a proper man to have at one's side in case of a fracas. He was old enough to have good judgment, but he had not run to fat like most of the Lisbonese men. His chest swelled reassuringly under his jacket, his belt was pulled into the last hole; he had the expression of a man who was well aware of his own worth.

"I, Affonso Fardo, will serve you," he said to Lee as if that settled all difficulties.

José, on the other hand, was as meager as a jockey. With his cap pulled rakishly over one eye, he looked like a street boy who had started to shrivel before he grew up. Not likely to be of much service in a mix-up, he was a heaven-sent chauffeur. He was a part of the car; he appeared not so much to drive it as to will it to do what he wanted.

They drove north out of Lisbon and turned east at Villa Franca to cross the Tagus. The Hispano-Suiza ran as smoothly as a watch. José was charmed with its performance. On a straight and moderately smooth stretch of road, he got her up to 120 kilometers for a short space. "She flies like a swallow," he said, patting the dashboard. The car belonged to General Aljubarotta, he further informed them in tones of respect, but His Honor was gracious enough to hire it out occasionally to a good driver.

"Extremely gracious of His Honor," said Lee, "at the price."

At Montemor Nova, an ancient place with a ruined castle beside a romantic stream, they paused to order a generous *almoco*. In order to save time they carried the food and wine with them to consume in the car.

The next considerable town was Arraiollos, another hoary and moldering place out of a picture book, with medieval walls and towers. As they crossed the little central praça, Lee suddenly clapped a hand on Luke's shoulder and pressed him to the floor.

"Down! Down!" he said, dropping to his own knees and bowing his head.

"What the hell!" gasped the astonished Luke.

"The Bulldog," said Lee grimly. "Standing at the door of the hotel picking his crooked teeth. His car is heading the same way we are."

Luke fervently cursed the Bulldog. "How many men did he have with him?"

Lee resumed his seat. "I couldn't see," he said. "They hadn't come out yet . . . At any rate, we're in advance of them now. And they don't know it!" He urged José for more speed. "It's all a question of driving. If you're just a little better than their chauffeur, José, they'll never catch us."

José patted the dashboard. "Best job in Portugal!" he said, grinning. Though the man's frame was small, his spirit was strong.

"It is good that I am with you," said Affonso.

All the ranges of hills and mountains in this part of the world run north and south, so that their progress was a series of long climbs followed by descents on the other side. On such a road, they could make no great speed, but neither could the car they supposed to be following them. At the top of the first height, Lee, looking back, glimpsed a tiny object crawling across the valley below.

"We have about ten minutes' start," he said.

These heights were covered with fine forests of the cork oak, and they could seldom see far behind them or ahead. They had no further sight of the following car, and could only hope they were gaining on it. As they proceeded eastward, the terrain became even more rugged and tumbled. The road was modern and well kept up. There were no road signs, but as the map indicated it was the only modern road in the vicinity, there was no danger of going astray.

With its wild heights and fertile valleys, it was a beautiful country, unchanged in many generations. Even the farm buildings and the villages had been there so long they had become a natural part of the scene. But the passengers in the flying Hispano-Suiza had little attention for natural beauties. The three on the back seat rode with their heads over their shoulders. Every time they screamed around a curve of the descent, Lee's heart rose in his throat. A burst tire in this solitude! José seemed to read his mind.

"All the tires are new," he said comfortably.

They had to slow up for other towns: Vimiera, Estremoz, Borba, all ancient, all with maddeningly narrow, crooked streets that had not been laid out for an elongated Hispano-Suiza. Finally, about two-thirty, they rolled into Villa Boim, which consisted of a big church, a small hotel, and a huddle of old houses around a little cobbled praça. They were heading north at this point, and on their right swept up a higher range of mountains than any they had seen. On the other side of this range, according to the map, lay Spain.

A romantic loafer lounged in front of the hotel. José stopped the car and asked him if he knew where Senhor Juan Barreto lived.

He did. Moving on past the hotel building, he pointed up a lane, seemingly to the sky. There it was, he said. A long, low, white building clung to the mountainside high above the town. It was about a mile distant as the crow flies, but undoubtedly longer by road. To reach it, the native said, they must follow that very lane to its end. Could a motorcar make it? Oh yes, the road was rough and crooked, but cars often went up and down. Senhor Barreto himself had a car.

"Ask him," said Lee, "if he is acquainted with the senhor and what manner of man is he."

This question produced the usual flood of Portuguese. When José sorted it out, Lee learned that Senhor Barreto was a Spanish Republican. He had come to Portugal after the civil war and bought land. He was a brave man. On more than one occasion, a party of Falangists had sneaked over the mountain with the intention of seizing him and carrying him back to Spain for trial. But his house was like a fort, and there he was still.

They turned down the lane, crossed a brook, and started to climb the other side. The narrow lane was stony and very rough, but offered no special obstacle to their progress. Small, neatly kept terraced fields spread away on either side. The higher they climbed, the farther Lee could see down the valley where the highway ran. No car was visible upon it.

Above the cultivated ground the stony track was swallowed in a cork forest. It climbed the steep slope sideways, back and forth, with a turn at each end so sharp that the Hispano-Suiza had to back and fill in order to get around it. Now they could see nothing below because of the trees.

"I wouldn't like to be chased down this hill," Lee remarked dryly.

Without warning they issued out on a grassy terrace lying in front of the house they were seeking. Behind the house the mountainside swept on up to the sky. There was no sign of human life visible. The house was built on a series of big arches which formed its foundation. Each archway was dosed with a pair of heavy wooden doors. These arches, they guessed, served the farmhouse as barn, stable, cattle byres, granary, etc.

The living rooms were above, with a long, narrow gallery running across the front ending in a curved stairway at each end, the whole making a pleasing, antique composition. All the doors and windows opening on the balcony were tightly closed and shuttered, except a door in the middle which stood open, revealing a black interior. Through the open door issued a grim masculine voice asking:

"Who are you and what do you want?"

Lee had learned that the best way to answer such a challenge is instantly to show yourself. He stepped out of the car and pulled a little American flag from his pocket. Luke, close behind him, spoke up to the open door:

"This is Senhor Mappin of New York. He wants to speak to your guests."

The response to voice—or flag—was instantaneous. A hard-bitten man of forty or so, with a rifle across his arm, stepped out on the balcony. Others pressed behind him; a half-grown boy, a blond young man, an old couple, children of assorted ages. They hastened along the balcony and down the stairs. The place came suddenly alive.

Lee remembered that his host was a Spaniard and restrained his enthusiasm. Measured, courteous greetings were exchanged on the terrace. Barreto, a tall, spare man, was a fine example of the antique Spanish virtues, grave, reticent, and hard. But it was the young blond fellow's hand that Lee clung to a little longer.

"So you are Walther Niebuhr," he said in German. "I salute a brave man!"

Niebuhr was an extraordinarily attractive young man, built like a hero of the *Nibelungenlied*, with wide-set, candid blue eyes and fresh, smiling lips. There was more in him, though, than youthful good humor; there was power and endurance behind his smiling eyes. He colored with pleasure as he said:

"What I have done is nothing. I am German, I have no choice; but you have come halfway across the world to help us, out of pure good will to mankind."

"We are working for the same end," said Lee.

"That is so; freedom for all peoples . . . So you got my letter. I dared not hope you would answer it in person."

"I got it," said Lee, "but I am afraid others may have got it for whose eyes it was not intended." He turned to Barreto. "We are followed, senhor. The party is led by Albrecht Stengel. I do not know how close they may be. If we leave instantly, perhaps we could reach the foot of the mountain and turn east before they arrive."

Young Niebuhr smiled and shook his head slightly. Lee did not get the significance of it until later.

Barreto also vetoed the plan. They all looked out over the valley. Half a world seemed to be spread at their feet. The highway from the west was visible for a distance of several miles. No motorcar moved on it.

"The risk is too great," said Barreto. "From the point where we can first see them they can reach the village in five minutes by car, whereas it would take you twenty minutes from here in that big car. It is too long for mountain work. You must wait for them here. You will be safe."

"Can you stand a siege?" asked Lee with a smile.

"It would not be the first time," answered Barreto gravely. "There is ample food and water—and ammunition."

Lee glanced at the house. It appeared well fitted to stand a siege; doors and shutters were of iron, an unusual feature; the roof was of red tiles. The only vulnerable spots were the wooden doors in the archways below. Barreto, following Lee's eyes, said quietly:

"They will never reach the doors. I have holes in the floor of the balcony to shoot through."

"Very well, we will take our chance with you," said Lee.

"My son Jaime will watch the road from the balcony," said Barreto.

Lee hung the strap of the binoculars around the boy's neck. "I suppose you know how to use them," he said.

The boy smiled and nodded.

"Jaime is an old campaigner," his father said, not without pride.

CHAPTER FOURTEEN

IN JUAN BARRETO'S HOUSE, Lee was introduced to the elder Niebuhrs. Like so many old couples, they resembled each other strongly; their faces were worn with care to an almost transparent fineness, but steady still. They were very quiet, scarcely ever spoke; their old eyes followed their handsome son in all his movements with an inexpressible wistfulness.

The visitors were invited into the house to take wine, José and Affonso being included since there were no distinctions of rank in this household. In the house Lee met the Senhora Barreto, another quiet woman who had borne much. The principal room revealed an aristocratic bareness; a few pieces of ancient, hand-carved oaken furniture, a holy picture, nothing more. Lee's glance around approved the absence of cheap machine-made stuff and dusty upholstery. Owing to the rising ground, the back windows of this room were only a foot or two above the grass.

When the wine was poured and toasts drunk, young Niebuhr and the grave Barreto exchanged a glance of understanding, and the former said quietly:

"I shall not be going on with you from here, Mr. Mappin."

"Hey?" said the startled Lee.

"I will put the old folks in your care," Niebuhr went on. "They will be safer if I am not with you, because I am the one they are after."

"What will you do?"

"I shall return to Germany."

153

"All the way across Spain and across France! You'll never make it!"

"I think I will," said the young man confidently. "It will be easier when I am on my own. One finds friends everywhere."

"I had hoped you would go to America or to England with them," said Lee regretfully. "You have done your share."

The smiling young man shook his head. "What would I do in America? America is for Americans. I am German. I am useful back there. They are waiting for me."

"I am sorry . . . !" said Lee.

"As long as the old folks were in Germany," said Niebuhr, "the Gestapo could get at me through them. They were continually hounded, and that was hell for me. They were too old to make such a journey alone, and so I have brought them thus far. I leave them with friends, and I go back with an easy mind."

Lee glanced at the old couple. The mother's head was lowered and the tears were falling silently in her lap; the old man was looking stonily ahead. This decision was no surprise to them.

Niebuhr went on softly: "I could not seek safety for myself, Mr. Mappin, and leave my friends in danger back there."

"It is for you to say," Lee said slowly. "I would not try to influence you . . . If you have made the decision, you should start at once before your enemies get here."

Niebuhr shook his head again. "Barreto and I have decided that," he said firmly. "If I wait until they come, I can draw them away up the mountainside while you escape below. They will never catch me on the mountain."

"Jaime will guide him over the mountain," added Barreto. "The boy knows every path."

Lee accepted the decision with a nod. One could as well have argued with a pair of flint stones. "At any rate," said Lee, "you must let me give you money for the return journey. It is subscribed by American sympathizers."

"I'll be glad to have it," the young man said, with his delightful open smile. "One can never have too much money for bribes."

Lee handed him a roll of notes. As Niebuhr started to count it, Lee put a hand over his. "Put it in your pocket. It's not a loan, it's a subscription to the cause."

Lee drew the young German aside. "Herr Niebuhr," he said, "have you and your fellow workers ever succeeded in planting a man in the Foreign Office?"

"Yes," was the smiling answer. "We have an observer there."

"If it is possible for you to procure for me copies of the Prince zu L—'s confidential reports to the Foreign Minister of his doings in Lisbon, it would help me very much in my work here. I would particularly like to see an account of his disbursements, if he makes such reports. It might even hasten the end of the war."

"I will do the best I can, Herr Mappin."

Jaime came to the open door to announce, without excitement, that there was a car on the highway, coming from the east. This tall boy, already toughened by danger, was going to be like his father.

The men went out on the balcony. The car could be seen, like an insect on the distant highway. Even through the binoculars it was impossible to distinguish any details. After watching it for a moment, one could see that it was moving fast.

"We will assume that it is our enemies," said Barreto, "and prepare."

"Should we hide our car in the woods?" suggested Lee.

The Spaniard shook his head. "It will be better in the stable. You can get away quicker."

There was an interior stairway to the lower level. The doors that filled the first archway were unbarred and thrown open, a space cleared inside, the Hispano-Suiza backed in, and the doors closed again, but not locked. The men returned to the room above.

Jaime reported from the balcony: "The car has arrived in the village. It is stopped in front of the hotel where I can't see it."

Juan Barreto looked over his little force appraisingly. There were four men in Lee's party of various sizes and degrees of muscularity. In addition to himself, Juan had Walther Niebuhr and Jaime, who was as good as another man. From a wall cupboard,

Juan produced a formidable armament consisting of four rifles and as many short guns with spare ammunition. Each man in Lee's party had a short gun.

Affonso said with hand on hip: "I am a sure shot."

Juan said grimly: "There is to be no shooting unless I order it."

The four children were placed in a far corner of the room and told to stay there and keep quiet. Even the children of this hard-bitten family did not appear to be unduly alarmed at the prospect of shooting.

Ten minutes passed before the car could be seen leaving the village and crossing the cultivated strip at the foot of the mountain. Lee said:

"By this time they must know that we have ascended the mountain before them. It cannot have been good news."

Barreto's house faced west and the afternoon sun was striking through the door and making a dazzling oblong patch on the cement floor. To the left of this patch, Juan sat in a chair tipped back against the side wall, with his hat pulled down over his eyes and his rifle across his knees. He coolly rolled a cigarette and lighted it. In this position, while sitting in the shadow, he commanded an oblique view through the door of the spot where the ascending car would issue from the trees.

The rest of the party grouped further back in the room, the younger members squatting on the floor since there were not chairs for all. Senhora Barreto moved about quietly, blowing up the fire, putting some small sticks on it, placing the coffeepot on a tripod. Astonishing family!

It seemed to take an endless time for the coming car to climb the mountain. Most of the men lit cigarettes. A thin cloud of smoke floated into the dazzling shaft of sunlight and out through the door.

While it was still some distance away, they heard the puffing of the exhaust as the car climbed in low gear. These were the hardest moments to bear. Lee arose and pressed himself against the wall in the shadow alongside Barreto, where he, too, could look out.

At last the car rose into view; a gray closed car, with faded paint and battered fenders. It rolled across the grassy terrace and came to a stop squarely in front of the open door, and about seventy-five feet away. The doors opened and men issued from both sides. The squat figure and repulsive face of Stengel first appeared, then the storklike Schoënhut, with the man they had christened Mustaches and the bestial visage of Scarface. From around the car appeared two uniformed policemen.

"Police?" murmured Lee, surprised.

"That's what they stopped in the village for," growled Barreto.

The men below looked up at the balcony. Framed in the doorway, the figures had a slightly unreal look like a scene reproduced on the screen—in Technicolor.

Barreto spoke the words they had first heard from him: "Who are you and what do you want?"

Stengel's hoarse voice answered: "We want the German that you are harboring. We have a warrant for his arrest."

"You can go back where you came from," said Barreto contemptuously.

"It's useless for you to deny that he's there," said Stengel.

"I do not deny it," said Barreto. "The man is my guest. I shall not give him up."

The Bulldog showed his ugly little teeth; even at the distance, they could see how his face darkened. "You can't defy the Police, Spaniard! We'll surround you and rush the house. We mean business."

There was a sharp report in the yard. A bullet flew through the open door and embedded itself in the ceiling. Bits of plaster fell to the floor. The women and the little children flinched.

Barreto noted that the two policemen were sent around the house to watch the rear windows. "Get ready to leave," he said quietly over his shoulder.

Walther Niebuhr embraced his parents. The tears ran down the cheeks of the old woman and the man, but they made no sound of grief. Jaime softly started to unfasten one of the rear shutters.

Suddenly the gaunt Spaniard appeared to go berserk. Leaping to his feet and shouting curses, he discharged his gun through the door as fast as he could pull the trigger. But he was not aiming at those below. Lee, understanding that he was to take part in this diversion, shouted, too, and fired his pistol over the heads of the men on the terrace.

The two policemen came running back around the house to see what the uproar was about. Barreto spoke over his shoulder. "Now go, quickly!" Niebuhr and Jaime slipped over the sill and those in the room closed and fastened the shutter after them. When the shooting began, Stengel and his men ran behind their car and returned a few shots which thudded harmlessly against the wall of the house. Realizing presently that it was a trick, they held their fire.

From the steep slope behind the house came two ringing young voices, baritone and alto: "Stengel, you butcher! Here we are! Come and get us if you're men enough!"

The two policemen started back around one end of the house; Mustaches and Scarface went around the other end. Stengel and Schoënhut remained hidden behind the gray car. From the rear the young voices continued to shout: "Here we are! This way! Can't you see us, bats?" There was actually a ring of laughter in the sound. Some scattered shots were heard. Barreto said to Lee:

"Take your people and go down and get in the car. Start the engine. When I fire my gun, drive out. Don't stop to open the doors; they are not locked; drive into them!"

After a quick handshake, Lee shepherded his people down the inside stairway and into the car. José started the engine. "Down in the bottom of the car, all!" commanded Lee. Presently they heard the crack of Barreto's rifle overhead, José let in the clutch, and they charged forward. The doors crashed open and the Hispano-Suiza sped out into the sun. The two Germans started firing over the engine hood of their car. A bullet splintered through a side window. Lee opened the door a crack and fired back—not at the men but at their tires. There were two sharp explosions, and he pulled the door to, smiling.

"*Duas roturas pneu!*" howled José in delight.

"I guess that will hold them for a while!" said Luke.

The two Germans started firing at their tires but it was too late. The Hispano-Suiza gained the shelter of the trees and slowed down.

Since there was now no possibility of immediate pursuit, they proceeded down the mountainside at a safe rate of speed, made their way through the village, and set off west on the highway. Only two hours had elapsed since their arrival. It seemed longer. Jose, Affonso, and Luke were in the highest spirits over their success, but Lee's heart ached for the quiet, gray-faced couple who sat on the back seat holding hands and paying no attention to the passing scene. They had said good-by to all they held dear and were setting their faces among strangers.

Lee speculated on the chances of pursuit. "It will take them at least half an hour to mend their tires and call in their men. Perhaps as much as an hour."

"We won't see them again this side Lisbon," said Luke confidently.

"I hope not," said Lee, "but as long as they have secured the support of the police, they may try to stop us by telegraphing ahead. Let us do a little telegraphing ourselves."

From the town of Borba Lee sent this message:

> Inspector da Gama,
> > Ministry of Police,
> Lisboa.
> Please to instruct local police at Estremoz, Vimiera, Arraiollos, Montemor Novo, and Vendas Novas to afford me and my party of five, including chauffeur, safe conduct to Lisboa, and disregard requests to the contrary from local officials to the east.
> > Amos Lee Mappin

Proceeding, they passed through Estremoz and Vimiera without hindrance. At the entrance to the walled town of Arraiollos, halfway, a closed barrier across the road forced them to stop. Two policemen came out of the guardhouse, one of whom held a telegram. Instantly there was a pandemonium of voices. No business can be transacted in Portugal without it. It was impossible to keep José and Affonso from making their contributions. José kept assuring the policemen in an indignant voice that this was General Aljubarotta's car. The policemen were impressed but adamant. Affonso described what would happen to them for stopping so great a man as Mr. Mappin.

Lee's and Luke's American passports were above suspicion, and the identification papers of the two Portuguese were in order, but the German couple had no papers; there was the rub. A crowd gathered, many of whom added their voices to the discussion. As Lee could not very well offer the policemen bribes in the sight of the crowd, he suggested an adjournment to the guardhouse, which was made. This was no better, because now the heads of the crowd filled the windows, and various persons of consideration crowded in until the air of the little shed became suffocating. So they all surged outside again.

The old couple, sad and resigned, remained sitting in the car holding hands. They did not know what it was all about and, apparently, did not much care. Everybody had to go and gape at them through the windows. The police remained polite but firm. The old people had no papers; therefore they could not pass until an investigation was made.

Time passed and they were getting nowhere. Lee kept glancing anxiously to the east. The road over which they had come dipped down into a valley and climbed a high mountain on the other side. A greater functionary was brought up; mayor perhaps, or whatever corresponded to mayor in this town. Lee dispatched Luke to the post office to see if a message from Inspector da Gama was not forthcoming.

For the benefit of the mayor, the whole story had to be told from the beginning. It was growing dark now, and Lee groaned inwardly. The mayor supported the police. He had a happy idea. The old people, obviously, could not be allowed to proceed, but if the American gentleman was in a hurry, let him drive on and he, the mayor, would take personal charge of his friends. They should be lodged at the hotel and every comfort provided until the matter was settled.

This did not help any. At the top of the distant mountain a pair of headlights twinkled and started to descend.

The discussion continued. Affonso now acted as Lee's interpreter. He loved the job and made the most of it. The headlights crept down the mountainside and Lee broke into a gentle sweat.

In the nick of time Luke came running from the center of town, waving a telegram over his head. The mayor opened it. Lee did not ask to see it. Judging from the general smiles and bows that everything was now all right, he hustled his men into the car. The pursuing car had reached the floor of the valley, not more than five minutes away.

"That car that is coming," said Lee to the police, "contains Germans, members of the Gestapo, who wish to seize this harmless old couple and carry them back to Germany!"

The crowd murmured in anger. "Drive on" Lee said, and left them with that.

In each of the succeeding towns they were stopped, but now Lee had only to identify himself and they were waved on with smiles. They saw no more of the following car.

After crossing the Tagus and heading south, Lee, fearing there might be an attempt to intercept them at the edge of the city, had José make a wide detour to the west. They entered Lisbon from that side. At ten o'clock Mr. and Mrs. Niebuhr were delivered safely to the *Senhora* at the Macaco Branco and whisked to their rooms upstairs. The four men enjoyed a belated dinner in the restaurant.

On a subsequent day, Lee contrived to have the Niebuhrs smuggled aboard an English ship in the harbor, without ever having been seen by Stengel or his men. Bosco reported that the Bulldog had been overheard to say in the Hotel Excelsior that the *verdammt* Mappin was a magician. "I never had a finer tribute!" said Lee, smiling.

CHAPTER FIFTEEN

THE NAME OF MONSIEUR GADE was announced on the telephone as calling to see Senhor Mappin, and Lee requested that he be brought upstairs. The tidy little Frenchman presented himself in the sitting room with a series of bows.

"Senhor Mappin," he said, "you engaged me to find if I could a certain covered truck in Lisbon such as undertakers use to transport bodies from place to place."

"Have you found it?" asked Lee eagerly.

"You described certain peculiarities in the tires. I have found a truck with such tires, but it bears a plate with the name of the proprietor, and you said the truck you were looking for had no such distinguishing mark."

"Such a plate could be screwed on and off, couldn't it? If a murder was contemplated, naturally they'd remove it."

"Assuredly, senhor." M. Gade furnished Lee with the name of the undertaking establishment where the truck was to be found. "Cavilho," he said. "A superior sort of place, patronized by the well-to-do. Do you wish me to accompany you when you go to look at it?"

"No," said Lee. "I am continually watched and followed about, and I don't want my ill-wishers to find out that you are in my employ."

"Very good, senhor. Have you any further commands?"

"Yes," said Lee. "Somewhere in Lisbon I want you to find me a long, low-hung gray sedan car. It bears a license with this number, but you will no doubt find that the license plates are stolen or

162

altered. The car has seen hard use, the fenders are battered, the paint faded, but mechanically it's in perfect order. I was unable to get the name of the manufacturer. I shot holes in the two right-hand tires yesterday. They may have new tires by now, but one of my bullets entered the right-hand side just above the running board. That will be an identifying mark. I'll know the car if you can find it. It is one used by the Gestapo outfit. I am also hoping that in the place where this car is kept, you may find a charcoal brazier such as plumbers use to heat their irons, and three irons that go with it. That would be vital evidence."

"I will do my best, Senhor Mappin."

Lee and Luke presently set out. The address given was in one of the newer streets to the west, and the place was not unlike a similar establishment in America, with this difference—that there was no chapel attached, since no good Catholic would think of being buried from such an unconsecrated place. The parlors were handsomely furnished, and the proprietor who came forward to greet them, a large, pale man with soft hands, wore the sort of bland, commiserating smile that is characteristic of undertakers everywhere.

"I am Senhor Cavilho," he said.

He lost his smile when Lee said bluntly: "May I see the motorcars in your outfit, senhor?"

"A very strange request, senhor! Do me the favor of explaining why you wish to see my motorcars."

"I am looking for a truck such as those used for transporting bodies from place to place, which has certain distinguishing marks."

"For why? For why? I demand an answer, senhor."

"You shall have it," said Lee. "On the night of September eighteenth this truck was used to transport an unconscious man to the place where he was murdered."

Cavilho turned as white as paper and dropped suddenly on one of his expensive chairs. "Who are you?" he stammered.

Lee presented his card. "I expect my name will mean nothing to you, senhor. If you require a reference, please call up the American Legation and ask His Excellency, the Minister."

The shaken man tried to bluff it out. "Senhor, I can tell you at once that no car of mine was out of the garage on the night of September eighteenth." The attempt was not a success.

"I fear the senhor is not being frank with me," said Lee sternly. "The car or truck has already been identified by a man in my employ."

Cavilho mopped his face with a white handkerchief. "He is mistaken," he stammered. "No car could be taken out without my knowledge."

"Exactly," said Lee dryly. "Let us have a look at the cars, senhor, and I can tell you instantly."

The undertaker led them towards the back of the building and down some steps into a garage. Among the vehicles there was only one truck of the sort that Lee was looking for. A small, black, covered truck, elegantly finished, it had a neat silver plate bearing the proprietor's name screwed to each side near the front. Lee showed Luke some scratches on the screws which showed they had lately been tampered with. He stooped to examine the tires.

"This is the car," he said.

The unfortunate undertaker wrung his hands. "No! No!" he lamented. "It cannot be! I know of no murder! My reputation is my life! You are seeking to ruin me, senhor! What reason have you for making such an assertion?"

Lee showed him the pages of his notebook on which he had sketched the tracks left by the car in the film of mud. "Drawn to scale," said Lee, "on the morning following the murder. Notice the clean, sharp design of the tread as left by new tires like those on your car. The tread is no proof since many tires of the same make are sold. But notice the irregular impression of this cut on the right-hand rear tire. The car was seen standing at the door of the house where the man was murdered. The proof is positive, senhor."

"I shall be ruined!" wailed Cavilho.

"No one has accused you of being a party to the murder," said Lee crisply. "The best way to clear your reputation, senhor, is to be absolutely frank with the authorities. Did you or did you not hire out this car on the night of September eighteenth?"

"How do I know you are an authorized person?"

"Call up Inspector da Gama at the Ministry of Police and ask him."

"No! I will tell all!" wailed the distressed man. "It is true, I did rent out this car on September eighteenth, senhor . . . But I am not guilty of any wrongdoing! I swear it. The man said, it was to be used in an innocent prank. The car was returned before morning. There was no . . . no blood. It was in perfect order . . ."

Lee interrupted him. "Wait a minute! Who hired it?"

"The name has slipped my memory. I have it written down somewhere. It was a cash transaction."

"Never mind. It was certainly a false name. Describe the man."

"A handsome young man, senhor. Full of spirits. He had the appearance of a gentleman. An American like yourself, senhor."

"Ha!" said Lee. He and Luke exchanged a glance.

"I saw no harm in it, senhor," the man wailed. "They say that Americans are very fond of practical jokes. One is never surprised at anything an American may do. Senhor, I have a blameless reputation."

"I suppose he paid you a very good price," put in Lee dryly.

Cavilho made no answer.

"And you undoubtedly exacted a large sum as a forfeit in case of damage to the car."

He miserably admitted it.

"Many days have passed," said Lee, "and the car is not likely to reveal any further evidence. Nevertheless, let us examine it. Have you a strong flashlight?"

Such a light was produced. Lee opened the back doors of the car and threw the flash inside. On the floor lay a folding stretcher. "This went with the car?" asked Lee.

Cavilho nodded miserably.

"Has it been used since?"

"No, senhor."

Luke pulled out the stretcher and set it up on the floor. Lee went over it inch by inch. It yielded no evidence. Lee then climbed into the car and with the flashlight searched floors, walls, and ceiling. When he climbed out he opened his hand to reveal a little flat stone lying on his palm. It was oval in shape, of a dark green color, with crimson flecks in it and highly polished.

"A bloodstone," said Lee. "Symbolic, eh? This may prove to be important."

The undertaker shuddered. "Shall you report this to the police?"

"Not at the moment," said Lee. "Not until I have completed my case." He borrowed an envelope from Cavilho and, stowing the bloodstone in it, endorsed it with the time and the place. "In the meantime, senhor, I recommend that you say nothing about it. Best for you and best for all of us. When an opportunity arises, I shall ask you to identify the man who hired this car from you. By doing so you can clear yourself completely."

Judging from the man's face, there was no danger that he would talk.

ARRIVING BACK IN THE HOTEL, Lee said: "Let's hang around downstairs a while."

They found seats in the lounge and watched the panorama of life in the Lisboa Palace during wartime. The old hotel was one of the principal centers of intrigue in that city of intrigue. The restaurant was filling up for lunch. Nationals of all the warring peoples met in the lounge, ignoring each other or nodding with fulsome, false smiles; English, American, German, Italian, Japanese, besides all the neutrals who were not neutral. Every man had a smile on his lips and a guard over his eyes. Lee suspected that many a treacherous deal was effected by the foxy merchants of all nations in the private rooms, and that the secret history of the Lisboa Palace, if it could be published, would surprise the world.

Ronald Franklin, smiling and debonair, came up the stairway. Lee waved a hand to him and he came up with a face full of gladness.

"You're looking very fit, Mr. Mappin. I missed you yesterday."

"Went for a little trip in the country," said Lee. "I must see something of the country, too, for my book, you know."

"For your book, of course," said Franklin without any suggestion of irony.

"Are you lunching alone?" asked Lee. "I should be glad if you would join us."

A spark of surprise appeared in Franklin's wary eyes. "Delighted!" he cried.

"We had better go right in," said Lee. "The restaurant is filling up."

Lee looked at Luke, and Luke understood him. "I'll join you directly," he said.

Lee took Franklin's arm in sociable fashion and they went into the restaurant. Luke disappeared in a telephone booth.

Presently the three of them were established at a table not far from the door.

"How is the book progressing?" asked Franklin.

"I am taking notes," said Lee. "I shall not attempt to write it until I get home. But what material! What material! This is a dreadful city! Sometimes it terrifies me!"

"Extraordinarily interesting, I admit," said Franklin. "But why terrifying?"

Lee blinked at him innocently through his glasses. "Take the wanton murder of my poor friend, William Miller. Do you know the police have not made the slightest progress towards solving it? I am driven to the belief that they don't want to solve it."

Franklin never batted an eyelash. "What possible reason could they have for not wanting to solve it?"

"Oh, it's the parochialism one finds everywhere in the world. They are afraid of bringing their city into disrepute."

"Well, with your record as a criminologist, why don't you set about solving it yourself?" asked Franklin.

Lee shook his head sadly. "My ignorance of the language, and of the whole situation over here is too great a handicap."

"You must have some theory."

Lee lowered his voice confidentially. "Well, William was a German, you know."

"No! I didn't know that."

"And I suppose it has something to do with the affairs of that unhappy country. Perhaps other Germans considered him a traitor because he worked for an American."

"It is possible," said Franklin with a serious air.

Luke, who was of too forthright a nature to enjoy this sort of verbal sparring, kept his eyes on his plate.

Kate McDonald entered the restaurant alone. She bowed smil-
ingly to Lee and to Luke, ignored Franklin; looked around for the
maître d'hôtel.

Lee sprang up. "Miss McDonald! You are alone. Pray join us."

The girl was startled. "Oh, thank you! I couldn't think of it!"

"You must!" said Lee. "Look at us, three bored men without a
lady to grace our table. It will make all the difference between mere
food and a banquet!"

His talk bore her down; she hung irresolutely. The maître
d'hôtel came bustling up. "The young lady will lunch with us if you
will have another place laid," said Lee.

Franklin was not at all put about by this encounter. He was so
pleased with his own cleverness it did not seem to occur to him
that Lee was pulling his leg. The girl's intuition told her better.
She sat down with an embarrassed air.

"Mr. Tremaine you know," said Lee. "This is Mr. Ronald
Franklin. He crossed with us, don't you remember? I always wondered why you two didn't hit it off together. The handsomest couple
on the ship!"

"Now come, Mr. Mappin!" protested Franklin. "I can only accept that for the feminine half of the couple."

So it went. Lee was enjoying himself; Franklin put on a good
show; Luke and the girl stole curious, sidelong glances at each
other.

In the middle of the meal Lee, who was facing the entrance,
saw Senhor Cavilho, the undertaker, come in. He passed their table,
proceeded to the end of the room looking from table to table; returned. Ronald Franklin was now facing him. Cavilho changed color
and bit his lip. He passed on out of the restaurant. Franklin had
paid no attention to him.

When they had finished eating, Franklin excused himself on
the score that he had an engagement. Lee caught Luke's eye, and
Luke rose, saying that he had telephoning to do. Thus Lee and the
girl were left together at the table with their coffee and cigarettes.

"Well, my dear," said Lee in a fatherly fashion, "you didn't
enjoy it very much, did you?"

She looked at him in a scared way. "Why yes . . . yes, of course!"

"I was just having a bit of fun with you," Lee went on. "I know that you and Mr. Franklin are very well acquainted indeed."

She stared at him, terrified and fascinated. "You are mistaken," she stammered. "I don't know why you . . ."

"I also know that it was you who arranged to have me seized and tied up in the most humiliating fashion and carried off in a motorcar at Ponta Delgada . . ."

The girl put her napkin to her lips. "No!" she whispered.

"But I don't bear you any ill will. I like you. I am only sorry to see the company you keep. Did they tell you what they did to my friend, William Miller? They murdered him, my dear . . . I see by your face that that is news to you . . . You are in a bad jam. If you confided in me I might be able to help you get out of it."

She pushed her chair back from the table. She was breathing fast.

Lee rose. "Well, at any rate, don't tell Franklin that we have reached a kind of understanding. That would only make it worse for everybody. And remember, if you want to come to me at any time, you can be sure of finding a friend."

She fled from the room.

Lee reseated himself. "Some fresh coffee," he said to the waiter.

When he got up to his rooms Luke was there. "Has Cavilho had time enough to get home?" Lee asked.

Luke nodded.

"Call him up."

After a brief telephone conversation, Luke reported that the undertaker identified the man lunching with Lee as the same individual who had hired his truck on the night of September eighteenth.

"You had not told him over the phone that he would find the man at my table?"

"No indeed. He picked him out of the whole restaurant. He was surprised and upset to find him sitting down with you."

"Good!" said Lee. "That ought to be sufficient to hang number five!"

There was a silence. Then Luke asked: "What are you going to do about him in the meantime?"

"Nothing just now. As long as he doesn't suspect how much we know, we can pick him up at any time. I don't want to alarm Stengel too much. He must already be somewhat disturbed."

THE TELEPHONE RANG. Luke answered it. "It's Inspector da Gama," he said.

Lee took the instrument: "Hello, Senhor da Gama?"

The inspector said: "I was expecting to hear from you this morning, senhor. I wanted to know what happened yesterday. What were the circumstances leading up to that message you sent me?"

"Do you really want to know?" asked Lee.

"Well, I leave that to your judgment," said the inspector cautiously. "Not unless you wish me to take further action in the matter."

"No further action will be necessary," said Lee. "We came through quite safely. But I must thank you for taking such prompt action. It's a long story, Inspector."

"Some day I shall expect to hear it all, Senhor Mappin . . . Your pursuers did not get off so easily," he added, and Lee thought he heard a chuckle in his voice.

"No? What happened?"

"It has been reported to me that their car was stoned at the town of Arraiollos, and when they got out of it they were roughly used by the crowd. The local police appear to have been helpless to protect them. The Embassy of Germany has lodged a protest. It is very regrettable."

"Very!" said Lee. "I feel for you, Inspector . . . How roughly were they used?"

"Bruised and cut by flying stones, I am told, and pushed around by the crowd. Only one was seriously injured. His leg was broken. They brought him into Lisbon and put him into the Bon Secours Hospital."

"Which one?" asked Lee eagerly.

"Not the leader of the party. The man's name is given as Diehlmann."

"Thank you, Inspector. I shall give myself the pleasure of visiting the poor fellow in hospital."

This time there was no doubt that the inspector laughed. "You're a terrible man, Senhor Mappin."

As they were preparing to go out, the telephone rang again. This was Bosco. He had lunched with his pals at the *leiteria* and they had reported to him that a strange quiet had lain on the Hotel Excelsior all morning. Neither Stengel nor the man Lee knew as Scarface had returned to the hotel the night before, nor had either been seen there since. Schoënhut was in the hotel as usual, and in a bad temper. He had had several telephone talks with Stengel, and apparently had caught hell, but the lift operator had not been able to hear anything. Bosco had a date that night with the hotel chambermaid, and hoped to have more to report in the morning.

CHAPTER SIXTEEN

LEE AND LUKE entered the long hospital ward, guided by a black-robed sister of charity with a gentle voice.

"He suffered much pain before they brought him here," she said. "Forced to ride in a crowded motorcar for a hundred miles. It was necessary to retract the broken leg before it could be put in a cast." She smiled compassionately. "Naturally after such an experience he is a bad patient. Nothing pleases him."

"Ah, poor fellow!" said Lee sympathetically. "How long will he have to stay in hospital, Sister?"

"Four weeks, senhor."

"Has he had any other visitors today?"

"No, senhor."

"Is there anything I can provide to relieve the tedium?"

"Ask him, senhor. Ask him yourself."

They were passing between two rows of white beds, some with dark heads lying quiet on the pillow; others with patients sitting up. The more fortunate ones, clad in rough bathrobes and slippers, were moving about and visiting from bed to bed. The entrance of the plump little American gentleman in a white waistcoat and his tall friend aroused a general interest. All heads followed their passage through the ward, curious to discover whom they had come to visit.

"Here he is," said the sister, stopping.

Lee and Luke saw at a glance that the patient was the man they had christened Mustaches, for lack of a better name. His elevated leg was being stretched in a contrivance with weighted ropes that passed over a pulley at the foot of the bed. He was a black German of about forty, with an ill-natured expression. The salient feature of his face was the pair of handle bars which projected beyond his cheeks on either side. Such a magnificent mustache had rarely seen. The wearer had included some of the hair of his beard to increase its volume. He was continually stroking and pulling this ornament.

"These kind gentlemen have come to see you," said the nurse.

"Good morning, Diehlmann," said Lee in German.

When his eyes fell on Lee, the German's face presented an extraordinary study of amazement, anger, fear. "What do you want?" he demanded.

"Only to pay you a little visit."

Diehlmann's face flushed darkly. "Go away!" he said. "I want no visit from you. Where is Algodão? Where is Luiz Rosado and his brother Antonio? You can't get hold of me! I'm safe from you here! Go away! You won't get anything out of me!"

The sister shook her head sadly. Lee said to Luke:

"Explain to her that the poor fellow blames me for his accident. He is not responsible for what he says. Pain has unnerved him." Luke repeated this in Portuguese.

Diehlmann turned to the sister. In his excitement, he was still speaking German. "Send this man away! Have I no protection here? He's no friend of mine. He has only come here to see what he can get out of me. He is an American! He is my country's enemy!"

Lee said to Luke: "Tell her she needn't wait. I'll try to soothe him. If my presence continues to excite him, I'll go."

She had many duties to perform and she softly moved away. Lee sat on a chair beside the bed; Diehlmann turned away his head and fell silent; Luke stood at the bed's foot.

After a while Lee asked mildly: "Is there anything you would like?"

"I want smokes," said Diehlmann sullenly. "My money is in the drawer of the stand behind you. You can get cigarettes in the entrance lobby."

Lee pulled out the little drawer. "There's only some change here," he said. "Is that all you had on you?"

"What is it to you?" growled Diehlmann.

"You will need many little things, smokes, fruit, wine. I will leave a hundred escudos in the drawer."

"Suit yourself," said Diehlmann gracelessly. "A hundred escudos won't buy me, nor a thousand, nor ten thousand."

Luke departed to buy the cigarettes. Lee sat quietly beside the bed, confident that he could bear the silence longer than Diehlmann could. He was right. Diehlmann presently rolled his head over and demanded:

"Who told you I was here?"

"A little bird," said Lee.

"Ahh! Go to hell!" said Diehlmann in good American.

There was another long silence; then he came back: "If you want me to talk, you tell me, where is Algodão? Where are the Rosados?"

"That seems to bother you," said Lee. "They're traveling—at my expense."

"Well, anyhow," said Diehlmann passionately, "we got the better of you yesterday. You didn't succeed in rescuing the German traitor. He is lying dead on the mountainside above Villa Boim right now, and the Spanish boy beside him."

"I suspect you're lying," said Lee calmly. "At any rate, I'll soon know."

Luke returned with cigarettes. Diehlmann's hand trembled with eagerness as he lighted up. After filling his lungs with smoke a few times and luxuriously blowing it out, he seemed to be in a better humor.

"There's one thing I bet you'd like to know," he said to Lee.

"Many things," said Lee.

"You'd like to know how we got the tip that Niebuhr was hidden at the Spaniard's."

"That's one thing I do know," said Lee. "German agents in Badajoz intercepted his letter to me, and after reading it, remailed it."

"And wouldn't you like to know how we secured the code that enabled us to read it?"

"You couldn't read it," said Lee calmly. "Only the address it contained. The code is known to about ten men only. It does not exist in writing."

"What good is your code to you when we can intercept your letters?"

"I have taken measures to prevent a repetition of that."

Diehlmann laughed scornfully.

The black-robed sister appeared at the end of the ward, bringing another visitor. Lee was the first to take note of the tall, lanky figure with tousled head; the Stork, otherwise Schoënhut. Lee smiled, anticipating further comedy.

When Schoënhut saw Lee, he jerked back as if he had stumbled on a snake in his path. So comical was his look of dismay that Lee and Luke laughed outright. Even Diehlmann was sufficiently recovered from his discomfiture to be amused. Schoënhut demanded in German:

"What is he doing here?"

Diehlmann answered: "Fishing; but he hasn't caught anything . . . Remember, he understands German."

Schoënhut wiped his agitated face.

"Sit down," said Lee affably. "Luke, fetch the chair from the next bed for Herr Schoënhut. Nobody is using it. Sit down, sit down. Herr Schoënhut, and let us continue our pleasant talk. We don't have to bring our enmities to the bedside of an injured friend."

Schoënhut dropped in the offered chair. Having less self-possession than Diehlmann, he had difficulty in commanding his features. With his eyes bolting this way and that, and his Adam's apple working convulsively up and down, he was a ludicrous figure.

"I was sorry to hear that you had trouble with the populace at Arraiollos last night," said Lee politely.

"That was your work!" growled Schoënhut.

"Really! All I did was to tell the people that the Gestapo was after us. Nobody loves the Gestapo!"

Schoënhut rose from his chair and cursed Lee thickly. His face was convulsed with rage.

"Watch yourself!" growled Diehlmann. "He is only baiting you."

Schoënhut dropped back on the chair. The men in the neighboring beds, suspecting that something humorous was going on, strained their ears to hear, but the German baffled them. They scowled and muttered.

"How is Fraulein the cigar-maker's daughter?" Lee asked wickedly. "Pray give her my regards when you call."

Schoënhut could bear no more. He jumped up, and saying to Diehlmann over his shoulder: "I'll see you later," marched out.

"Too bad he is so easily discomposed," said Lee, shaking his head. "As a leader of the dreaded Gestapo, he is a disappointment to me."

"He's a fool!" growled Diehlmann. "Better not judge the Gestapo by *him*, Herr Mappin."

After a little further sparring with Diehlmann, Lee said to Luke: "We'd better go now. If we stay too long, Herr Schoënhut may round up his friends to wait for us at the door."

"Tell me," said Diehlmann, scowling, "why did you come here this afternoon?"

"You have already guessed why," said Lee, smiling. "It was to pick up any ill-considered trifles of information that might offer themselves."

"But you didn't get anything!"

Lee's smile broadened. "Oh, I wouldn't say that! . . . Come, Luke! I'll be seeing you, Herr Diehlmann."

On the way out, they were followed by the scowls of the other patients. "They think we're Germans, too," said Lee. Meeting the black-robed sister at the door, Lee said to her with a shake of the head:

"A hard customer, sister!" He pressed a donation for the poor upon her.

In the taxicab on the way back, Luke asked: "Did you have a special object in going there?"

Lee shook his head. "I told Diehlmann the truth. I just went on the chance. You never can tell how a man will react to pain."

"Well, it was amusing," said Luke, "but it didn't profit us much."

"You're wrong," said Lee, smiling. "Look!" He thrust thumb and forefinger in his vest pocket and, opening his hand, showed Luke a pair of gold cuff links lying on his palm. They were of the type that is set with a jewel on one side and has a curved, solid shank ending in a gold button. One link was set with an oval bloodstone. In the other, the setting was empty.

Luke whistled. "My God! where did you pick those up?"

"In the drawer of the bedstand among his change and other little objects of value."

"This will convict him of being present that night!"

"Surely! This accounts for number six!"

CHAPTER SEVENTEEN

When Lee and Luke entered the hotel, they found Kate McDonald waiting in the lobby. There was a change in her appearance; she was not so perfectly turned out as they were accustomed to see her; the beautiful eyes were stormy, their lids swollen as from weeping. At Lee's approach, she instinctively put up a hand to cover her cheek.

"Here I am," she said falteringly. "I want to . . . you said to come. I suppose you didn't expect to see me so soon . . ."

Lee gently drew down the hand from her face. There was a bruise on her cheek bone that told its own story.

"Come upstairs," said Lee.

As soon as the door of the suite closed behind them she dropped in a chair and broke into a quiet, piteous weeping. The tears stole between her angers. She struggled breathlessly to apologize for the breakdown.

"Let it come! Let it come!" said Lee. "You'll feel better for it."

She pointed blindly at Luke. "Send him away . . . please!"

At a glance from Lee, Luke went into the bedroom and closed the door.

"You can trust him just the same as you would me," said Lee.

"I know," she said brokenly. "He's a good, decent fellow. He's a man! That's why. That's why. It shames me to have him see me."

Lee waited for her to recover control.

"I haven't had any luck," she said piteously; "Ronnie Franklin is a brute and a scoundrel. I've known it for a long time. But I hadn't

178

the strength to leave him. Today he struck me. It was the first time. That ends it! Oh, help me to have the courage not to go crawling back!"

"I'll help you all I can," said Lee. "But in the end that courage can come only from yourself."

"I know! I know! Oh, it's hell on earth to be fond of somebody whom you know is bad. When I am away from him I can see him as he is. I hate him then. But in his presence I am enslaved! When he touches me I go to pieces. Why is that?"

"It's common enough," said Lee. "They call it infatuation."

"Oh, help me, help me to get the better of it!"

"I think the cure has already begun," said Lee dryly.

She shook her head hopelessly. "No! Even now something is drawing me back to him. Something stronger than I. I am lost!"

"Nonsense!" said Lee. "You don't have to go back unless you want to. Let's drag the whole matter out into the light. There is no cure like letting in light. Have you told him you're through?"

She nodded. "Yes, but he didn't believe me. He only laughed. I have said it before. He is so absolutely sure of me he despises me."

"Well, let's give him the shock of his life this time," said Lee cheerfully. "Tell me about yourself and how it began."

"I am Italian," she said. "My father and mother are dead. For many years before the war I worked in England. That is why I speak the language without an accent. I was a governess in different English families. I was treated like an upper servant. It was an intolerable existence. I felt as if life was passing me by.

"I met Ronnie in England before the war. He sought out because I worked in a cabinet minister's family, but I didn't know that until long afterwards. I was a Fascist—at least, I imagined I was. Anything to be different from the arrogant English. I know better now. Little by little, Ronnie let me understand that he was a German agent. I thought that was wonderful. Such a charming fellow he seemed then, full of pluck and kindness and laughter!

"I didn't know anything about English government affairs, but I made believe I did, just to lead Ronnie on. I tried to find things out for him, and I did to a certain extent. In the end I was discovered and the English threatened to send me to prison. Ronnie saved me from that. Don't ask me how. He had powerful friends in England. Nobody suspected what he was. It was he who got me the English passport.

"So I went with Ronnie. Day by day I became more infatuated. The life he offered me was intoxicating; secrecy, excitement, danger, continual travel. We have been all over the world together, always traveling as strangers. Ronnie seemed to me like a superman, the way he could fool everybody and get what he wanted out of them. There was a hardness, a cruelty in him that made a slave of me. But I welcomed it. Can you understand that?"

"It is very understandable," said Lee.

Her tears had dried, leaving her white and exhausted-looking. "That's my story," she said, spreading her hands. "He doesn't trust me completely. I've always known that. I knew nothing about a murder, but since you told me I have been putting two and two together. I understand more now. Some of his associates here in Lisbon are horrible men!" She shuddered.

"Did your quarrel today have anything to do with us?" asked Lee.

She nodded. "Ever since *he* started to work for you,"—she nodded towards the bedroom door—"Ronnie has been after me to work on him, to lead him on, to get him in my power." She hung her head. "I have done that for him before. I am ashamed of it now! I didn't mind with the others, because they were just as crooked as we were. But this one is different! he's a decent, honest fellow, and somehow I couldn't do it!"

"I told you the cure had begun," said Lee.

"That's why I've been hanging around the hotel," she continued. "Ronnie sent me here today to get you to ask me to lunch with you and Mr. Tremaine. I didn't expect to find Ronnie himself lunching with you . . ."

"He hadn't expected it either," murmured Lee.

"That upset me and made me self-conscious. I could scarcely bring myself to look at Mr. Tremaine. I couldn't open my lips. Ronnie was getting angrier with me every minute, and that made me worse."

"And you quarreled when you met afterwards?"

She nodded. "Somehow I found the courage to talk back to him—for the first time; I said too much. He struck me!"

"Where are you living?" asked Lee.

"At the Victoria."

"Together?"

She hung her head. "We have rooms on the same corridor. We are never seen together."

Lee began to pace the room. "Kate," he said, "—I suppose I should continue to call you Kate?"

"That is my name, though my parents spelled it Caterina."

"I shall call you Kate. It comes naturally to an Anglo-Saxon tongue . . . You can't shake off this obsession without making an effort. Have you the courage to fight it, to fight Ronnie Franklin?"

She paled. "You mean work to obtain evidence against him, evidence of murder?"

"No. I shan't ask that. But to help me to convict the chief of the murderers, Stengel. That is the one who looks like a bulldog."

A shiver passed through her. "I have seen him."

"And another whose name I don't know. He has a scar down the side of his face and we call him Scarface. I have reason to believe that it was he who plunged a knife into my friend's breast."

"I don't know him."

"Apparently I've thrown a scare into these two and they've gone into hiding. I must find out where they are. Will you help me?"

The girl said nothing.

"You say you have seen the folly and the falsity of Fascism; do it for freedom's sake, Kate."

She still hesitated.

"Well, if that leaves you cold, you have suffered; do it for revenge!"

"I'll try," she murmured.

"Not good enough," said Lee coolly. "If you cannot do it with your whole heart, better leave it alone. You would only be defeated . . . But think, Kate, this is your chance to free yourself. If you don't take it, a worse hell than any you have known is waiting for you."

"What do you mean?" she asked, startled.

"This man will soon cast you aside."

She stared ahead of her as if there were a ghost there. "You're right," she whispered.

"Are you going to wait like a tame woman until that happens?"

She stood up suddenly. "No! I'll do what you want."

They shook hands on it.

"How should I begin?" she asked.

"By making up with Ronnie."

Her face fell.

"Wouldn't it be fun," suggested Lee, "to be the one who was doing the fooling for a change? . . . Is there a tearoom in your hotel?"

"Yes."

"Well, take Luke and give him tea there. Let Ronnie see you with him. You are obeying him, you are doing what he wants. That will be sufficient without saying anything."

A slow smile spread across her pale face. "You're a devil!" she said. "You know exactly how to get around a woman!"

"Only so far!" said Lee, with a rueful shake of the head. "Only so far!"

"No man would be attracted to me with this," she said, indicating the bruise.

"Tut!" said Lee. "A little liquid powder and rouge will soon fix that up. Don't tell me you're not familiar with the possibilities of make-up!"

She took a hasty survey of herself in a wall mirror. "I look awful! What must he think of me? Ask Mr. Tremaine to meet me in the foyer of the Victoria in half an hour. You explain everything to him."

CHAPTER EIGHTEEN

AT DINNER TIME Luke had not returned, and Lee set out on foot alone for the Macaco Branco. He was not followed. A strange boy was selling papers at Bosco's post on the Rocío, and Lee smiled to himself, thinking of Bosco's date.

Soon after he had ordered his dinner, Luke joined him. "Everything went off all right," he said with a broad smile.

There was a brightness in his eye and a warmth in his voice that caused Lee to look at him sharply. "Did Franklin see you with the girl?"

"Yes. He came into the hotel while we were sitting in the tea-room and took in the situation. It was all right with him. He went upstairs."

"What did you talk about?" asked Lee.

Luke laughed. "There was no lack of talk. She told me about her childhood in Italy." The young man's eyes were reminiscent.

"I didn't want you to go *too* far," said Lee, frowning.

Luke was amused by his anxiety. "Why not?"

"We . . . you know the situation."

"Certainly I know it. That's just it. It's the first time in my life, I think, that I ever began with a girl on a perfectly honest basis."

"Dangerous!" suggested Lee.

"I can't see it, Chief. My life has not been exactly a clean page either. However far it may go, my eyes are open and so are hers, so where's the danger?"

Lee, afraid of saying too much, let the subject drop.

Luke wouldn't let it drop. "And I haven't forgotten my job, either," he added. "Nor has she. The only way we can win her over is by being fond of her, Chief. You may not think so, but she's very lovable. Well, I suppose every woman is lovable when she's honest. And she thinks I'm a wonderful person, simply because I'm honest with her. It's a big change for her. For me, too. I never realized before what a satisfying feeling it gave you to be honest with a woman."

"Damn it!" muttered Lee. "We fall from one situation right smack into another."

Luke laughed. "Well, I don't care how it looks, or what an outsider might say; judging from my own feelings, this is one of the best situations I ever fell into!"

Their talk was interrupted by a slight commotion at the door of the restaurant. A small, ragged, and extremely dirty bootblack came in with his blacking-box over his shoulder. He was scared and trying to brazen it out. The *Senhora* flew at him like an angry hen and shooed him out. He came in a second time, and again she flew at him, crying: "You can't shine shoes in here!" The boy was strangely persistent. A third time his grimy face appeared around the door, and this time he stood his ground. He said something to the *Senhora* that made her pause. Telling him to stand by the door, she came back to Lee's table.

"This boy says he has a message for you, senhor. Such impudence! Shall I send him away?"

"Certainly not," said Lee. "Bring him back."

She led the boy down the room at arm's length. Impudent, grinning and triumphant, he said to Lee in his hoarse gamin's voice:

"Send her away, senhor."

Lee said apologetically: "He says he must speak to me alone, senhora. Please to excuse us."

She flounced back to her desk.

"What's your name?" asked Lee.

"Johnny," said the bootblack, "like an American boy. Are you Senhor Mappin, the patron of Bosco?"

"Yes," said Lee. "What of it?"

"Bosco needs help," said Johnny simply.

"Where is he?"

Johnny named a humble eating-house in a nearby street. "He has a girl with him. Two men are laying for him outside."

Lee threw down his napkin and got up. "Come on," he said to Luke.

They left the restaurant. Turning out of the little square, they entered a darker street leading east, and hastened along the pavement. Johnny chattered and Luke translated.

"He says Bosco told him he was going out tonight with the girl who works in the Hotel Excelsior. Bosco told Johnny to watch the hotel and if any of the men came out to try to find out where they went. The girl came out shortly after six, and one of the men followed her, unknown to her. So Johnny followed them both."

"Tell him to describe the man."

"A long-legged guy, Johnny says, with a big nose and wears glasses."

"Schoënhut," murmured Lee.

"The girl went home," Luke continued, "with the man following her and Johnny following the man. The man waited outside the house where she lives, and after a while she came out all dressed up for the evening. Johnny doesn't think much of her looks. He calls her a crow, just the same as us. Man and boy then followed her to the eating-house in the Rua Escova, where Johnny is taking us now. When the man saw that the boy and girl were going to stay there, he went into a tobacconist's and telephoned, and in a few minutes another man joined him."

"Describe the second man."

"A slick young fellow," Johnny says, "dressed fine like an American."

"Franklin!"

"Johnny left the two of them watching the eating-house while he came to get you. Johnny's slang is a little hard to follow. He's telling me, I take it, that Bosco was giving the girl a heavy line."

"I hope to God they're still in the place," said Lee anxiously.

"If there are two men, shouldn't we have more help, Chief?"

Lee shook his head. "Our appearance on the scene will be sufficient to prevent trouble."

They turned a corner into a little street of shops that Johnny said was Rua Escova. The boy pointed out the eating-house, and they eagerly peered through the windows. A rough interior, hazy with tobacco smoke, with people sitting around plain tables, a bar at the side. The birds had flown.

Lee swore helplessly under his breath. "We're stopped!" he said.

Johnny spoke up. Luke said: "He says Bosco was going to take the girl to his room afterwards. He knows that, because he heard Bosco making a deal with the fellow he lives with to stay out tonight." Luke laughed. "That's where your money goes!"

Lee clucked his tongue. "Lisbon boys are so precocious!"

"But he doesn't know where Bosco lives."

"I do," said Lee, fishing out his notebook. "It's at Calcado Poço, 7."

Luke and Johnny consulted. "Five minutes' walk from here," said Luke. "Johnny knows the way."

"Tell him to lead on!"

They started. Luke glanced anxiously down at the plump little figure toddling beside him. "Ought to have more help!" he grumbled.

"Can't stop for that now!" said Lee.

Continuing to the eastward, they struck into the maze of lanes encircling the principal hill of Lisbon, crowned with its castle. For a while they climbed a steep *calcado*, lined with little shops and full of noise and movement; then Johnny led them off to the left through a dark and unfrequented lane, and from that to another and another lane, always darker and more solitary. They lost all sense of direction. The boy finally stopped before a door.

"This is it."

It was the basement entrance to a two-story house. There were a couple of half-windows, flush with the sidewalk, tightly shuttered. All the windows of the house above were dark. Lee threw his flashlight on the door. Luke said in surprise:

"This door has already been forced!" He tried it softly. "Seems to be barricaded inside." He laid his ear against the crack. "There are people inside," he murmured. "Sounds like a woman crying."

"See if you can force the door," said Lee.

Putting his shoulder to it, Luke launched his full weight against the door. It gave way with a sound of rending wood. They had a glimpse of a dimly lighted interior, then the light went out. Luke started in.

From behind him came a warning cry from Bosco. "Wait!" said Lee sharply. "Take a look first!"

It was too late. Luke ran down half a dozen steps at the side. There was a crash, a grunt, a heavy fall on the floor. Somebody brushed past Lee and got the door closed again. The light went on, and Lee found himself looking into the barrel of a gun in Ronald Franklin's hand. Lee's hand was on his own gun, but the other man had him covered. "Drop it!" said Franklin, and Lee obeyed. He had no choice.

Luke lay unconscious on the floor beside Lee, bleeding from a scalp wound. Beyond him a smashed chair showed how he was struck down. Schoënhut, coming up behind, picked up Lee's gun with a triumphant grin. The small boy had disappeared. At the other end of the room there was a bed, with a woman lying on it, sobbing pitifully. She raised her swollen, stained face for a moment, and hid it again, weeping afresh. A dozen feet from the bed sat Bosco, lashed to a chair. His young face was convulsed with rage; he twisted in his bonds and cursed savagely.

"Well, Mr. Mappin, you walked right into it!" said Franklin. "This is almost too good to be true! My cards are on the table now. Are you surprised?"

"Not in the least," said Lee.

"Search him!" said Franklin to Schoënhut. "Maybe he has another gun."

Lee had no other gun. Schoënhut took his wallet and dropped it in his own pocket.

"Take the gun from that guy on the floor," ordered Franklin.

It was done.

Lee looked about him. A long, sparsely furnished room, lighted by a single unshaded bulb hanging from a cord. There were two half-windows high up on the street side, and two full-sized windows on the opposite side, with casements standing open. Through these windows Lee could see lights sparkling below; evidently the hill went down precipitously on that side. The house was an ancient one; the floor worn and uneven; the low beams overhead blackened with soot. At the far end, there was a rude fireplace with some primitive cooking utensils scattered on the hearth. A table and four rush-bottomed chairs completed the furniture. From a line of wooden pegs hung the spare clothes of the two youths who shared the room. Schoënhut had refastened the door by dropping a chair between door and stair rail.

Franklin was in high spirits. "Push up a chair for Mr. Mappin," he cried. "There's no necessity for you to tire yourself out, sir. There's nothing you can do about it. Better make the best of things. I hope you're not going to make it necessary for us to tie you up like young Lothario here. Cruel, wasn't it, to interrupt love's young dream? However, we're not going to hurt either of them. After we make our getaway, they can continue their dalliance . . . How did you find this place?"

"I knew Bosco lived here," said Lee. He took the offered chair and lighted a cigarette.

"That's right!" said Franklin heartily. "Smoke up! You are a philosopher! I am sorry that the war has separated us into different camps. I should like to work under you. I have read some of your books."

"Indeed!" said Lee. "If you don't mind," he went on politely, "I should like to wash the wound on my friend's head, and bind it up. I have a clean handkerchief that will serve."

"Go ahead, if it will make you feel better," said Franklin. "Won't make any difference to him. He will never leave this room again."

There was a bucket of water on the table. Lee carried it to where Luke lay, and kneeling, washed the blood from his head and face. Then, rinsing the handkerchief, he tied it around Luke's head. The wounded man stirred at the touch of the cold water and opened his eyes. Lee, keeping his body between Luke and the watching Franklin, touched Luke's lips with his fingers. A look of understanding came into the young man's eyes, and Lee, bending closer over him, whispered: "Keep your eyes closed and don't move until I give the word."

Luke nodded slightly.

Lee made the operation last as long as possible. They never saw Johnny, he was thinking; if the boy has his wits about him he'll bring the police.

Franklin finally became impatient. "That's all you can do for him," he said. "Come and sit in this chair."

Lee obeyed. Franklin had placed a chair on the hearth with its back towards the fireplace. He had a piece of rope in his hand.

"I have to tie you up just for a moment," he said, grinning, "so I can close the door after my friend. He's going out to telephone for a car."

Lee allowed his hands to be tied behind him. "The gray car?" he asked.

Franklin laughed. "Sure! The gray car. You know it, don't you?"

When the two men went up the steps to the door, Lee whispered to Bosco, who was now beside him: "Keep your spirits up, Bosco!" He added the words "Johnny" and *policia*.

Bosco shook his head gloomily and answered something which Lee took to mean that Johnny would not dare apply to the police; that the police had it in for Johnny, because he shined shoes without taking out a license.

The steps went up alongside the wall of the room. After Schoënhut went out, Franklin again closed the door by jamming a chair between the door and the rail of the landing.

He returned, stuck another cigarette in Lee's mouth, lighted it and one for himself. "I'll untie your hands as soon as I let him in again."

"Give the young fellow a cigarette," said Lee.

"The hell I will," said Franklin coolly. "I offered him one and he spat in my face."

"So I am to be taken for a ride," said Lee.

"Sure. We've got a nice place in the country now," said Franklin. "Herr Stengel will be delighted to have a talk with you."

"You tried that before," said Lee. "What's the use?"

Franklin laughed evilly. "You don't know the half of it, Mr. Mappin. We've got many other methods of persuasion."

"Let us go together," said Lee with a nod towards Luke.

Franklin shook his head. "He's no further use to us," he said. "We are going to leave his body here. The kid can explain it as best he can."

Bosco broke into shrill vituperation. The words were strange to Lee. Obviously the boy was fishing up the dregs of language to empty on Franklin's head. The latter got up coolly and slapped the helpless boy's face, first with one hand, then the other. Bosco's voice rose higher, and Franklin slapped him again, harder. Lee, sickened by the exhibition, cried:

"Stop it, Bosco! Stop it!"

Bosco fell silent and Franklin returned to his chair. The girl on the bed broke into a renewed wailing, and he shut her up with a coarse threat.

Presently there was a scratching at the door and Franklin went and let Schoënhut in. The latter said:

"Car will be here in half an hour."

Franklin untied Lee's hands and he had a chance to stand up and stamp his feet and swing his arms to restore the circulation. He went to Luke and dropped beside him.

"Are you all right?" he whispered.

Luke nodded slightly.

"Whatever happens don't move until I give the word."

Franklin, suddenly suspicious, cried out: "What are you doing there?" Jumping up, he thrust Lee aside with his knee and bent over to examine the wounded man. He turned Luke's body over with his foot, but Luke gave so successful a representation of an unconscious man that he was satisfied and left him.

Lee, having returned to his chair, was amazed to see a blackened face suddenly appear outside an open window and vanish again. Then another face showed and disappeared. Franklin and Schoënhut saw nothing. Bosco grinned. There was a heavy knocking at the street door and a young voice crying:

"Bosco!"

"Come in!" shouted Bosco.

Franklin dealt him a savage backhanded blow. Bosco laughed and continued to shout: "Come in! Come in!" The door was violently shaken and Schoënhut instinctively ran towards the steps. Franklin, saying to Lee: "If you move or speak, I'll shoot you," followed the other man.

An amazing sight followed. Lee could scarcely believe his eyes. Figures began coming in over the sills of the two back windows, one after another, landing silently on the floor, boys with blackened faces and hands like commandos, each with a grin that revealed his gleaming teeth. They were mostly well-grown boys, fifteen or older, but little Johnny was among them, too. They came too fast for Lee to count.

The two men at the door, hearing a sound, looked behind them. Seeing what was happening, they ran down the steps, Franklin pulling his gun. Bosco shouted a warning. Several boys dived simultaneously for Franklin's legs and he crashed to the floor. The gun was discharged harmlessly. A boy stamped on Franklin's wrist; another snatched the gun from his hand. Schoënhut, less quick-witted than his mate, gaped at the boys clownishly. He was quickly borne down. Luke Tremaine rolled out of the way of the melee and, scrambling to his feet, leaned against the wall. He was fully conscious, but still weak and shaky.

One after another, the boys flung themselves on the heap in the middle of the floor. There was a furious threshing of bodies back and forth, arms and legs flying. The Gestapo men were at the bottom of the heap. Cries, groans, curses, and shouts arose from it, ranging the scale from bass to treble. Along with other sounds could be heard the hollow thudding of two skulls on the floor boards. The girl on the bed sat up and watched with staring eyes. Her hair was coming down, her dress torn at the neck.

"Quiet! Quiet!" ordered Bosco without the slightest effect. "Untie me!" he shouted.

A boy detached himself from the heap and, running to Bosco, untied the knots that bound him to the chair. Snatching up the

rope that had lately bound Lee's hands, the two ran back to get in
the scrimmage, Bosco commanding and imploring his friends to
make less noise. Another boy ran up the steps and, lifting the chair
that held the door, admitted several more boys from the street.
The chair was then jammed back in place.

The heap of boys in the middle of the floor separated and fell
quiet and busy. Nothing but an occasional groan from the Gestapo
men could be heard now. Finally, Franklin and Schoënhut were
hoisted to their feet, half led, half carried to the two chairs near
the hearth, and dropped upon them. Both groggy from the treat-
ment they had received, their heads rolled on their breasts. They
were lashed to the chairs with their hands behind them. Lee re-
trieved his wallet from Schoënhut's breast pocket. He also recovered their guns. Bosco stood back and spat in Franklin's face, then
slapped him with all his might, first on one cheek, then the other.

"Not when he's tied up!" remonstrated Lee.

Bosco turned around in pure surprise to protest. It was clear
that he was telling Lee this was what the man had done to him
when he was helpless.

"I know! I know!" said Lee. "But you don't have to act like the
Gestapo."

Bosco didn't get it. He continued passionately to justify himself, indicating first himself, then the girl. Luke put in dryly: "Chief,
he's telling you what this swine did before we got here."

Lee, seeing the uselessness of objecting, walked away to the
window while the boys continued to bat their prisoners around.
Certainly, it was no more than the Gestapo men deserved, but it
was a little too much for Lee's nerves. Moreover, he was afraid the
men might die if this was kept up long enough, and he designed a
different fate for them. After a bit, he had an idea and said:

"Let Luke take the girl home now. This is no sight for a woman.
It will do Luke good to get a breath of fresh air."

Some of the bigger boys, with sly, sidelong glances at the girl,
were inclined to protest; but Bosco had assumed the leadership
and Bosco approved the suggestion. As Luke started to lead her to
the door, she hung back and held out her arms to Bosco. She was

an unattractive girl at the best, dull of face and shapeless of body, and now in her torn finery she looked like a caricature. The boys howled with laughter, and Bosco, flushing, turned his back. Finally Luke and the girl were let out into the street and the door fastened behind them.

The baiting of the two prisoners continued. Lee looked out of the window and tried not to hear the sounds behind him. After the boys had begun to tire of batting the Gestapo men around, Lee heard a scratching at the door. Whirling around and holding up his hands for silence, he said:

"Boys, there's an automobile at the door. Seize it, and bring the chauffeur inside."

Bosco had enough English to understand this. He translated it and the mob started for the door, with wide grins in their blackened faces. It was surprising how softly they could move when they had an object in it.

The chair was lifted and the door opened. There was an astonished cry, a brief scuffle, and the boys reappeared dragging a helpless figure between them. His heels thudded down from step to step. Bosco darted outside. He reappeared, and the door was closed and fastened again. Bosco brought the key of the car to Lee.

The chauffeur's face was new to Lee. He was a small man wearing a suit that was too big for him; terror had reduced him to a gibbering state. The boys planted him in a chair and lashed him to it like the other two. When he saw the state Franklin and Schoënhut were in, his pleas for mercy were pitiful. The boys laughed at him and pulled his nose. "Can you speak English?" demanded Lee.

He dumbly shook his head.

Lee said to Bosco: "I want to find out where this car is stabled."

Bosco understood. "I make tell," he said, grinning.

Lee walked to the far end of the room, not anxious to witness the means of persuasion. What they did to the little chauffeur he never knew. He squealed like a pig, while the boys roared with laughter. When Lee came back, Bosco had the address written for him on a dirty scrap of paper. Bosco also handed Lee a key they had taken from the chauffeur, which he said would open the garage.

Since Bosco and his friends had no particular feeling against the chauffeur, they then let him alone. A shrill discussion arose as to what was to be done with the other two. Lee could not understand a word of the rapid Portuguese argot. Finally, to his astonishment, they began to untie the ropes that bound Franklin to the chair. They laid him on his back on the floor and a boy fetched the pail of water that was tinged with Luke's blood. Franklin appeared to be half conscious.

"What are you going to do?" Lee demanded of Bosco.

Bosco grinned like a young fiend. "We give water cure," he said. "Make feel better."

"No, by God!" said Lee. "I'm not going to stand for that! He's a swine all right, but I'm not going to see him tortured! Put him back on the chair, you devils, and let him alone!"

They couldn't understand Lee's words, but it was clear to all that he was trying to stop their fun. They protested angrily and volubly. One boy dipped a cup in the pail and, dropping to his knees beside Franklin, prepared to administer it.

"Open his mouth," he said.

Lee sent the cup flying out of the boy's hand. "Stop it!" he cried. "He's had enough."

For a moment, flat rebellion faced Lee. The half-savage young creatures gathered in a group facing him, scowling and muttering in an ugly fashion. There were close on twenty of them. Bosco's face presented a study of conflicting emotions. He was remembering that Lee was the source of all the good things he and his pals had enjoyed during the past days.

Finally, Bosco made up his mind and, ranging himself alongside Lee, started to harangue the boys. Presumably he was reminding them of what Lee had done for them all. Lee breathed more freely. He and Bosco lifted Franklin under the arms and, dragging him back over the floor, dropped him in the chair and made him fast to it.

The other boys looked on, silent and scowling. One of the biggest tried to incite the others to rebel. Bosco singled him out with a forefinger and silenced him with a curse. Lee had a happy idea. Taking a bill from his wallet and handing it to Bosco, he said:

"Send a couple of boys out for food and wine. *Vinho*, Bosco, *pao, carne.*"

It acted like a charm. Scowls turned into smiles; the tension relaxed.

Two boys were sent out with the money. The others lay about the floor singing and slanging each other. There must have been a store close by, for the messengers soon returned, laden with loaves of bread, bottles of wine, also meat, cheese, and other things. It was all spread out on the table and the boys gathered around, wolfing the food and passing the bottles from hand to hand. In a twinkling Lee had become the prince of good fellows. He glanced at his watch surreptitiously. It lacked a few minutes of ten.

Lee was the first to hear the distant sound of the police sirens. His heart began to beat fast. One by one the others heard it, and mouths stopped thawing. All knew what that sound meant. It drew closer and louder, and a look of fear appeared in the boys' faces. The approach of the time-honored enemy! The sirens stopped a little way off, but presently, through the shutters on the street side, they heard unmistakable sounds of a crowd gathering outside. A whispered word went from mouth to mouth: "*Policia!*"

There was a pounding on the door. Lee silently pointed to the open windows. Pausing only to sweep the table bare, the boys went out over the sills as silently as they had entered, clutching the bread and the wine under their jackets. All one could hear was a soft thudding as they dropped on the ground outside! It was as silent and as swift as a flight of birds. In an instant they were gone.

There was a renewed pounding on the door, and Luke's voice calling: "Chief! Chief!"

"Coming!" said Lee blandly. He scampered up the steps and, lifting the chair, let them in: four policemen, followed by Luke. Lee shut the door in the faces of the populace, and dropped the chair back in place.

Luke looked around him with a smile. He guessed what had happened. "Inspector da Gama will follow shortly," he said dryly. "He was attending a party at the Chinese Legation."

Lee, with Luke's assistance, described the situation briefly to the officer. "This is the room of a young man who is employed by me. He is known by the name of Bosco. These men"—pointing to the helpless three—"are agents of the Gestapo. They followed Bosco and his girl here, tied them up, and mistreated them. Another boy rounded up Bosco's friends, brought them here and released Bosco and tied up the Gestapo men in their places."

"What has become of these boys?" asked the officer.

"When they heard the police approaching, senhor, they went out of the window."

The policemen laughed. "Can you identify the boys, senhor?"

"Only Bosco, the one employed by me."

"Where's the girl?"

"I sent her home."

"How did you get in this mess, senhor?"

"I was on my way here with my secretary to warn Bosco that the men were laying for him. But they got here first."

When the policeman's questions became too searching, Lee merely suggested that they wait for the inspector.

Inspector da Gama presently arrived, bringing a couple of additional men, these two in plain clothes. Lee told him the story in greater detail. In conclusion he said, pointing to Schoënhut and Franklin:

"These two men are implicated in the murder of William Miller. I can produce the evidence to prove it. I have no charge against the third man, but as he is a chauffeur for the Gestapo, I suggest that he had better be detained as a witness."

The inspector nodded.

Lee continued: "You have said from the beginning that you would act as soon as I could present you with a case. It is almost complete."

"I stand by that," said the inspector.

"Da Gama," Lee continued in a lower voice, "Schoënhut is the local chief of the Gestapo. Are you man enough to lock him up?"

The inspector looked startled. "It will cause an uproar, senhor. The Embassy may force us to release him. High politics are outside my department."

"That's all right, said Lee. "If you are forced to release him, that won't be your fault. All I ask is that you let me know in advance, so he can't escape us altogether."

"Senhor, I give you my personal assurance that you shall be notified in advance."

They shook hands on it. Lee handed the inspector the address of the Gestapo garage and the key to it. "It will help us both, Inspector, if you will put seals on this building until I have a chance to search it. I hope to find additional evidence of great value there."

"I will not only seal it, senhor, I will put a guard on the building until tomorrow." The inspector jerked his head toward the three captives. "Take them out to the car," he ordered.

As Ronald Franklin was being led out, he held back in front of Luke. "You think you're quite a fellow, don't you, Lady Killer?" he sneered. "Taking my girl and all that. She doesn't mean a thing to me. She never did. She was nothing but a useful tool. Now that her usefulness to me is ended, you're welcome to her—*if you can find her!*" He went out, laughing.

CHAPTER NINETEEN

LEE AND LUKE WERE DRIVEN back to the Lisboa Palace in the Gestapo car by a policeman. Franklin's words rankled in Luke's breast.

"Perhaps it is just a bit of German frightfulness," suggested Lee.

"It must be more than that," said Luke. "It is clear that he knows she has betrayed him to us."

"Not necessarily. He might have been trying a shot in the dark. From your face, he knew that he had hit something. That's why he laughed."

In order to allay Luke's anxiety, Lee had their driver stop before a tobacconist's, and Luke went in to telephone the Victoria Hotel. He returned gloomier than ever.

"Kate went out an hour ago and has not returned. A private car called for her," he said.

"Don't despair!" said Lee.

When they entered their own hotel, the porter handed Lee a note addressed in an angular feminine hand. Since it was on Lisboa Palace paper, it must have been written right there in the hotel.

Dear Mr. Mappin:
I cannot be sure whether or not Ronnie has found me out. When he left me he was more than usually affectionate and that has aroused my suspicions. A while ago he called up to say I must carry a message to the Chief—he did not name him. He said there was no

198

telephone in the house where the Chief was stopping, and that was why I must go to him. The message was that Ronnie had received a call for help from "S" and therefore he could not come out as expected. He expected to come an hour or two later, and might perhaps bring guests. When I asked Ronnie where the house was, he said he was sending a car to take me there, and the driver knew the directions.

I realize that if Ronnie does smell a rat it is dangerous for me to go on this expedition; on the other hand, if I defy him, it would end my usefulness to you. I don't want to risk that. So I told him I would go, and shortly afterwards the car called for me.

Luckily, the driver of this car is a stupid fellow, and by making out that I was afraid he might lose his way in the dark, I tricked him into telling me where he was taking me. It's up the main north road and through Campo Grande to Lumiar. Beyond the town we take the second road to the west (that is second to the left) and after two miles a road to the north (right-hand side) marked by a tall eucalyptus tree shattered at the top by lightning. Half a mile up this road, at a spot where there is a wayside shrine, a stony track leads off to the west (left again) and the house we are seeking is at the end of this track. It is an ancient villa in the Manoeline style, pretty badly run down.

I hope you will approve of what I am doing. Give my best to Luke.

In haste,
Kate

"Oh God!" groaned Luke, running his fingers through his hair.

"Call up José at the garage," said Lee crisply. "Tell him to pick up Affonso and to get here as quick as he can. Both men should be armed and both bring flashlights."

Luke presently reported that José was starting immediately.

"Now call up the Ministry of Police and tell da Gama what we have learned."

Inspector da Gama, Luke was told, after having locked up his prisoners, had returned to the party at the Chinese Legation. Luke requested his clerk to get hold of him as quickly as possible, and to say that Mr. Mappin had a matter of the utmost importance to communicate, and would the inspector please remain within call until he heard from Mr. Mappin.

In a few minutes there was a call from the hotel bureau to say that Mr. Mappin's car was waiting. Before setting out, they called the Ministry of Police again. Inspector da Gama had not returned.

The shabby little car with José and his three passengers sped up the Avenida and on to the north out of the city. The taxi had been overhauled at Lee's expense and was in first-rate mechanical condition. Affonso supplied what conversation there was.

"We don't know how many men there may be waiting in this house. It doesn't matter. I am ready. It is lucky that José found me at home. The little fellow is brave but he lacks weight. I, Affonso, am afraid of nothing!"

In Lumiar they stopped again to telephone, and Lee had the satisfaction of getting da Gama on the wire. He quickly explained the situation, and the inspector said:

"I'll follow you as soon as I can get a few men together. I shan't be more than half an hour behind you."

"A lot can happen in half an hour," said Lee grimly.

Owing to Kate's explicit directions they had no difficulty with the road. Five minutes beyond the town they turned to the left, and a couple of miles farther the shattered eucalyptus tree marked the road to the north. Opposite the roadside shrine, with its bunch of faded flowers, they turned into a stony track which climbed steeply. It was a clear, still night with a sky full of stars. A dozen miles to the south glowed the lights of Lisbon.

When the dark mass of the ancient villa rose above them against the stars, Lee ordered José to stop. The track here ran between low stonewalls, and while José's car rested in the middle, there was no room for another to pass.

"You stay with the car, José," said Lee. "They might give us the slip. If they come this way, sound your horn and fire a shot in the air."

Lee, Luke and Affonso continued to ascend the road. The ornamental grounds of the villa, having been neglected for years, had grown up like a jungle. Yet a tree which had fallen across the road had been chopped in two and carried to one side, showing that the road was used. The villa itself, a long rectangular building with a balustrated roof, was built on a terrace above. As they drew closer, they saw that it was designed like a fortress, having no entrances in the outer wall. The outside windows were small, and too high from the ground to be reached without ladders. No spark of light showed anywhere. It was like a palace of the dead.

The road brought them to an elaborately ornamented, arched entrance leading to an interior patio or court. It was closed by a massive iron grille, which let down from the top like a portcullis. The three men surveyed this formidable barrier in dismay. A big bell hung close to the gate, with a rope dangling from it.

"If we rang the bell, they would think it was their folks coming back and come down and open up," suggested Affonso hopefully.

Lee shook his head. "If they did come to the gate, they wouldn't open it until they had identified us. All we would gain would be the pleasure of looking at them through the bars."

Affonso cast his eyes upward. "It could be climbed," he said. "There is room at the top for a man to squeeze through."

"Sure," said Luke, "but in that case we'd have to leave the chief outside."

"Nothing of the sort," said Lee sharply. "If it can be climbed, I can make shift to climb it, too."

Affonso climbed with no special difficulty and let himself down on the other side. "There is a winch for hauling it up," he reported in a whisper.

"Don't touch it!" warned Lee. "I'm sure it hasn't been oiled in years. The screech of the iron would wake the dead."

"Chief, if you're determined to try it, you go before me," said Luke.

It was many a year since Lee had done any climbing. There were plenty of protuberances on the ornamental grille to afford foot-holds. He painfully hauled himself up a few inches at a time, Luke close beside him, ready to lend a hand. Nobody ever knew what the effort cost Lee. He made the top at last, and paused to recover his breath. Going down on the inside was easier.

Presently the three of them were standing together in the arched, tunnel-like passage leading to the interior court. Lee curiously examined the rusty apparatus for raising the gate.

"It would take two men to work that," he said.

A small door opened off the passage, with a window beside it. Lee opened the door and cast his light around the small, bare chamber within. It had no connection with the rest of the house.

"Porter's lodge or guardroom," said Lee. "Come on!"

Architects and sculptors had lavished their art on the inside face of the building. There was a covered passage or arcade all around the court. The main rooms, projecting overhead, were carried on a series of slender arches, decorated with stone carvings as delicate as lace. Every window, every balcony, seemed to flower in stone. A strange, beautiful, silent place in the starlight; the only sign of human occupancy was a dim light showing behind the middle three of the tall windows looking down on the court from the left.

"At any rate," murmured Lee, "there doesn't appear to be an army quartered here."

In the middle of the court rose a fantastically decorated fountain, dry now; the driveway encircled it. Some of the convoluted balustrades were broken, the statues thrown down, the planting was running riot; still it was obvious an effort had been made to put this part of the villa in order. In all the weird scene, the strangest object was a modern motorcar, standing abandoned in the driveway.

Pointing to the car, Lee whispered to Luke: "If the key is in the switch, bring it; if not, cut the wires."

Luke opened the car door noiselessly. He returned with the key.

Under the arcade they searched for a means of entrance to the villa. All the windows of the lower floor opening on the arcade had shutters closed and barred from within. In the middle of this side under the arcade, they came to a great door studded with nails. This appeared to be the main entrance. It was locked. Near the rear of the same side there was a smaller door, also locked. A complete circuit of the arcade revealed that every door was locked and every window shuttered.

Baffled for the moment, they backed into the driveway and gazed up at the three dimly lighted windows. One of the elaborately carved stone balconies ran along outside these tall casements, but the casements themselves were shut. While they looked, they heard a muffled cry from the room within; a dreadful, faint sound in the stillness.

"Oh God!" groaned Luke.

Lee clapped a hand over his mouth. "Quiet, for God's sake!" he said in Luke's ear. "If they hear your voice, they'll kill her!"

Luke shook as if seized by an ague. "The brutes! The brutes!" he groaned.

"Keep your wits about you!" urged Lee. "Run to the gate and stick your arm through, and ring the bell. Ring it twice, then pause, then twice again, pause, and twice more. That's their signal."

Luke disappeared in the darkness. Presently the sound of the bell clanged out; three measured double strokes. There were no further cries from the house.

Luke returned. The three men pressed forward under the arcade and flattened themselves against the wall beyond the door. They heard the sounds of bolts being withdrawn inside. The door swung in, letting out a shaft of light, and two men emerged. The light revealed the broad, squat figures of Albrecht Stengel and the tall, broad-shouldered Scarface. Lee pressed Luke's hand.

The two hastened away in the direction of the gate. When they had passed out of hearing, Lee said: "They have no servants here or they would not have gone to the gate themselves."

Lee, Luke, and Affonso slipped through the open door and, softly closing it, worked the great bolts across. They found themselves in a monumental stair hall with stone floor, stone walls, and vaulted ceiling. Electric lights had been installed in this part of the villa. A broad, curving stair led upward. They ran up. Opening off the landing at the top was a great pair of carved oaken doors to the left; another to the right. A line of light showed under the left-hand doors; they were locked, but the great key stood in the lock; they had only to turn it and enter.

A long, nobly proportioned chamber faced them, empty except for some temporary objects; several cots with tumbled bedding, chairs, a folding table. Opposite the tall windows was a row of smaller windows in the outside wall of the villa. Kate lay stretched on the floor of the room with her face hidden. She supposed it was her tormentors returning and did not look up. Luke murmured her name.

"Kate!"

She jerked up her head and Lee saw such joy break as he had never before seen in a human face. Luke ran and gathered her in his arms.

"Are you hurt?" he demanded in an agonized voice.

Kate shook her head. "No! But I had given up all hope!"

Luke carried her to one of the cots, and sat holding her as if he would never let her go.

Lee attempted to open one of the casements. He had to call on Affonso for help before he could move the long-closed frame. He stole out on the balcony to listen, taking care to keep below the balustrade.

Soon he heard the two Gestapo men coming back under the arcade. Stengel, in his hoarse, guttural voice, was scolding the other. Suddenly the voice was cut off in the middle of a sentence. They had come to the door and found it closed. Lee smiled to himself. Stengel exploded in wrath, shook the door and kicked it, shouted for Kate. Remembering that he had locked her in above, he suddenly fell quiet, as if afraid.

"Hello, Herr Stengel," said Lee in German. It was imprudent perhaps, but the temptation was too great.

Stengel apparently started to run out from under the arcade and was dragged back by the other man. "He'll shoot!" warned Scarface.

Stengel stood back out of sight and cursed Lee from a heart that seemed about to burst with rage. Lee enjoyed it.

"I'm learning some new German words," he said.

At length Stengel succeeded in controlling his rage. "Well, you've trapped yourself nicely," he said, attempting to laugh. "How the hell do you think you're going to get out?"

"I can stand it if you can," said Lee.

"How many men have you got up there?"

"More than you have."

Stengel laughed again. "My friends will be here directly."

"Sorry," said Lee "but the friends you are expecting are lodged in jail. That is to say, Schoënhut and the man who calls himself Ronald Franklin. The newsboy was too much for him."

"You're a liar!" said Stengel.

There was a silence from below. Lee pictured them with their heads close together, whispering. Then Stengel's. voice rose again:

"Are you there, Mappin?"

"Right here."

A new and silkier note came into the German's voice. "Look here, we've reached a deadlock. We can't get in and you can't get out. Let us declare a truce."

Lee smiled to himself. "All right. What are your terms?"

"We're willing to let you leave without hindrance and take the girl, if you'll return the key to our car."

"Very well," said Lee. "As an evidence of good faith, throw your guns up in the balcony."

There was a brief silence below. "That would be too one-sided," objected Stengel. "You could shoot us on your way out."

"Remove part of the firing mechanism, and we'll do the same before we throw our guns down."

"Agreed! Wait there until I fix the guns."

Stengel's voice was as false as hell, and Lee knew that this offer was preliminary to some trick. Stengel was playing for time. Lee

crept back through the window into the big room. He said: "I'm
satisfied they can't force that door at the foot of the stairs, but there
may be some way in at the rear. Come with me Affonso, and we'll
explore. Luke, lock that door at the end of the room and watch the
balcony. If you get in a jam, fire your gun."

Beyond the long room lay another of the same size. This was a
banqueting room; the long table was still in place, no other furniture. They proceeded through the dark rooms, flashlights in hand.
Beyond lay a serving pantry. There were no locks on the doors between these rooms. From the pantry a stairway led down to an
immense, stone-paved kitchen. There was another heavy, bolted
door from the kitchen to the arcade, and a row of shuttered windows.

Lee opened a casement and laid an ear against the crack between the shutters to listen. Outside he heard little sounds like
mice behind a wainscot, and smiled. He had guessed right. Retreating a few steps, he flattened himself against the wall and stood
with searchlight and gun ready. In a few minutes, there was a crash
that splintered the shutters. Lee stood waiting while they pulled
away the pieces of broken wood. Then suddenly he flashed his light
alongside the wall just as a leg came over the window sill. Lee fired,
and the leg was jerked out of sight.

A long silence followed. Finally a round bull's eye of light was
thrown into the room from outside. It searched around the floor,
but Lee and Affonso were safely out of its range. It was shut off,
and the silence and darkness closed in again, hard on the nerves.
Lee stole forward to the wrecked window and, without exposing
himself, cast his light outside. It did not succeed in drawing their
fire, and as the moments of silence accumulated, Lee felt that the
men were no longer there.

Far away two shots were fired, so close together they were almost one. Lee ordered Affonso to keep watch across the window
with his light. He ran upstairs and back through the rooms as fast
as he could go. The great room where he had left Luke and Kate
was dark now. His heart sank. He could hear a suppressed sobbing. He hesitated to switch on his light.

"Luke!" he said.

Luke's voice came to him, resonant and full, through the dark: "All okay, Chief!"

Lee's heart rebounded with joy. Switching on his light, he saw Luke lying on the floor looking around the open casement. Across the room lay Kate, trying to stifle her hysterical sobs.

"I got one of them," said Luke.

"Which one?"

"Stengel."

"Is he dead?"

"Dead as mutton."

"Well . . ." said Lee, "I had hoped to give him a more public execution."

"They placed a ladder at the end of the balcony where I could not see it," Luke went on. "And Stengel snaked along the balcony to the open window. The first I knew of it was when his head and arm appeared at the window. We fired almost simultaneously, but he missed and my bullet found its mark. The ladder is still in place. I couldn't push it over without exposing myself too much. I have Stengel's gun."

Lee took Luke's place at the window. "Go to Kate," he said.

"She's been through too much today," said Luke apologetically. "Her nerves are completely shot."

"She's got reason enough," said Lee.

He flashed his light briefly out on the balcony. Stengel lay sprawling on his back. Luke's bullet had caught him in the middle of the forehead, and there was no doubt that he was dead. Death revealed him with hideous clarity as the brute he was; bulldog; butcher.

Lee switched off his light. There was a long silence in the dark room, with faint starshine showing through the windows. No sound of movement reached Lee's ears from below. Kate's sobbing had quieted. Finally Luke said:

"What's the next move, Chief? I know you won't be satisfied with just lying here waiting for Scarface to attack."

"No," said Lee. "And neither will Scarface sit still and wait for us to make the first move . . . Scarface is the man who killed William

Miller, and we must take him alive. I have been trying to dope out how his mind would work. Come and take my place here. I have an idea."

Lee went to one of the smaller windows in the outside wall of the villa and, opening the casement and the shutter outside, cast his light on the ground below. "Eighteen feet, I should say," he said. "At any rate, not more than twenty. There are plenty of these thin blankets; let's knot them together and make a getaway out of the window."

"Oh, yes!" breathed Kate.

"What about Scarface?" asked Luke.

"I haven't forgotten him," said Lee, smiling. ". . . Come, Kate, help me with the blankets."

The distraught girl was delighted to have work for her hands to do. They laid the flashlight on the floor to give them light and gathered up the blankets. Luke watched and listened at the open window.

When the blankets were knotted together, corner to corner, and the knots thoroughly tested, Lee hung his rope from the window. It was long enough. He said:

"I will go now and fetch Affonso."

In the kitchen, Affonso reported that he had neither seen anything nor heard anything since he had been left on watch. He and Lee hastened back to the big room above.

They folded one of the cots, tied the end of the rope firmly around the middle, and placed the cot across the window frame. Lee was the first to descend. The night air was fragrant with cedar; the cool, starry sky like a benediction. The rope was hauled up again, and tied around the body of Stengel. Luke and Affonso lowered him to Lee, who untied the rope and dragged the body out of the way. Kate was then lowered into Lee's arms; Luke and Affonso descended after her. Affonso, according to instructions, had turned on the lights in the big room before climbing out of the window.

When they were reunited on the ground, Luke and Affonso picked up the body of Stengel to carry it towards the road. Kate, once she was safe out of that house of terror, was herself again.

She accompanied the two men, and Lee was left to watch the dangling rope.

Lee's instructions were: "It is time for Inspector da Gama to get here. If you meet him, tell him to make a noise like the police, sirens, horns, etc. Tell him to send his men to the gate of the villa and jangle the bell. Luke and Affonso are to come back to me as quick as they can."

Lee settled himself behind a thick clump of cedar to watch the window above, and the dangling rope. After a while, the lights in the big room went out, and his heart beat faster. Scarface was in there. He thought a shadow darkened the open window, but could not be sure. Then Scarface's light flashed on. It searched the ground all around the foot of the rope. Lee was well hidden.

Scarface, still full of suspicion, would not trust himself to the rope. He snapped off his light and withdrew inside the window. Darkness again took possession of the scene.

Alter another lapse of time, Lee heard the welcome hooting of sirens near by. Judging from the sounds, the police car had been halted in the road by José's car. José then moved aside to let it pass, for the sirens were next heard around at the gate. Meanwhile, Luke and Affonso joined Lee behind the cedars. The great bell at the gate of the villa clanged imperiously.

"That sound will put the fear of God into him," murmured Lee.

Scarface came back to the window above and cast his light down. But still he hesitated and went back. The bell set up a renewed clangor, and the clumsy, knotted rope began to shake. Scarface was climbing out of the window. They watched the dark, swaying shadow slowly descend against the paler wall of the villa.

The three men crept noiselessly to the foot of the rope. The swaying Scarface, fully occupied in lowering himself, could not see what was immediately under him. If he had seen, he could not have drawn a gun. When he was near the ground, he sensed that there was somebody below him; his hold of the rope loosened and he dropped. Instantly they got him. Scarface was a powerful man, but so were Luke and Affonso. Turning him over on his face, they tied his wrists behind him with a handkerchief. Luke held a light.

Scarface's hands, as usual, were gloved. Commanded to get up and walk, they marched him around to the gate of the villa.

Da Gama's men stared. A couple of them had already gone over the top of the gate and were busy hoisting it from within with a screeching of rusty iron. Scarface was handed over to the care of da Gama, and the handkerchief exchanged for handcuffs.

"There were only two members of the gang here," said Lee. "You'll find the house empty."

Da Gama congratulated him. "I'll search the premises anyhow," he said. "There will be evidence."

"You can get in the house," said Lee, "by a ladder to the balcony outside the main chamber, or by a smashed window in the kitchen. Pull in the rope and lock the windows in the great room. Take careful note of everything you see, as I shall need your evidence to corroborate my story of what happened. Here's the switch key to their car that is standing in the court . . . There's only one more thing I want you to see, Inspector . . . Hold out your hands!" Lee commanded Scarface.

Luke threw a light on the man's hands, and with his free hand pulled off the left-hand glove. The end joint of Scarface's third finger was missing.

Da Gama exclaimed in surprise.

"Notice," said Lee, "that the glove finger is stuffed out to hide the disfigurement. With your permission, I'll keep the gloves for the moment . . . Number seven and last," said Lee to Luke.

LATE AS IT WAS, when they got back to Lisbon, Lee would not go to bed until he had called up the United States Legation. He insisted upon having his friend the Minister awakened, and gave him a brief account of what had happened.

"Full particulars tomorrow," said Lee. "They are quite amusing. Will you do me the kindness to cable Westerholm on the island of Fayal tonight, and instruct him to turn Pedro Chavez and his passengers back to Lisbon, the moment he arrives."

"Right!" said the Minister.

"Sorry to cause so much bother at this time of night," Lee continued, "but a showdown cannot be delayed for long now. Will you also request the British Ambassador to ask the authorities at Gibraltar to return the prisoner Algodão to Lisbon at the earliest possible moment."

"I'll see to it," said the Minister.

CHAPTER TWENTY

A WEEK PASSED. Bosco reported that all members of the Gestapo had abandoned the Hotel Excelsior and the house was closed. In the course of the week, Algodão from one direction was mysteriously set ashore in Lisbon, and from another direction the Rosado brothers, Luiz and Antonio. Lee handed them over to the police. Every day Inspector da Gama urged Lee to bring charges against these and the other prisoners he was holding.

"You can depend upon it," said da Gama, "the Embassy of a certain country unfriendly to yours is exceedingly busy in the matter. Representations have been made to the chief persons in my government, and I must take action of one sort or another."

Each day Lee begged for twenty-four hours more.

VERY LATE ONE NIGHT, when Lee was preparing for bed, the telephone rang. Luke was already in bed, and Lee answered the call. A fresh young male voice, speaking Portuguese with an accent, asked:

"Is this Mr. Mappeen?"

"*Si, Senhor*," said Lee.

"This is Jaime Barreto. Do you remember the Spanish boy?"

"I certainly do!" cried Lee, forgetting his Portuguese. "Wait a minute until I call my secretary. He will understand you better."

Luke was quickly hauled to the telephone. Lee stood by.

Said Luke: "He apologizes for disturbing you at such a late hour. He says he couldn't set out from his father's house until after dark,

212

and must be back there before daylight. He wants to see you on a matter of great importance."

"Where is he?" asked Lee.

"He asks if you will meet him at the north side of the Rocío beyond the National Theatre. He will be waiting there in his father's car."

"What does he want to see me about?"

"That he won't tell me because, he says, he is afraid somebody might be listening in." Luke covered the transmitter with his hand. "Is it safe, Chief?"

"Why not?" said Lee. "If it is really Jaime Barreto, I would trust that boy anywhere. If it's a crook, he would hardly appoint the Rocío for a meeting; the most brilliantly lighted spot in town, with people passing back and forth all night."

"Okay," said Luke. "What shall I tell him?"

"Tell him we'll be there in ten minutes."

Jaime Barreto's little old car waited beside the curb beyond the National Theatre, and the slim Spanish boy stood beside it, looking for them. Lee and Luke shook his hand warmly. He opened the rear door.

"There's a friend inside," he said, smiling.

The light revealed a figure on the back seat, a frank, smiling young face, an outstretched hand.

"Niebuhr!" breathed Lee in astonishment.

The young German laid a finger on his lips as he drew Lee in. Luke climbed after. Niebuhr said to Jaime: "Drive around the Square two or three times. We won't keep Herr Mappin more than ten minutes. We must be getting back!"

"The danger is not so great tonight," said Lee. "You could have driven right up to the hotel. Stengel is dead and most of the local Gestapo's in jail!"

"Still, I must be careful," said Niebuhr, smiling. "Every Nazi carries my picture in his wallet—not because he loves me, but because he hopes to win the reward."

"They told us," said Lee, "that both you and the boy had been shot on the mountainside."

"A typical Gestapo lie," said Niebuhr. "They never got near us."

"Where have you been?" asked Lee.

"To Berlin and back."

"Good God!" said Lee. "You have made that dangerous journey twice more!"

"Each time I make it, it is a little easier, a little quicker. I know the ropes. I find new friends to help me along."

The car was slowly encircling the Rocío. Taxis still whisked here and there, groups moved along the sidewalks, the sound of singing and the plucking of guitars was heard; Lisbon never went to bed. The passing lights flashed on and off in Niebuhr's fresh-colored, handsome face. Lee, deeply moved by his grave smile, was impelled to throw an arm around the young fellow's shoulders.

"What brought you back to Lisbon?" he asked.

"You!" said Niebuhr. "You told me that if I could secure certain papers for you, it might have the effect of shortening the war. What greater incentive could a man have than that? Even to shorten it a single day! As soon as I arrived in Berlin, I applied myself to getting what you wanted and I was successful."

"Wonderful!" cried Lee.

Niebuhr passed over a raincoat. "The papers are sewed inside the lining of this coat," he said. "I couldn't carry away the originals. It would have meant discovery and death for the friend and fellow worker who got them for me. These are photostat copies."

"Just as good," said Lee.

"There was nobody in the world I could trust to carry them across Europe," Niebuhr said simply, "so I brought them myself."

"I hope that the use I make of them will justify you," said Lee gravely.

"Now we must start back," said Niebuhr. "Let Mr. Mappin out at the spot where we picked him up, Jaime."

"So soon!" said Lee. "Can't you stop and rest? Won't tomorrow do as well for the return journey? Luke and I will hide you close."

Niebuhr shook his head. "My timetable has been carefully worked out. In Bajadoz a man is waiting with a car who will drive me to the French border."

"You and the boy need food," protested Lee, "and a bottle of wine to drink to victory."

"We have food and wine in the car. As soon as we get out of town I will drive and the boy can sleep."

The car stopped; Luke and Lee got out. Lee clung to Niebuhr's hand for a moment, hating to let him go. "Well . . . good luck, my boy!"

"Good luck! Good luck!" answered Niebuhr. "The sky is already beginning to lighten in the east."

The little car drove away.

NEXT MORNING, Inspector da Gama called Lee on the telephone. "I am afraid you have waited too long," he said gloomily. "Charges have now been made against you. I am sorry you didn't bring your charges first. You are required to appear in the office of the Minister of Police at half-past ten this morning. A car will be sent to the hotel for you."

"Very good," said Lee. "I shall be ready."

Lee and Luke dressed with care for the occasion. Luke at the best had a sort of rough-and-ready good looks, but Lee was turned out like a little fashion plate.

The private office of the Minister of Police was a much more imposing chamber than that allotted to a mere inspector. Several officers and gentlemen were in attendance, including da Gama and various secretaries and amanuenses. The Minister, a handsome, grave man in fashionable civilian costume, greeted Lee and Luke courteously, waved them to chairs, offered them cigarettes, started a polite conversation about the United States.

After this had continued for a little, Lee asked courteously: "May we proceed to business, Your Excellency?"

"We are waiting for the complainant," answered the Minister.

Very soon the doors were thrown open and an orderly sonorously announced, "The Prince zu L—." That personage strode in as if he had swallowed a ramrod, monocle firmly screwed into place. Today he was attended by several stooges carrying stuffed briefcases. The Prince bowed stiffly to the Minister, looked over the heads of everybody else in the room, and condescended to take the chair that was offered to him. His stooges sat in a row behind him.

Meanwhile, Lee noted that one of the Portuguese attendants unobtrusively opened a door behind the Minister's chair, and left it standing a few inches ajar. From that he judged that an even more exalted personage than the Minister of Police was listening to the proceedings.

"Senhor Mappin," said the Minister, "before we begin I should inform you that this hearing is of a quasi-judicial nature, and you are therefore entitled to be represented by an advocate if you so desire."

"I thank Your Excellency," said Lee. "To me it does not appear to be necessary at this juncture. As to the future, I will be guided by what transpires here this morning."

"Very good, senhor. Firstly, you are charged with being responsible for the death of Albrecht Stengel, a subject of Germany."

Lee looked at Luke, and Luke arose: "By your favor, Excellency, may I say at once that it was I who shot Albrecht Stengel; thus I may save time."

His Excellency was surprised by this prompt confession. "So!" be said, stroking his chin. "Was it by the order of Senhor Mappin?"

"No, Excellency. Senhor Mappin was not present. I shot Stengel because he had a pistol leveled at my head. A second later he fired. We have a witness to the actual shooting, Your Excellency. Also, Senhor Mappin and another man, a citizen of Lisbon, were within hearing and can testify that the two shots were fired almost simultaneously. Senhor Mappin was provoked with me when he found the man was dead."

"Why?" asked the Minister with undisguised curiosity.

"Because it was his wish to see Stengel brought to trial."

"Ha!" said the Minister, stroking his chin. ". . . Well, let that go for the moment. There is another charge against Senhor Mappin. He is accused of having brought about the death of William Miller, also a subject of Germany."

Lee and Luke looked at each other in purest surprise. "Well, I'll be damned!" murmured Lee. To the Minister he said: "Is the man who makes this accusation present, your Excellency?"

"He is not," said the Minister dryly—"for a very good reason . . . A deposition will be read." He looked at the German party. One of the stooges fished a paper out of his brief case and, rising, commenced to read. The Minister interrupted him.

"It is in German," he said to Lee. "Shall I have it translated for you?"

"Thank you, I speak German," said Lee.

The German read:

Albrecht Stengel, aged 43, a subject of Germany, upon being sworn, deposes and says that:

William Miller was known to me for five years past as a loyal subject of *der Fuehrer* and for the same length of time has been employed by me as agent of the German Intelligence. I was his superior officer. In the United States there is an organization known as the Association for Aiding Anti-Nazis, which is engaged in subversive activities in Germany, and in neutral countries. Early in 1943, I sent William Miller to the United States to investigate these people and to supply me with information that would enable me to block their underground work in my country. Miller was admitted to the Association, he won the confidence of the officers, and when the Association appointed Amos Lee Mappin as their general agent in Europe with headquarters in Lisbon, William Miller came with him as his secretary.

Immediately on his arrival in Lisbon, Miller got in touch with me and with the local office of German Intelligence, and thus, day by day, we were kept informed of every move made by Mappin. In some manner unknown to deponent, Mappin discovered that his secretary was an agent of German Intelligence. He decoyed Miller to his office at Rua Cachimbo, 23, on the night of September 18, and there with the assistance of other persons, foully murdered him. Mappin is what is called in America a criminologist of long experience. Ever since the murder he has been engaged with devilish ingenuity in manufacturing evidence tending to prove that it was other members of German Intelligence in Lisbon who were guilty of the murder of their friend and loyal fellow worker, William Miller.

(Signed) Albrecht Stengel

Lee laughed a little when the man finished reading.

The Minister was affronted. "This is hardly an occasion for levity, Senhor Mappin."

Lee apologized. "Stengel is dead, Your Excellency," he added.

"I am aware of it, senhor. It is the contention of the complainant that he was killed to prevent him from giving this evidence. However, fearing such a fate, he had already made his deposition."

"By your favor, Excellency, he furnishes no evidence, but only an unsupported statement," said Lee.

"Do you wish to answer it now," asked the Minister, "or will you take legal advice?"

"I will answer it now, Excellency."

"I must warn you that anything you say can be used against you later."

"I am prepared for that, sir."

While Lee talked, an amanuensis took down his statements.

"Your Excellency," he began, "I can easily show that the claim that William Miller was a loyal agent of the Gestapo is completely false. Soon after we arrived in Lisbon, I was engaged in the delicate matter of bringing the famous anti-Nazi author, Friedrich Erbelding, and his family out of Germany, where they had been persecuted, and in finding transportation for them to the United States. William Miller assisted me at every step in this matter. If he was in touch with the Gestapo, why did he not tell them? The Erbeldings left Portugal on September thirteenth, five days before William Miller was murdered. The Germans were making every effort to stop the Erbeldings, as Inspector da Gama can testify. As you have no doubt read in the dispatches, Herr Erbelding and his family have now arrived safely in the United States."

The Minister nodded.

"As to the charge of murder," Lee continued, "that, if Your Excellency will permit me, is what we call in America a red herring drawn across the trail. I am prepared to describe to you exactly how William Miller came to his end. And, furthermore, every statement I make will be supported by legal evidence."

The Minister signed to Lee to proceed.

"My arrival here in Lisbon," Lee began, "was considered a menace by the Gestapo. They had not much confidence in Schoënhut, their local director; and Albrecht Stengel, the famous—or infamous—Butcher of Paris, was sent to Lisbon to deal with me. Within twenty-four hours of his arrival, he had perfected a plot to liquidate William Miller, because, it was supposed, I could not function without him. I was to be put out of the way later, that is, as soon as they had secured from me information vital to them concerning our friends in Spain, France, Switzerland, Germany, also the code by which we communicated with each other, and so on.

"In addition to Stengel, there were seven men concerned in this plot, six of whom are now in the hands of the Lisbon Police, while the seventh, known to me as Diehlmann, is a patient in the Bon Secours Hospital with a broken leg. Stengel's first act was to plant one Algodão, your prisoner who bears a Portuguese name but carries a German passport, in the hotel room adjoining my suite. Algodão had a passkey made by which he could enter my room at his pleasure. Early in the evening of September eighteenth, he entered my suite in my absence and doctored the water bottle beside my bed with a solution of Duotol, a powerful soporific, also the water bottle beside William Miller's bed in the adjoining room."

"What evidence have you against Algodão?" asked the Minister.

Lee checked it off on his fingers: "(a) A chambermaid in the Lisboa Palace Hotel will testify that he tricked her into lending him her passkey; (b) a respectable locksmith in the vicinity of the hotel will identify Algodão as the man for whom he made the passkey; (c) he left fingerprints on the necks of both water bottles; (d) his fingerprints were also found in the room where William Miller was killed; (e) a bottle containing Duotol tablets was found in his suitcase subsequent to the murder."

"Proceed," said the Minister.

"The next step was to secure a small covered truck, such as undertakers use for transporting bodies. The prisoner named Ronald Franklin was assigned to this task. Franklin, I regret to say, is a citizen of the United States. He carries a bona fide United States passport. No doubt he has a German passport also. If the government of Portugal desires to surrender him, my government will try him for treason. On the night of September eighteenth, he hired such a truck from Cavilho, the well-known undertaker of West Lisbon, and returned it before morning. He represented to Senhor Cavilho that it was required for an innocent prank. Cavilho will testify to this effect. He has identified Franklin.

"Thus, on the night of September eighteenth, having thrown Miller and myself into a profound drugged sleep, the gang entered our suite. Miller wag bound and gagged (in case he should awaken too soon), laid upon a stretcher which came with the truck, and covered with a blanket. Four men carried him out of the hotel by way of a rear stairway and a service entrance. The watchman at this entrance was either put out of the way or bribed. He has disappeared. The truck was waiting to receive the body."

"How do you expect to prove these statements?" asked the Minister.

"In this manner, Excellency. The stretcher was recovered in Senhor Cavilho's garage. The truck has been positively identified, owing to certain peculiarities in the tires. A guest in the hotel saw the body being carried through the corridor. He very naturally supposed that a death had occurred in the hotel, and that the body was being removed in this secret manner to avoid distressing the other guests."

"Do you know the identity of the four men who carried the stretcher?"

"Yes, sir; Diehlmann, the two Rosados, and the prisoner who was booked by the police under the name of Evart Stahl. Until I learned his name, I called him Scarface. According to this guest who saw them, a fifth man led the way through the corridor. This must have been Algodão."

"Continue, senhor."

"William Miller, then, was carried to the Rua Cachimbo. A householder in that street saw the truck standing at the door of number 23. But not for long. Franklin returned it to its garage as soon as he could. There is no evidence that Franklin was present at the scene of the murder. He may have returned to the Rua Cachimbo after returning the truck; in any case, he is an accessory before the fact.

"They broke into that room in the Rua Cachimbo which I rented for an office. In the effort to extract information from William Miller, they cruelly tortured him with irons heated in a sort of bucket of burning charcoal. This so-called bucket has been recovered and has been identified by Luke Tremaine, who was subsequently mistreated by the same gang. That is another story. The bucket is now in the possession of the police.

"Stengel and Schoënhut were either waiting at the Rua Cachimbo for the others or they joined them there . . ."

"You have proof of this, senhor?"

"As to Schoënhut, absolute proof, senhor. Although they were seven against one, Miller succeeded in freeing himself partly and put up a magnificent struggle. The room was wrecked. Schoënhut lost his glasses in the melee and they were stepped on and broken. He neglected to pick up the pieces of glass. I was able to have them put together and so establish the oculist's prescription from which they had been made. I am prepared to prove that Schoënhut sent to an optician on the next day but one, and ordered a pair of glasses from the same prescription."

"What about Stengel?"

"It is only by inference that I know he was present, Excellency. He was always present at such scenes of questioning and torture. That was his specialty."

"I suggest that you avoid drawing inferences, senhor. Please continue."

"In the end," said Lee, spreading out his hands, "my poor friend was stabbed to the heart and left lying there. In the morning a voice called me on the telephone to say he was waiting for me in my office."

"Such evidence," said the Minister, "would directly connect Algodão, Schoënhut and Franklin with the crime. What about the others you have named?"

"Clutched between the dead man's thumb and forefinger," said Lee, "I found certain hairs which have been identified under the microscope as having been pulled from Luiz Rosado's beard. Antonio Rosado, besides fingerprints, is connected with the crime by the finding of the false passkey among his effects. As to Diehlmann, in the truck used to convey William Miller to the place where he was killed, I found a jewel, specifically a bloodstone, which had fallen from a pair of cuff links that Diehlmann was wearing."

"You mention fingerprints; what about them?"

"The Gestapo men were either very careless, Your Excellency, or they were unfamiliar with modern methods of detecting crime. There were fingerprints everywhere about the room where William Miller was killed. I collected and have preserved full sets and partial sets, which have been identified as belonging to Schoënhut Algodão, the two Rosados, and Diehlmann,"

"Not Stengel?"

"No, sir. Stengel took no part in the dirty work."

"Not Evart Stahl, or Scarface as you called him?"

"No, sir."

"Then you are not prepared to say who struck the fatal blow?"

"By your favor, Excellency, I am prepared to say."

"Who was it?"

"Evart Stahl."

"What proof do you offer?"

"Stahl left no fingerprints because it is his habit at all times to wear gloves, brown cotton gloves. An odd fancy for a man in hot weather. The reason he does so is to conceal a disfigurement. He has lost the top joint of the third finger of his left hand. He keeps this glove finger stuffed out to the end with cotton. When I examined the body of William Miller, I found his teeth tightly clenched. Force was required to pry them apart. Within his mouth I found a scrap of brown material with a seam in it; in other words, the end of a finger of a cotton glove."

"This is proof that he was present, but not that he stabbed Miller."

"No, Excellency. I should inform you that I had found the print of other fingers on the dead man's breast. These were bloody prints. I did not refer to them as fingerprints in the usual sense, because they showed none of the lines to be found in the skin of naked fingers. All revealed an identical texture; it was that of a cotton material. The knife had been driven to the hilt in the dead man's body, and considerable strength was required to withdraw it. I figure that the killer had to place the fingers of his left hand against the breast to obtain the necessary leverage . . . I have the pair of gloves taken from Stahl's hands the night he was arrested. It is the same pair. Probably he could obtain no others, so he washed and mended them. The mended place is apparent . . ."

The Prince zu L— arose and screwed in his monocle. "How much more of this nonsense am I expected to listen to?" he demanded arrogantly. "It is not only false but frivolous! A torn cotton glove, forsooth! Some hairs from a man's beard! Mr. Minister, I wonder that you are content to listen to such a farrago. All it amounts to is a confession that the witness has shamefully abused your country's neutrality. Please do me the credit of remembering that I warned you he was tricky and ingenious. But really, I must say I expected something better!" He turned to leave the room.

Lee was saying blandly: "I have not quite finished."

The Minister said very politely: "Your Highness, I beg of you, let the witness finish his story."

Prince zu L— remained standing with a scornful air, his hand on the back of his chair. He glanced impatiently at his watch, like a busy man detained against his will.

Lee drew a long envelope from his breast pocket. "These papers," he said, "contain evidence going back of Albrecht Stengel in establishing the responsibility for this murder. They are photostat copies of confidential notes from His Highness, Prince zu L— to his principal, the Minister of Foreign Affairs."

The monocle flew out of the Prince's eye. "What!" he cried furiously.

"The earliest note speaks of my arrival in Lisbon," Lee continued in a level voice, "complains of Schoënhut's incapacity, and requests that Albrecht Stengel be sent to Lisbon to deal with the situation. A note of later date reports that William Miller has been liquidated, and intimates that the Foreign Minister may expect to hear soon that a similar fate has befallen me. In the same communication, His Highness speaks of the great expense he has been put to, and asks for a grant to cover it."

Prince zu L—'s voice broke, rose almost to a shriek. "Outrageous! Impudent forgeries! No such notes were ever written!"

"They are written in the Prince's own hand," Lee persisted without raising his voice. "I am sure there must be many specimens of it in the Portuguese archives, and I invite comparison."

The Prince was speechless now.

Lee went on, handing the envelope to the Minister. "There are a number of other letters which reveal His Highness' tender regard for the neutrality of the Republic of Portugal."

The Prince, who had flushed a rusty color, now paled in ghastly fashion. He found his voice again. "Ask him where he got these pretended letters of mine."

"From the archives of the Foreign Office," said Lee coolly. "They were handed me by a special messenger from Berlin."

"Preposterous!" cried the Prince. "I shall listen no longer to this mountebank! As for you, Mr. Minister, you shall be taught that Portugal is in no position so to insult the conqueror of Europe! I will consult with the head of your government!" He stalked out of the room, followed by his stooges.

Quiet followed. The Minister was studying the papers Lee had handed him. Finally he lifted an amazed face. "My God, senhor! These papers, if bona fide, are of supreme importance!"

"So I assumed," said Lee demurely.

"They must instantly be laid before a higher authority than mine. I have your permission?"

"Certainly," said Lee blandly. "What is your pleasure as regards myself, senhor? Am I under arrest?"

"No! No! No!" said the Minister impatiently. "The men you have charged shall be brought to trial immediately, and you will be required to testify. All I ask, senhor, is that you give me your word not to leave Lisbon."

"No danger of that, Excellency," said Lee, smiling. "I give you my word of honor that I will not leave Lisbon."

With hasty bows, the Minister of Police disappeared through the door behind him.

Lee and Luke made their way out of the building.

NEXT MORNING, at the earliest hour that could be considered diplomatically decent, Lee and Luke made their way to the United States Legation to report. They found the Minister striding up and down his study in a high state of excitement.

"Congratulations, Mappin!" he cried. "Congratulations!"

"On what?" asked Lee, with make-believe innocence.

"The Prince zu L— has been fired! Not in the usual fashion by a polite note to his government, but escorted to the railway station on twelve hours' notice! Fired! Fired! They say that the note to Germany is a scorcher, but that has not been given out. It has been intimated to me that this is the result of your work."

"Well, fancy that!" said Lee.

"And there is better news, better news to heap on that!" the Minister continued. "The British Ambassador has just telephoned me that the government of Portugal has graciously consented to allow His Majesty's Government to establish naval bases in the Azores Islands! There's a smack in the eye for the U-boat campaign! As far as Portugal is concerned, it is the beginning of the end, Mappin! Portugal will soon be in it on our side up to the neck!"

"WELL," SAID LEE TO LUKE, when they had returned to their hotel, "there will be another Ambassador from the enemy, and another branch of the Gestapo established in Lisbon. So let us make hay while the sun shines. Spain, too, even Spain, will be greatly influenced by these happenings. We must proceed at once to have that refugee family in Barcelona sent on to us. We can tell Switzerland, too, that we are ready to receive others . . ."

COACHWHIP PUBLICATIONS

ALSO AVAILABLE

1

HULBERT FOOTNER
THE ADVENTURES OF
MADAME STOREY

ISBN 978-1-61646-236-9

COACHWHIP PUBLICATIONS

COACHWHIPBOOKS.COM

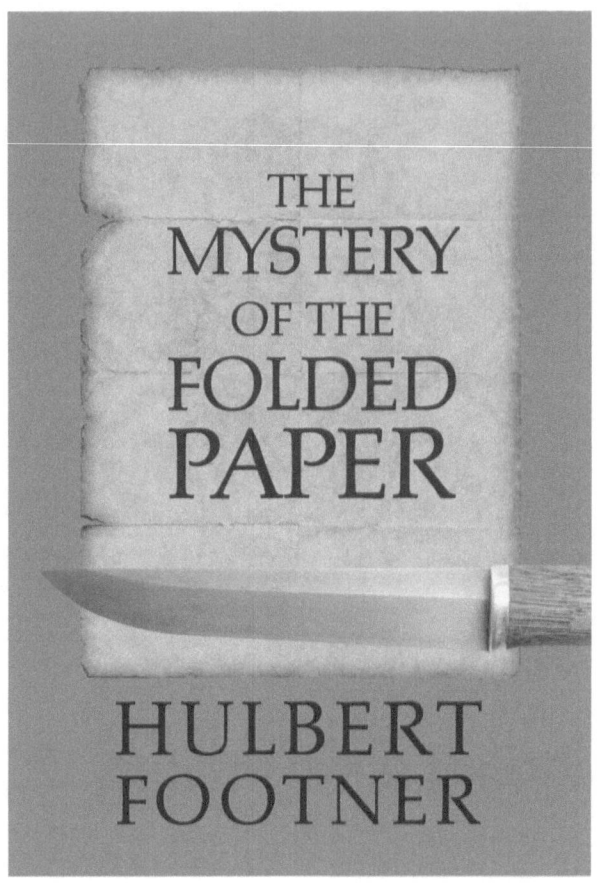

ISBN 978-1-61646-255-8

ORCHIDS TO MURDER

HULBERT FOOTNER

ISBN 978-1-61646-262-8

COACHWHIP PUBLICATIONS

COACHWHIPBOOKS.COM

WHO KILLED THE
HUSBAND?

HULBERT FOOTNER

ISBN 978-1-61646-256-6

THE MURDER
THAT HAD
EVERYTHING!

HULBURT
FOOTNER

ISBN 978-1-61646-258-2

Coachwhip Publications

CoachwhipBooks.com

THE HOUSE WITH
THE BLUE DOOR
HULBERT FOOTNER

ISBN 978-1-61646-261-1

THE
DEATH
OF A
CELEBRITY

HULBERT
FOOTNER

AN AMOS LEE MAPPIN MYSTERY

ISBN 978-1-61646-263-5

COACHWHIP PUBLICATIONS

COACHWHIPBOOKS.COM

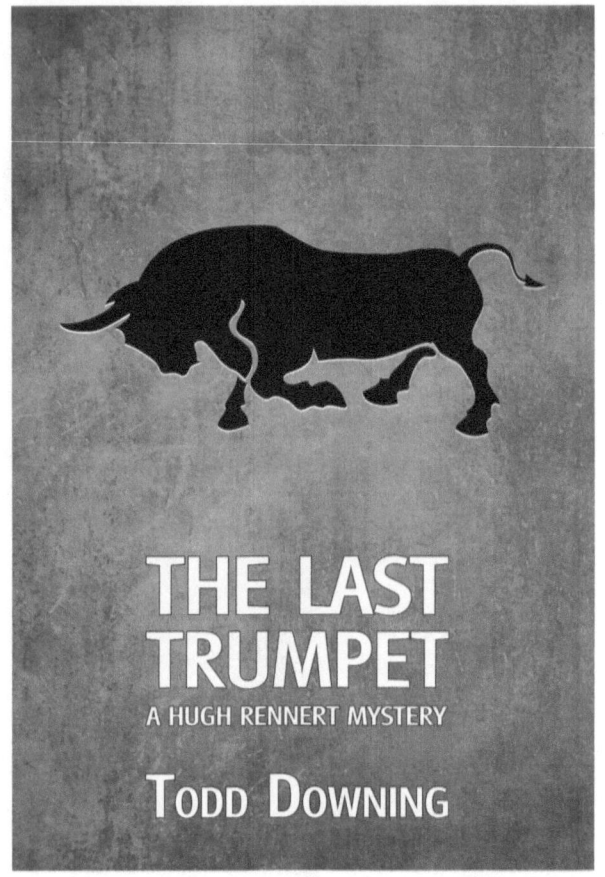

THE LAST
TRUMPET
A HUGH RENNERT MYSTERY

TODD DOWNING

ISBN 978-1-61646-152-2

THE QUINNY HITE
MYSTERIES
CHINESE RED · HERE LIES THE BODY

RICHARD BURKE

ISBN 978-1-61646-247-5

COACHWHIP PUBLICATIONS

COACHWHIPBOOKS.COM

MURDER OF
THE HONEST BROKER

WILLOUGHBY SHARP

ISBN 978-1-61646-211-6

THERE IS
NO RETURN
THE ADELAIDE ADAMS MYSTERIES
ANITA BLACKMON

ISBN 978-1-61646-223-9